KU-545-618

JUDGEMENT CALL

JUDGEMENT CALL

A Detective Superintendent Henry Christie Novel

Nick Oldham

This first world edition published 2013
in Great Britain and 2014 in the USA by
SEVERN HOUSE PUBLISHERS LTD of
19 Cedar Road, Sutton, Surrey, England, SM2 5DA.

Copyright © 2013 by Nick Oldham

All rights reserved.
The moral right of the author has been asserted.

British Library Cataloguing in Publication Data

Oldham, Nick, 1956- author.
  Judgement call. – (A Henry Christie mystery; 20)
  1. Christie, Henry (Fictitious character)–Fiction.
  2. Police–England–Blackpool–Fiction. 3. Detective and mystery stories.
  I. Title II. Series
  823.9'2-dc23

ISBN-13: 978-0-7278-8333-9 (cased)

Except where actual historical events and characters are being
described for the storyline of this novel, all situations in this
publication are fictitious and any resemblance to living persons
is purely coincidental.

All S⸏ ₍rn House titles are printed on acid-free paper.

₍vern House Publishers support the Forest Stewardship Council™ [FSC™],
₍he leading international forest certification organisation. All our titles that
are printed on FSC certified paper carry the FSC logo.

MIX
Paper from
responsible sources
FSC
www.fsc.org   FSC® C013056

Typeset by Palimpsest Book Production Ltd.,
Falkirk, Stirlingshire, Scotland.
Printed and bound in Great Britain by
TJ International, Padstow, Cornwall.

Falkirk Council	
BN	
Askews & Holts	
AF C	£19.99

To my former partners in the pursuit of crime:
Dave Briggs (RIP), Ian Carney, Graham Street and Greg Plummer.

ONE

1982

'Seriously, I don't want much,' Henry Christie mumbled to himself. 'All I want is a job, one measly deployment . . . anything'll do . . . sheep straying . . . sheep-rustling . . . sheep-shagging . . . a murder, even,' he said hopefully. 'Literally anything, please.'

He was at the wheel of the unmarked dark-blue Mark 1 Vauxhall Cavalier, one of the two crime cars that worked the Rossendale Valley, and he was alone, so no one heard his mutterings. His usual partner in pursuit of crime had reported in sick that morning – from over-indulgence, Henry knew – so twenty-three-year-old PC Henry Christie was out on solo patrol on the steep streets of the valley in one of Lancashire's far-flung corners. And so far, over two hours into his shift, nothing of great interest had come his way. Unlike in Blackburn, that incredibly busy industrial town a few miles west, where Henry had just had a short and bitter-sweet secondment as a CID aide, which was a place where every cop was run ragged from start of their shift to finish, whatever time of day. Here in the sleepy valley, by comparison, jobs were few and far between – or at least that's how it seemed to Henry, who champed at the bit for something to get his teeth into.

And, to add insult to injury, he was back in uniform.

He'd been cruising the town centre and council estate streets of Rawtenstall and Haslingden, covering the western half of the Rossendale Valley, the side he had been allocated to patrol that day with the call sign Hotel Romeo Seven – 'HR7'. He'd come on duty at eight o'clock that morning and after having attended a couple of burglaries first thing, other than being roped into the fiasco that was the court run – escorting overnight and remand prisoners from the police station to Rossendale Magistrates' Court – he'd had nothing. He'd been so bored that he'd randomly pulled two cars and issued the drivers with HORT1s – document 'producers' – requiring them to take their driving documents to a police station of their own choice within five days.

Both drivers had whinged and asked why they'd been stopped and the young PC had snarled, 'Because I can,' a claim which in law was totally valid, though not really an excuse to stop/ check people because of feeling mean. He had also stopped and checked a prolific valley criminal he'd spotted sauntering inno- cently along the main shopping street in Rawtenstall, got the man to empty his pockets and patted him down, but found nothing of interest. He did manage to wind the guy up, though, which was quite satisfying.

And now he found himself in the slipstream of a tatty flat-back Transit van, stacked with scrap household goods, driven by Lancashire rednecks, certain the only way he was going to uncover anything of interest that morning was by self-initiated work.

The van coughed out plumes of purple diesel exhaust as it dropped down a gear and the whole load on the back shifted dangerously.

Henry's right forefinger slid into the key ring dangling just above the side window which was attached by a thin cable running under- neath the roof lining to the 'police-stop' pop-up sign hinged face down along the back parcel shelf. A not very hi-tech contraption, requiring the driver to pull the key ring (which often, mysteriously, got stuck) and draw the stop sign upright, hook the key ring around the protruding head of a screw that had been driven into the door stanchion, then flick the switch on the dashboard to, hopefully, illuminate the sign, which sometimes didn't work.

Henry pulled up the sign, looped the key ring around the screw head. His intention was to overtake the Transit van at an appro- priate place, pull it and see what transpired. Vans and lorries carrying scrap were always worth a tug any time of night or day as theft of metal was still rife in the valley.

He waited for a break in the approaching traffic and eased the nose of the Cavalier out for an overtake . . . at which moment the half-brick sized Burndept personal radio slung on a harness around his neck, tucked under the front of his tunic, came to life.

'Romeo Seven?' It was the communications room at Rawtenstall calling him up, using the abbreviated form of his call sign.

Henry eased off the gas, dropped back, and pressed the transmit button. 'Receiving.'

'You free to attend a job?'

He stifled a guffaw at the stupid question. 'Yes – go ahead.'

The house was on the largest council estate in Rawtenstall, within walking distance of the town centre. It wasn't the most notorious estate in the valley, though. In fact Henry thought most of the estates in Rossendale were pretty tame in comparison to the ones he had wistfully left behind on his short – and ultimately sour – secondment to the CID in Blackburn.

He found the address and pulled up outside. It was a well-constructed fifties semi-detached in a fairly pleasant setting on a hillside with great views across to the flat-topped hill that was Musberry Tor, Rossendale's mini answer to Table Mountain. But the house had a kicked-down garden fence with the gate still standing uselessly, and a debris-strewn garden.

His mouth twisted sardonically.

He was four years into his police service and in that time had already visited numerous houses like this one, the stock in trade properties that cops regularly found themselves inside, or trying to enter. Henry was not fatigued by this because he was always curious as to what slice of humanity he might find behind the door.

He clambered out of the Cavalier and fitted his chequer-banded flat cap that somehow always seemed to tilt backwards on his head like a joke bus conductor's. He ensured his handcuffs were tucked into his waistband and that his trusty staff – which he'd hit only two people with so far, without much damage – was slotted down the specially sewn-in pocket running down the side of his right thigh, inside his uniform trousers.

So, fully kitted out and with one tug of the hem of his tunic, he walked up to the front door, which opened on his approach.

A young woman stood there, dressed in a baggy, low-cut T-shirt, equally loose-fitting shell-suit bottoms, huge fluffy slippers and nothing else. The usual fashion for young ladies of leisure on the estate. They often also sported black eyes – as did this lady. Hers was accompanied by a matching lip, swollen like an inner tube sticking out of a split bicycle tyre.

'Sally Lee?' Henry asked, feeling a tremor of rage course through him at the sight of her injuries. Already he wanted to arrest the person responsible . . . the *man* responsible.

She nodded and dropped her gaze, a bit shamefaced, Henry thought. She stepped aside, opened the door wider and flicked her fingers for Henry to enter the house. He did, removing his cap. She closed the door behind him then slid ahead and led him into the lounge, which was scattered with baby clothes, empty cups, overflowing ashtrays. There was a big-screen TV in the corner, a monstrosity of a thing, and a Betamax video-cassette player underneath it.

'Sit down if you want.'

Henry moved aside a grey-hooded parka jacket and found space on a ragged armchair whilst Sally Lee sat on the settee amongst child's clothing. It was only then that Henry spotted the actual baby, lying camouflaged by the clothes, sleeping soundly, a dummy in its mouth. He couldn't quite decide what sex it was, but it was very young, a matter of months at most. Henry's eyes flickered to the woman's face, assuming she was the mother – but not taking it for granted. Anything was possible on this estate.

'You've been assaulted.' He stated the obvious.

'My boyfriend.'

'And you want to make a complaint about it?'

Her eyes fell again. 'Not just about him hitting me,' she muttered.

'What else?'

She swallowed. 'He raped me, too.' She eased her hand between two cushions in the settee and came out with a crumpled packet of cigarettes. She shuffled one out with a shaky hand, lit it with a throwaway lighter that she then inserted back into the pack.

'Do you mind telling me what happened?' Henry said softly. 'Or if you prefer you can speak to a policewoman.'

'You'll do . . . I don't mind . . . I've just had the kid – *his* kid – four months ago and you know what,' she said defiantly, 'I don't want sex. Don't feel like it. It hurts. Just don't want it . . . but he does . . . He just got angry with me, knocked seven bells out of me.' She tilted her head so Henry could see what he'd already seen. Then her eyes did meet his. 'And he raped me . . .

here, on the baby clothes . . . in front of the kid, a kid he doesn't give a monkey's about, anyway.'

Henry nodded as she spoke.

'You believe me, don't you?'

'Course I do,' he said, puzzled by the question. He squinted. 'Look, the best thing would be for you to come down to the nick so we can talk without any interruption. It'll be better if there's just you. Is there anyone who could look after the kiddie for you?'

'Aaron? Uh, yeah, suppose so.' She took a deep drag of the cigarette and exhaled. A cloud of smoke hung listlessly a few inches above the child's sleeping face. Henry wondered if little Aaron would grow up psychologically damaged with the image of his mother's rape permanently etched into his little brain, and with ravaged lungs from inhaling someone else's smoke. The little guy's future, he thought, was already bleak.

Henry thought he heard a noise at the back of the house. A click. A scrape. A creak. Maybe a soft footfall. He thought nothing of it.

'Who is your boyfriend?'

'Vladimir Kaminski . . . you'll have heard of him.'

He had. 'Vlad the Impaler' was his nickname. He was allegedly the cock of the town, a young man with a fearsome reputation as a very dirty fighter. No doubt he would have been christened the 'Impaler' anyway, but there was a certain truth to it. He had once impaled a lad's hand onto an iron fence post. Henry had yet to come across him, but he knew it would only be a matter of time.

'Real violent bastard, he is,' Sally confirmed.

There was another creaking noise from the hallway, a definite sound of movement. This time Henry knew for certain there was someone else in the house. He went still, then turned his face slowly towards the closed living-room door. He saw a shadow move in the gap at floor level.

He glanced at Sally. The colour had drained from her already pale face, a look of fear in her eyes. He placed a finger across his lips – *shhh* – and pointed to the door and mouthed, 'Is that him?'

'Think so,' she mouthed back, nodding.

Henry stood up slowly, reaching his full height of six-two. He reached for the leather strap of his staff and looped it around his hand, ready to draw it if necessary.

Suddenly the door was booted open, clattering back on his hinges, crashing all the way to the wall.

Henry Christie was approaching his sporting prime. He was broad-shouldered, physically fit, a sports fanatic. He played rugby for Lancashire Constabulary, swam for them too, played squash three times a week, seven-a-side football once. He lifted weights and ate like a horse that loved curries. He was pretty big and handy, his police lifestyle – rotten shifts, fast food, greasy pies, beer and little sleep – not yet having taken a toll on him, and he was proud of his physique.

However, the man who had just kicked open the door of Sally Lee's living room, whilst about the same age as Henry, was wider, slightly smaller, but much stronger-looking – and he had a mean disposition that often resulted in violence, whereas Henry was quite mild-mannered and it took a lot to ignite him.

'Vladimir Kaminski?' Henry said unnecessarily.

'Who wants to know?' His beady eyes bore into Henry's.

'Me. My name is PC Christie,' Henry said evenly, trying to work out how he was going to flatten this muscle man, because even before things had got going he knew it would come to a rough and tumble.

'I don' give a flying fuck who you is,' Kaminski spat. His accent was an uncomfortable blend of East Europe and East Lancashire.

'You're under arrest on suspicion of rape and assault. You're not obliged to say anything . . .' Henry began to recite the caution and took a step toward his prisoner to be.

'You come near me, I kill you,' he warned Henry and pulled his shirt sleeve right up to his bicep to reveal a huge arm with muscles like Popeye's and an array of interlinking tattoos, instantly making Henry think, 'Steroids.' No one got muscles like that legitimately.

Henry gave him a lopsided 'Sure you will' grin. He was no fighter, but his strength was the ability to overpower people without the need to punch their lights out. But above all, he wasn't afraid. 'Like I said, you're under arrest,' Henry told him again. He didn't bother mentioning the 'easy way/hard way' option. Everything emanating from this guy screamed, 'Hard way!'

So be it.

Henry wrapped the truncheon strap tightly around his hand as he worked out the best place to whack Kaminski with his rather pathetic light wood stick. At training school he had been taught to go for the upper arm or leg, but he was already thinking, from the bulges under Kaminski's clothing, this would be useless. It would be like hitting a side of beef. It was going to have to be a head shot, even though the guy's skull looked pretty dense, too.

But then Kaminski did the last thing that Henry expected.

He turned and legged it.

Still gasping and gulping for breath, Henry repeated the word.

'Rape.'

'Excuse me?' The bulky station sergeant blinked, took a carefully measured sip from his apparently endless steaming hot mug of tea, adjusted his pince-nez and his slightly bemused focus to examine the young, bedraggled constable standing on the opposite side of the charge-office desk. The PC was breathless, almost to the point of exhaustion. His uniform trousers were ripped, Doc Marten boots sodden, he had lost his clip-on tie somewhere down the line – but to his credit, was still tightly gripping the arm of the prisoner, his prize, who was equally out of breath and knackered.

To the sergeant, the tale that this little scenario told was obvious.

During the course of the arrest, the prisoner had done a runner at some juncture ('juncture' being one of the sergeant's favourite words). The constable had given chase ('Ah, the eagerness of youth,' the sergeant had thought patronizingly. He had not demeaned himself to run after anyone since the summer of 1962. So undignified, especially in uniform) and the foot pursuit had taken cop and fleeing felon through fields and puddles, maybe a farmyard, and had ended up in a messy rugby tackle and scrum.

'Yes,' Henry reiterated. 'I've arrested this man on suspicion of rape.' He drew breath.

The sergeant was correct. It had been a long chase on foot and at one point a nasty little very determined Jack Russell terrier had appeared from nowhere, snapping ferociously at Henry's heels, complicating matters even further when it sank its fangs into Henry's trouser bottom and hung on for dear life. It had taken a well-aimed, brutal kick to send the little beast squealing and cartwheeling over a low wall.

'Rape,' the sergeant said, drawing out the word and lowering his jaw so his triple chins expanded like a toad.

'Yes, sarge,' Henry said respectfully.

'Mm.' The sergeant's lips rubbed together, but in opposite directions, like a loom. 'OK,' he said at length, and turned to the prisoner. 'Anything to say about that?'

'Not guilty.' Kaminski shook himself free from Henry's grip and sneered contemptuously at him. He had stony eyes and a pinched, rodent-like face, his cheeks pock-marked and pitted. Henry glared back with equal contempt, not fazed by the hard man, but aware it had been an uphill battle to subdue him and if the double-crewed section van hadn't turned up when it did, he might have had to admit defeat and let the bastard go.

'Circumstances?' The sergeant directed the word at Henry.

'Attended the report of a sexual assault, took the report – and this man is the alleged offender. Ran off when I told him he was under arrest.'

The sergeant pushed his half-glasses back up his bulbous, booze-reddened nose. 'You're sure about this?'

'Yes, sarge,' Henry answered, puzzled, wondering why he wouldn't be.

The sergeant's lips now tightened into a disapproving knot, but he reached under the desk and came out with a blank charge sheet which he placed with a flourish on the desktop. He extracted a torpedo-shaped fountain pen from his shirt pocket, unscrewed the lid and dipped the nib into the already open bottle of Quink and refilled the pen using the lever on its side. All the while he kept a beady eye on the two people in front of him. He tapped the tip of the nib on the rim of the ink bottle and was now ready to write and record details.

'Name,' he said to the prisoner, even though he already knew it.

'Vladimir Kaminski.'

Once the name, address and date of birth were recorded, then the prisoner's property, the sergeant instructed Henry to take him down to the cells and put him in number one. He could have used any of the cells that morning because they were all empty. It was a quiet morning at this end of the valley.

'This way,' Henry said. He placed a hand on Kaminski's huge right forearm to direct him to the cell corridor.

Kaminski spun fiercely. Henry reared back, expecting to be attacked as the prisoner bunched his immense fists. 'Don' you fuckin' touch me again,' he growled.

Suddenly, behind Kaminski there was a blur of speed and power as the sergeant leaned over and smacked the prisoner across the ear with a grizzly bear-like, open-handed blow that sent him spinning across the tiled floor, up against the wall.

Henry knew what he had witnessed, knew he'd seen it, something he'd only ever heard whispered about before – but the stunning blow had been delivered so quickly and accurately and apparently effortlessly that it was almost impossible to actually say it had really happened, other than for the sound of the smack and the prisoner hitting the wall a moment later.

Sergeant Bill Ridgeson's legendary forehand smash.

Kaminski was bent over double, his hands clamped over his head like a protective helmet, glaring at the officers.

The sergeant hadn't moved from his position. Calmly he repositioned his glasses on the bridge of his nose, picked up his mug of tea and said, 'I do not allow any form of aggression in my police station . . . except from me.' He took a slurp of tea, nodded at Henry. 'Cell one, please.'

'Yes, sarge.' He walked over to Kaminski. 'Up,' he said, jerking his thumb.

Scowling through a pain-ravaged face, hand cupping a throbbing ear, his head ringing like a church bell in a vestry, he rose and this time allowed Henry to steer him down to the cells and into number one, which was clean and ready for its first occupant of the day. Henry told him to remove his trainers and leave them in the corridor before entering the cell.

Henry slammed shut the self-locking steel door. Kaminski shoved his head at right angles into the inspection hatch.

'You make big mistake, cop,' he said, exaggerating his Eastern European accent for best effect.

'Vot you mean,' Henry mimicked him, 'Igor?'

'She vill not make a statement. She vill not take me to court. She knows she vill be dead if she does.'

'Now you shouldn't have said that. Threats to kill can put you away for ten years.' Henry crashed the up-sliding hatch into place and locked it.

'Ve'll see,' Kaminski's muted voice cried.

Henry jerked a middle digit up at the peephole in the cell door behind which he could see Kaminski's eye and returned to the charge office where Sergeant Ridgeson was inserting the forms into the binder. He glanced at Henry, shook his head sadly and said, 'Why have you arrested him?'

'Rape. He raped his girlfriend. Beat her up, too.'

'Sally Lee, you mean? Sally "Jugs" Lee?' Ridgeson scoffed.

'Yes, that's her . . .' A sudden lurch of dread gripped Henry's guts in a clawed hand.

The sergeant's head continued to shake pityingly. He blew out. 'You'll learn . . . I took the liberty of calling the DI, just to let him know.'

'Why?'

'His patch, laddie. He likes to keep abreast of all serious arrests. What are you going to do now?'

'Get a statement from Miss Lee . . . police surgeon and all that, Scenes of Crime . . . Hopefully she should have landed at the front desk by now.'

'You'll be lucky if she has,' the sergeant muttered. 'Just don't let her jerk you around.'

At that moment a policewoman appeared at the charge office door. She looked at Henry. 'A Miss Lee at the desk for you,' she announced. She kept her eyes on him.

'Thanks . . . be there in a moment, Jo.'

The policewoman gave him a slightly quirky half-smile, lowered her eyes coyly and returned to the front office with just another almost imperceptible second glance at Henry, who didn't notice a thing. The sergeant did. He was one of this police station's fixtures and fittings, a font of all knowledge, professional and tittle-tattle, and he rarely missed a trick.

'What do you mean, sarge?' Henry asked, referring to Ridgeson's last remark.

'You'll come to realize,' he said patiently, leaning forwards, 'that there's two sides to every coin and everything is not as it seems. I suspect that Miss Lee simply wants Vlad the Impaler out of her hair for a while. Probably wants some other bugger to shag her without poor Vlad finding out, then when the deed is done, she'll drop the charges, or you won't be able to find her to get her to court and next thing you know, it'll be all lovey-dovey . . . until next time. You'll look like an unwiped arse and the prosecutions department will not be happy with you.'

'So you're saying we don't protect her?'

'Don't waste your time on her . . . she howls wolf.'

'But he's beaten her up as well as raped her.'

Ridgeson shrugged. 'You'd be better off chasing the tail of that bonny police lass . . . you'd get a result there.'

'Uh?'

'Didn't you see the lustful, come-hither look she just gave you?'

'No.'

'Having said that, I hear you're courting.'

Henry grinned and reddened up. 'Wouldn't say courting.'

'Anyway . . .' The sergeant waved him away. 'Get your statement if you must, but I'm telling you from experience . . .'

'Waste of time?'

'And money and resources . . . and by the way, before you appear in public again, get yourself sorted out. You look like you've been dragged through a hedge backwards.'

After a hasty swill, brush up and tie replacement, Henry walked to the front office of the police station. It was a fairly small room, consisting of a radio console, a telephone switchboard, a tele-printer machine tucked away behind a clear Perspex screen, a narrow public enquiry desk with the foyer beyond, and little else. Not much room to manoeuvre for such an important location – the communications hub for the whole of the Rossendale Valley. It was staffed by a civilian phone/radio operator and a station duty constable who was presently having his refreshment break – refs – in the first-floor dining room. His job was being covered by Jo, the policewoman, whose eyes widened, then narrowed momentarily, as Henry entered.

'I've sat her down in the waiting room,' she told him.

Henry eyed her discreetly, a once-over. 'How did she seem?'

'The usual.'

'She's a regular?'

'Oh, yeah, seen her a few times . . . Is it true you flattened Vladimir?' Her gaze played rather obviously over Henry.

'Uh, sort of.'

'He's the cock of the town, you know?'

'Doesn't mean he doesn't get arrested,' Henry said brazenly. 'Maybe he needs locking up more often.' He grinned at her, sidled past, catching a faint aroma of pleasant perfume on her. At the front desk Henry stood aside to allow the station duty PC to enter the room. He was returning from his refs having visited the staff toilet accessed through the secure doors on the other side of the public foyer. He winked conspiratorially at Henry, folding a *Daily Express* under his arm and refitting his clip-on tie. Henry knew this PC was a bit of a legend and it was one of his horrible habits to leave what he called a 'baby's arm' in the toilet bowl for the benefit – and horror – of the next user who, invariably (as this loo was a shared sex one), would be one of the young ladies from the admin office. Screams of disgust were regularly heard throughout the station in the mornings and had generated frequent memos from the superintendent, most of which ended up defaced and stuck on the toilet wall.

Henry ducked through the hatch and turned right into the waiting room. Out of the corner of his eye he caught sight of a ferocious red-faced man entering the front door of the station, carrying a dog in his arms. A Jack Russell terrier. Henry recognized the nasty little canine as the one he'd brutally kicked out of the way after it had attacked him whilst chasing Kaminski. The dog saw him, made eye contact, must have recognized him, as it bristled, snarled, baring its teeth, then started yapping. Henry quickly went into the waiting room before the owner jumped to any conclusions.

Miss Lee had taken a seat on which she perched with her hands clasped between her knees, her head drooping, tears streaming down her battered face. She glanced up as Henry came in, and gently wiped her swollen cheek dry with her fingertips. Henry noted that her nails were long, sharp and painted bright red.

'How are you feeling?' He lowered himself onto the chair on the opposite side of the screwed-down table.

She looked broken-heartedly at him. 'Is he locked up?'

'Yes.'

The news had an instant effect on her. 'Brilliant.' She sat upright. She was still wearing the low-cut T-shirt exposing the upper half, or more, of her breasts. They wobbled whitely in a bra that was clearly a tight size too small for the job. Henry saw a tattoo on the right one: 'VLAD'. It looked home-inflicted. There was also an evil-looking discoloured love bite on the right side of her neck.

'Will he go on remand?' she asked hopefully.

Henry pouted. 'That won't be my decision. I need to gather evidence first, then interview him. Then see.'

'What do you mean, gather evidence?'

'A statement from you . . . photos of your injuries . . . you'll have to be examined by a police doctor . . . that sort of thing.'

'Oooh – I don't know about that.' Her face scrunched up sourly at the thought.

The detective inspector pushed away the prosecution file he'd been checking. He stood up and walked over to the full-length mirror hung discreetly on the back of his office door and gave himself a once-over.

As befitting the man who exercised the most influence in the station – regardless of what the uniformed superintendent and chief inspector might think – he, the highest ranking detective in the valley, was, as always, dressed immaculately. The suit he wore, from Slater's menswear in Manchester, where good deals could be had by savvy detectives, was of a light-grey Italian cut, with wide lapels. His slightly ostentatious tie was fastened with a massive Windsor knot against a dark-blue shirt, his highly polished black winkle-picker shoes had Cuban heels.

He looked the part.

His nostrils flared as he angled his face so that he looked down his nose at his reflection, a haughty smirk of superiority on his face. This was the look he gave most people, the ones he considered underlings: the look of contempt. Of course it would have been better had he been taller. Five-eight was only just high enough for him to join the cops, but the heels on his winkle-pickers did notch him up an extra inch and a half. It would also have been more effective if he wasn't so chubby, weight being a constant battle for him. CID boozing and bad food didn't help matters: the detective's lifestyle. A significant double jowl was also forming but he found that if he jutted his jawline out far enough, he could disguise it . . . to an extent.

He smiled at himself because he knew that although appearance did matter, what was more important was attitude. You could look good but you needed that something more to carry it off – and this detective inspector had it bursting out all over, all the way up from his heel protectors hammered carefully into his Cuban heels (that clicked arrogantly as he strutted along the tiled corridors of the cop shop), right up to his meticulously trimmed moustache and nasal hairs, and the thick head of hair and long Dickensian sideboards curving down in front of his ears.

He looked the part, acted the part, but above all, and as far as he was concerned, was the real deal.

He shrugged himself into his jacket, pulled down his shirt cuffs to display the platinum cufflinks and stepped out of his office into the corridor.

It was time for DI Robert Fanshaw-Bayley to implement some clout and see what that jumped-up PC was up to. He tried to recall the lad's name but for the moment, couldn't.

'If you'd be more comfortable speaking to a WPC, I can arrange that,' Henry suggested again.

'No . . . like I said, I like you. I don't mind talking to you,' Sally Lee said. 'You take me seriously . . . I don't mind you knowing intimate things about me.'

'OK,' Henry said.

Her bottom lip quivered.

'No need to cry, Miss Lee. We'll get this sorted.'

'Thanks. I'm really grateful,' she gulped. She had changed her mood again and now her handkerchief was damp with tear stains. Her mascara had run around her uninjured eye, adding to the mess her face had become, with the swollen, ugly-looking left eye and puffed-out lips that looked like fat earthworms.

'Could you manage a cup of tea?'

'That'd be good. Four sugars and milk, please, full fat if you've got it.'

Henry rose and Miss Lee gave him a contorted smile. 'Look . . . Sally . . . don't take this the wrong way, but I need to ask you something straight. Did Vladimir really rape you?'

'Yeah, course he did, the bastard,' she said, insulted. 'Last night.'

'He's done it before, I believe? And assaulted you before?'

Suddenly she wilted visibly, realizing where this might be leading. Henry squinted at her and lowered himself back into the chair.

'Don't you believe me?'

'Yes, I do, and I'll do everything I can to help you. That's a promise, but you have to know this is a two-way street.'

'Meaning?'

Henry chewed his bottom lip, wondering how to phrase the words, but before he could speak she said, 'I live in fear of him, OK? Y'know? He beats me up, regular like . . . and rapes me . . . one day I reckon he'll bloody well kill me.'

'*Oh, boo-hoo-hoo!*'

Henry and Sally jerked their faces around to the door which had opened so silently neither had noticed, and where DI Fanshaw-Bayley now stood, pretending to rub away tears from his eyes with his knuckles. He had obviously heard and disbelieved every single word of her story. He dropped his hands to his sides and said callously, 'Boo-bloody-hoo!'

He jabbed a thick finger at Henry. 'My office.' Then he jerked his thumb over his shoulder to underline the instruction. He looked at Sally Lee. 'You stay here. I'll be back soon to talk to you, Miss Jugs.'

'Sit down,' the DI said whilst easing his bulk into his office chair behind his impeccably neat desk. Henry sat on the indicated chair which, he could have sworn, had an inch shaved off each leg.

Fanshaw-Bayley shuffled his backside comfortable, like he was settling into a nest, leaned forwards and interlocked his fingers and gave Henry a tight, unpleasant smile.

'What's your name again?'

Slightly taken back – nay, offended – Henry said, 'PC Christie, Henry Christie.' His shock was because not very long before he had assisted the DI with a murder case and the two of them had had a lot of interaction – up to the point at which Henry had been cut adrift.

'Ahh, that's right. You gave me a chuck-up with that young lass who'd been murdered, didn't you?' the DI confirmed.

'Yeah, boss.'

The DI's eyes narrowed. 'Aren't you the one who's just come back from a CID aide secondment in Blackburn . . . under a cloud?' Henry swallowed drily, said nothing. 'Something about locking people up you were told not to? Had a big fallout with one of the DIs?'

'Uh – sort of,' Henry acknowledged, but thought, 'There's two sides to every story,' only problem being that with the CID being the most powerful, most 'other sides' were squashed like bugs.

Fanshaw-Bayley nodded knowledgeably. 'You raised your fist at him, didn't you?' Henry stayed dumb. 'Bit of a loose cannon, a hot-head by all accounts. Lucky you're still in a job.'

'Not really,' Henry said.

'Mm,' the DI said dubiously. 'Anyway . . . what you need to know now, lad, is that the Valley is my patch, yeah?'

'Yes, sir.'

'My patch. My way.' His eyes locked onto Henry's. 'So before we discuss what's going on here, let's just cover the rules of the game. If you want to thrive, there's a few things you need to have sorted up here.' He tapped the side of his own skull. 'First off, don't go thinking that just because I'm not the highest-ranking officer in this station, that I'm not in charge. In all matters of a criminal nature, I am. I,' he said forcefully, 'am God and the devil. What I say, goes.' He paused. Henry blinked. Fanshaw-Bayley took a breath, then said, 'And don't you forget it.'

Henry's time in Rossendale as a young cop had been one of learning, feeling his way, getting used to dealing with the public and working out which path his career might take. He had embraced everything and not shied away from any aspect of the job, but had gradually come to realize that what he enjoyed doing best, what gave him most pleasure, was locking people up. He had been prolific in terms of arrests, from drunks to thieves, and it had been his reputation and record that had got him a place on Task Force with only three and a half years' service. TF had been the traditional stepping stone to a career on CID, which was Henry's ultimate aim.

But Task Force had been disbanded almost as soon as Henry was on it and he'd found himself on the newly formed Operational Support Unit, OSU, which was a divisionally based resource. It was similar to TF in some ways, but with one big exception. It was controlled and operated at a local level, whereas Task Force had been a force-wide resource, run from headquarters.

Henry had tried to get a transfer to Blackburn OSU because he thought it offered more scope for eventual career development, but was unsuccessful, though he did manage to get a secondment to the CID in Blackburn, which had ended dismally, with him landing on his backside back in the backwater that was Rossendale.

Up to then Henry hadn't had too much interaction with the DI. It had been more by luck than judgement that he'd helped out on the young girl's murder (the ramifications of which would come to haunt both men much later in their careers, although neither of them could realize that at the time). But now he sat meekly in front of a DI who professed to hardly know him, getting a sinking feeling about the way this man operated. '*My patch, my way*,' he'd said ominously to Henry, who wondered just what that was supposed to mean when applied to that morning and the arrest of Vladimir Kaminski. Surely Henry had done nothing wrong by arresting an alleged rapist.

As if reading his thoughts, Fanshaw-Bayley said, 'Which brings me to this morning's debacle.'

'Debacle?'

'I think that fairly sums it up.'

'I'm not with you, boss. I'm investigating a rape.'

'And that very word – *rape* – should always ring warning bells with you.'

Henry's uncomfortable body language communicated that he did not understand.

'You don't go, willy-nilly, locking people up on claims of rape made by hysterical females.'

'I think you'd be hysterical if you'd been raped,' Henry countered and immediately wished he hadn't.

'I'll keep my cool, PC Christie,' the DI said formally, 'because that's the way I am, but don't you ever talk to me in that tone of voice again, do you understand?'

Henry swallowed. His throat was really dry now.

'You need to realize that you're embarking on a fruitless exercise here, because Miss Lee has a history of making allegations and then withdrawing them and we, as police officers, cannot be seen to be wasting our precious time on petty domestic disputes.'

Henry tugged his collar. 'So we don't do anything?'

'Not with people like her, PC Christie. She's a time-waster.'

'I think she's telling the truth.'

'PC Christie . . . she's a slapper.'

'And?' Henry wasn't sure he was believing his ears. 'Even slappers get raped.'

'They bring it on themselves,' Fanshaw-Bayley said painfully, as if he was imparting some deep-rooted truth.

Henry's fists were now bunched by his sides. He was close to raising them to this DI now, thinking how much this situation mirrored his experience in Blackburn.

Fanshaw-Bayley glanced down, again seeming to read Henry's mind. 'And if you're thinking of raising them to me, you'd better think again. Now go and get a statement from her saying she is sorry for wasting our time and that she wasn't in fact raped, and then release Kaminski . . . Actually, do it the other way around. Release him, then get her statement of retraction.'

'What if she won't make one?'

Fanshaw-Bayley looked at Henry as though he was a dim child. 'Oh, she will. Trust me.'

TWO

With Kaminski's bright blue and white Adidas trainers in his hand, Henry slid the key into the cell door and turned it hard, the mechanism grating rustily as the door unlocked. He pulled the heavy steel door open – outwards – as most cell doors were designed. One that opened inwards could lead to all sorts of problems with a non-compliant prisoner. Opening out gave the incumbent no hiding place.

This prisoner wasn't hiding.

He was sitting on the bench directly opposite the door and Henry could see him clearly. Henry stood on the threshold, framed by the door.

Kaminski looked coldly at him. 'What? You come to beat me up?'

Henry allowed a beat to pass. 'I wish,' he said, and even as he spoke he could feel a tremor throughout his body at the rage he was experiencing at the prospect of letting this man walk free. He didn't care that the prosecution against him might come to nothing. That was the way of the world. But he wanted to subject Kaminski to the process: interview, charge, remand in custody. Get him standing in front of a court. Let him know that the cops meant business, even if subsequently his girlfriend didn't have the will or courage to see it through. Henry wanted to interview him, throw the allegations at him, take his fingerprints and photograph, and do what he had promised for the girl who, whether or not she was lacking morals, he was certain had been raped. It was probably all part of her existence, but a crusading Henry wanted to show her that it didn't have to be like that.

Just to let the smug bastard have his liberty, to be able to do it again – and again – was screwing the young constable up. Tight.

Kaminski's face turned to a grin.

Henry took a step back into the cell corridor, made a sweeping 'after you' gesture with his right arm.

Kaminski got to his feet and walked, bare footed, up to Henry, so they were standing only inches away from each other. Kaminski was slightly shorter, maybe five-eleven, but he was broader, his muscles bigger and more defined from countless hours spent with weights and steroids. Henry realized he had done well to pin him down earlier and he could see why Kaminski was the so-called cock of the town. His physical presence aligned with a violent streak would be enough to intimidate and beat anyone.

'I told you, you can't keep me.'

'Maybe not this time,' Henry said unsteadily. 'But I'll be back for you. And in the meantime, don't be surprised if your hard-man reputation gets a big fat dint in it.'

'How you mean?'

'Trust me . . . people will find out that you're a rapist and that you beat up women.'

An expression of sheer ferocity filled Kaminski's face – one of those expressions Henry had seen often in disaffected young men like Vladimir. Intense, primal hatred. Henry wasn't fazed and he returned Kaminski a lovely smile. At the same time he imagined head-butting him to put him down. Not that Henry had ever head-butted anyone in his life. It was just a pleasant thought, that was all. He knew he would probably misjudge it anyway and end up breaking his own nose.

'It's incredible how such things can get out,' Henry said.

Kaminski's body relaxed. 'No one would care, anyway.'

'The ladies might,' Henry said. But he knew the truth. The level of Rossendale society in which Kaminski lived and operated would probably regard him as a hero.

Henry and Kaminski broke their deadlock glare and turned towards the station sergeant who had just entered the charge office, mug of tea in one hand. 'I take it he's en-route?' the sergeant said of the prisoner.

'Unfortunately,' Henry said, a word that made Kaminski smile victoriously. He handed Kaminski the trainers, pushing the foot-wear roughly into his chest. The prisoner bent over and slid his feet into them.

His property was returned to him and he was released. Henry followed him to the back door, glaring at the tattoo etched across the back of his neck, then ensured he left the premises completely, including getting out of the rear yard and car park. Then he went back to the charge office.

'Don't worry, lad,' Sergeant Ridgeson said. 'He'll come a cropper one day . . . but just for the moment you'll have to remember the bigger picture.'

'What do you mean, sarge?'

'Sometimes you need a sprat to catch a marlin, if you get my drift?'

Henry puckered his brow at the older, much more laid-back man. He reminded Henry of a genial Buddha, all seeing, all knowing, and full of bullshit philosophy. 'All I know is that he raped his girlfriend and he's walking away from it, sticking two fingers up at us as he does.'

Ridgeson sighed heavily. 'Maybe I'm not explaining myself properly . . . never mind.' He gave the impression that Henry was a bit of a lost cause. He tapped his bulbous nose, making it wobble slightly obscenely. 'Just forget him and concentrate on doing what young men of your age should be concentrating on – chasing tail – and make an older man vicariously very happy.'

'I'm really sorry—'

Henry had been quickly rehearsing the words he was going to have to say to, he suspected, a rightfully irate Sally Lee when he returned to the waiting room. He'd been concentrating on his little speech, but not to the exclusion of catching the eye, again, of the policewoman who was sitting in the front office by the radio unit. She swivelled slowly on an office chair and tracked his progress across the floor, as he mumbled angrily to himself.

Their eyes met and at the back of his brain, Henry registered the appraisal and half-smile she gave him.

But then he was at the door of the waiting room, about to jump in and offer an immediate apology to Sally for allowing her violent rapist boyfriend to walk free, but that it wasn't his fault, that blah! blah! blah! – but he was stopped dead in his tracks by the sight that greeted him on entering the room. He shut his mouth with a 'pop'.

DI Fanshaw-Bayley was leaning across the table, his face only inches away from Sally's. His left hand supported his weight whilst his right, forefinger pointed, was jabbing at her.

Sally looked at him horrified and distraught.

Fanshaw-Bayley stopped abruptly in mid-rant and his head rotated slowly towards Henry, then swivelled back to the young woman who was staring open-mouthed at him. The DI said, probably reinforcing his message, Henry assumed, slowly and quietly now, 'So you don't go wasting our time . . . have you got that?'

Cowed, she nodded. A tear trickled down her cheek.

Fanshaw-Bayley stood upright and tugged his jacket straight, his point clearly having been made and understood. To Henry he said, 'Take this little cow home.'

Henry drove her in the unmarked Cavalier, turning out of the back yard of Rawtenstall nick, then right onto Bacup Road and up to the traffic lights at the big roundabout that was Queen's Square. Much to his annoyance he saw Vladimir Kaminski standing at the bus station by the cinema, but Kaminski didn't clock Henry's car and seemed to be looking around for someone or something. He hadn't gone far from the police station and Henry was past him in an instant, glancing into his rear-view mirror as Kaminski sprinted across the road to a car pulling in opposite him.

By that time Henry was at the lights, which were on green, and his attention was pretty firmly fixed on the blubbering Sally Lee in the passenger seat alongside him, whose vision was blurred with her tears.

A couple of minutes later, Henry drew up outside her house on the estate.

'I'm sorry,' he said weakly.

'It's not your fault, it's not your fault,' she said, her face buried in the palms of her hands. She dragged it out, stretching her tear-stained features and smudging her heavily applied mascara even more.

'Look,' Henry began, feeling utterly useless.

'No,' she cut in, stifling a body-wracking sob. 'You can't do anything, you can't change anything, so don't bother trying . . . it's just how it is.'

'Doesn't have to be,' Henry insisted.

'Just forget it,' she said hopelessly. 'I'm just a nuisance, I know. I just feel so . . . fucking trapped.'

'Why don't you leave him?'

She snorted sarcastically. 'You have no idea, do you?'

'Try me.'

'I've got a babbie, I'm on benefits, my mum hates me, so I can't go there . . . I have literally nowhere to go.'

'Tell him to leave,' Henry said, thinking it sounded reasonable.

She looked at him in hysterical disbelief. 'Ooh, that's a good idea, I never thought of that.'

'OK,' he relented, getting the message.

'You live in another world, mate. You come on duty and dip into my life and make judgements and interfere, but you haven't got a clue in hell what it's like. I'm fucking trapped,' she said again. 'I have no way out.'

Henry closed his mouth and swallowed, his eyes playing over her realizing she was feisty, very intelligent in a feral way – and, as she said, trapped.

'And it doesn't help that you think we're second-, no, third-class citizens without any rights. So go on, bog off, go and catch your burglars and maybe me for shoplifting, cos you'll do that, won't you? And guess what, I'll get hammered again and maybe I'll call the cops and maybe I won't. And he'll rape me again . . . but let's just hope he doesn't kill me, eh? Then the shit would hit the fan, wouldn't it? Eh?' She sneered accusingly at the last syllable, opened the car door and without a backward glance stomped off towards her house.

Henry watched her, feeling empty and ineffective. He knew he was an integral part of the vicious circle of violence in the home. Like the DI had said, it was just too much like hard work where the police were concerned because most of the complaints were subsequently withdrawn. Henry had to ask himself why that was, but he knew the answer – because the cops and the social services and the justice system had allowed it to get that way. Their stance had never been firm enough and victims rarely had the support they needed. He also understood it was way more complicated than that, but he knew one thing for certain. Although he didn't have a lot of service in the cops – coming up to four years – he had already developed a strong sense of justice and had come to realize how unfairly and indifferently victims and witnesses were treated and not just in relation to domestic violence, it was across the board. He also knew he couldn't change the world, but perhaps he could just chew away at his own little orbit of it.

He jumped out of the car. 'Sally,' he shouted.

She had reached her front door. She stopped, turned to watch him approach.

'That retraction statement I just took from you . . . I'm going to rip it up. I want to come and get a proper one from you.'

'Why, what are you going to do?'

'Uh . . . not completely certain, haven't quite figured that one out yet.'

She regarded him thoughtfully. 'OK.'

'And, look, don't be frightened to call in if anything else happens. In fact, you must.'

She shrugged.

'I'll come back soon and we'll sit down to get a statement, OK?'

Another unconvinced shrug.

His mind churning, Henry drove away. He headed straight back to the police station, where he made his way up to the DI's office, the door of which was closed.

He was glad of this. It gave time for one more run through things. He would have liked to have stormed in, but he reigned in his innate hot-headedness, knowing that such action would be counterproductive. He still wanted to be a detective and upsetting another DI was not the way to go about it because if the CID didn't like you, you didn't get in.

He tapped on the door.

And waited.

He'd heard that Fanshaw-Bayley never answered a knock on the door straight away. He was a 'One, two, three, four, someone's knocking at the door; five, six, seven, eight, I think I'll make 'em wait' kind of boss. So Henry counted and as predicted the 'Enter' order came and he stepped inside Fanshaw-Bayley's den.

He was sitting at the desk, looking at some paperwork. He did not even glance up, but gestured with a ripple of his fingers for whoever it was to take a seat. He signed the bottom of a report with a flourish of his fancy fountain pen – an affected trademark – which he then laid down with a hint of ceremony, and only then raised his eyes to Henry.

'Thought it would be you.'

'*Thought right, didn't you?*' Henry almost retorted, but didn't snap. He knew he was on precarious ground, had to tread carefully, so he just nodded affably, remembering how nasty the DI had been earlier.

'I'd just like to know why Kaminski walked, that's all.'

'The trouble with the uniform branch is that they're too . . . touchy-feely . . . always wanting explanations and reasons . . . Those days may come, PC Christie, but not today, which is why you should simply accept what I tell you. He walks, end of story.'

Henry felt his heart rate increase dramatically. Fanshaw-Bayley was beginning to have that effect on him.

'You want to be a jack, don't you?'

'Y-yes, that's all I want.'

'Then learn to take orders, lad, and learn something from this. Man up, is what I say.'

'And I learn what?'

'That you have to schmooze and weave.' The DI began to move in his chair like a huge fat snake being charmed. 'That sometimes you have to let things go, that it isn't all black and white . . . That the world of crime and villains is a murky fucking place and as a detective you occasionally have to chew on your principles and sometimes they're like swallowing a brick.'

'She was raped.'

'Quite probably,' Fanshaw-Bayley said blandly.

'That seems pretty black and white to me, and even if she eventually decides not to go through with a prosecution, we should at least go through the motions with Kaminski. Send him a warning shot across the bows at least. Grind him.'

Undaunted, the DI said, 'And sometimes the bigger picture is more important than the suffering, albeit self-inflicted, of a slag like Sally Lee, PC Christie.'

Henry stood up. 'Fuck the bigger picture,' he snarled and stalked out of the office before he hurled his chair at Fanshaw-Bayley.

THREE

The Vauxhall Cavalier wasn't the fastest or sleekest of cars but it was possible to coax a decent enough turn of speed out of it when the accelerator pedal was floored gradually, the engine sweet-talked slowly through the gears.

Furious at his encounter with the unwavering DI, Henry headed for the Rawtenstall bypass. This was the dual carriageway that bore due south out of Rawtenstall and eventually became the M66 at Bury.

He steered through the town with one hand on the wheel whilst leaning across to the glove compartment into which he had fitted, quite unofficially, a tape cassette player, and rigged up a couple of small speakers behind the door panels. He switched it on and slotted in a tape he had made direct from the record of a live Rolling Stones album. As the opening riff of 'Jumpin' Jack Flash' blasted out, he veered onto the bypass from the Queens Square roundabout and to the accompaniment of Mick Jagger's sneering lyrics sped towards Greater Manchester in an effort to alleviate the stress he was feeling. That tightness in his chest, like a devil with sharply filed fingernails was squeezing his heart and lungs.

Taking a cop car for a razz with the Stones blasting out was always a good way of easing stress and tension.

Unfortunately when he was two hundred yards up the bypass and committed to driving away from the town, unable to turn off for at least three miles, an urgent voice from Rawtenstall comms came over the PR, that of WPC Wade.

'Report of an armed robbery in progress at Crawshawbooth Post Office, Burnley Road . . . shots fired. Patrols to attend,' Jo said, sounding shaky and excited, trying to hold it together. This was a big ask for any young officer.

Henry immediately responded – with a bit of a white lie. 'Romeo Seven from Rawtenstall town centre. ETA three minutes.' He knew the exact location of the post office – in the little village of Crawshawbooth which straddled the main road between Rawtenstall and Burnley. This location was a good thing in some respects, mainly because it meant that the villains could only escape in a car in one of two directions – north towards Burnley, or south, back towards Rawtenstall – and Henry had a good idea they would be coming in his direction. That said, he needed to get off the bypass somehow and get back to Rawtenstall.

Other patrols shouted up. There were only two single-crewed mobiles available and both were en route, as was DI Fanshaw-Bayley, who was turning out from the police station with a detective constable.

'Shit,' Henry said, frustrated by his geographical predicament.

But a lot of other things were also going through his mind.

Firstly, there was every chance that this robbery was being committed by a violent gang of very mobile armed robbers who travelled up from Manchester and targeted business premises in the Rossendale area. So far they had hit six shops and post offices and had used stolen vehicles, later found abandoned and set alight, before – and this was an assumption, not a certainty – piling into a legitimate or maybe another stolen car or cars to make good their escape. The police believed that the gang, consisting of four or five very hyped-up men, had always returned to Manchester after committing their offences. This meant there would be a good chance of them coming back in Henry's direction.

Next, in concurrent thought, Henry wondered about the delay. Often, something reported as being 'in progress' had already happened because of the time lag between someone actually picking up a phone and calling in. So he wondered if there was actually any point in tear-arsing up to the scene when it might be more prudent to hang back and take up a position from which he could monitor all the traffic coming through Rawtenstall centre and going onto the bypass. Even if the robbers had swapped cars, even if they had split up into more than one legit vehicle, Henry could at least try to spot possible offenders and if nothing else, he could note down car makes and numbers.

Not as exciting as rushing to the scene, maybe, but just as important.

Then a calm voice came over the air – that of Ridgeson, the station sergeant, whose deep, calming, authoritative tones of vast experience echoed Henry's thoughts.

'Romeo Seven,' he told Henry, 'do not attend the scene. Take up a checkpoint on Queens Square and await further instruction . . . The two other section mobiles continue to the scene . . . We are currently in telephone contact with the person reporting the incident . . .'

Henry acknowledged this and put his mind to exactly how he was going to get off the dual carriageway as quickly as possible and get back to town. First he needed a blue light – which was sitting in the front passenger footwell. Winding down his window first, he then reached over for the light and plugged the cable from it into the cigarette lighter. He then clamped the magnetic light itself onto the roof of the car with a heavy clunk so the coiled lead stretched diagonally across in front of him. The light came on and started to revolve sluggishly. Then he wound the window back up to trap the lead and thought about a U-turn, keeping an eye out for a likely gap in the central reservation crash barrier through which he might attempt this dangerous manoeuvre.

Amongst his other problems was the speed of traffic in both directions – particularly from Manchester – because as they passed over the boundary into Rossendale, the gradient of the road fell sharply and traffic built up speed very quickly, so if he attempted what he thought he was going to do, he would be putting himself and others in a lot of danger, flashing blue light notwithstanding.

But the danger didn't deter him in the slightest.

Being the age he was, he believed he was doing right, believed he would never come to any harm, that he had an important job to do and that he was indestructible. So doing a scary U-turn on a fast, busy dual carriageway was just another of those things.

He sped up the outside lane, coaxing seventy out of the reluctant Vauxhall, looking well ahead to see if there were any gaps in the barrier. He spotted one. He did a quick mirror check – no one too close behind – and slammed on, yanking the steering wheel down to the right, skidding the car through the gap and right across to the inner lane of the opposite carriageway and, more by sheer luck than judgement, slotted into a long gap in the oncoming traffic.

The back end of the Cavalier slewed wildly across the surface. Henry struggled to control it, fighting the very skittery car which, even in normal circumstances, did not behave well on the road and resented being thrown unwillingly into a fast U-turn under harsh braking and then acceleration.

He was thankful he made it without stalling, although he did hear a scraping noise across the car roof and realized as soon as he accelerated back towards town that the blue light, in spite of the magnet clamping it to the roof, clearly not powerful enough for purpose, had slid right off. It was now dangling by its lead from the driver's door window next to his shoulder, banging on the glass.

He cursed, wound the window down, hauled the useless light in and tossed it into the passenger footwell where it continued to rotate and flash until he yanked the plug out of the cigarette lighter and threw the lead down by the light. He wound the window back up.

Within a minute he was back on Queens Square, wondering where best to park for a good view. He circled it and pulled into Queen Street, a minor side street, parking quite illegally right on the junction with the roundabout so that every vehicle coming from the direction of Crawshawbooth wanting to get onto the bypass would have to drive past within twenty feet of him. Even though it was a good position to be in, it was still always possible for someone with knowledge of the local back streets to sneak past without being spotted, but he knew he couldn't be everywhere.

He called in his position, sat back, watched, listened and waited.

FOUR

P atrols had arrived at the scene of the robbery, confirming the offence had taken place, a firearm had been discharged, but no one had been hurt. A gang of four masked men had terrorized the little post office and the proprietor and two customers had been put in fear of their lives. A handgun had been fired twice into a wall, the gang had shrieked and yelled demonically at people, two had leapt over the counter and forced their way into the secure area behind. Then, with about three thousand pounds in cash, they had fled in a car, details of which were sketchy. The car – Henry was pleased to hear – had been seen heading in the direction of Rawtenstall, though that didn't actually mean it had come into the town.

The call alerting the police had been made by a neighbour from a house opposite.

Henry fidgeted as he listened to all the details as they filtered over the air bit by bit, all the while concentrating on the cars passing him, trying to pick one that could be the one the gang had escaped in, or might have transferred to. It was only a pure gut thing, scanning for likely looking young men, but nothing that went past seemed to fit the bill.

Checking his watch he realized it was now over ten minutes since the original call had come over the PR. That was easily enough time for the offenders to make it from the scene into town, particularly if there had been a delay in reporting the incident. Henry was getting ants in his already itchy uniform trousers. He became more impatient at the thought that if the car was going to zip past him, it would have done so by now.

He decided to move, believing he was wasting his time sitting there. He thought it would now be better to do a short cruise around and maybe he would come across the gang ditching their car, torching it and leaping into another motor.

He also knew this was probably a vain hope. But he was a young cop and still believed that luck was on his side and all he had to do was keep his eyes open and villains would just fall into his hands. He had learned that cops can make their own luck to a great extent, so he was going to give it a go, disobey orders, and leave the checkpoint he had been told to stay at until further instructions.

If he ever had to answer a question about it – which he doubted – he would argue that he'd made a judgement call based on what was happening and his knowledge of the MO of the gang and thought he was just being conscientious.

He crunched the Cavalier into gear and poked its nose out onto the roundabout, turned left and headed up onto the estate he'd been on earlier attending the report of the rape on Sally Lee, and through which he had chased Vladimir Kaminski on foot. There were tracts of wasteland all around the estate which were likely places to abandon and set fire to stolen cars. He was going to do a quick tour of these 'bomb sites' and see what he could find, if anything.

He came off the roundabout, crossed the bridge over the River Irwell, with a large ASDA superstore to his left, then did another sharp left onto the road which led up onto the estate, a road that rose steeply up the hillside, then began his search, combing the avenues and crescents and cul-de-sacs. He loved cruising slowly around the highways and byways, one of the great pleasures of being a cop in a car, eyeing people and being glared at, and maybe dropping on something of interest.

Nothing much seemed to be happening on the estate.

He drove up to its highest point, just below Balladen Hill, from where he got a magnificent view all the way across the bypass where he'd done the U-turn. This road was settled deep in the valley, rising as it left Rossendale. Running parallel to it was the single track of the disused East Lancashire Railway, connecting Rawtenstall to Bury. Henry had once, foolishly, driven a police Land Rover for almost the full length of the train line, a precarious and very dangerous journey that had forced him to drive over almost derelict bridges spanning the River Irwell, and never to be repeated.

As he looked across, the wildness of the upper moors took his breath: Cribden Moor to the north and Musberry Heights across to the west. But he didn't get much time to consider their grandeur because a plume of black smoke rising from an industrial area on the valley bottom caught his eye, in the space between the railway line and the bypass. And it wasn't smoke rising from a chimney. It was a bonfire of sorts, but its actual source was impossible to see from his position high on the estate, about a mile distant.

He knew it could be nothing, probably just junk being destroyed out in the open. Illegal, but not his problem.

Or it could be a car on fire.

Henry slammed the Cavalier into first and hurtled downhill, taking chances at some of the junctions on the estate, but as he came to Bury Road, previously the main road south out of Rawtenstall before the bypass was built, he had to anchor on. He needed to do a left turn, then a right onto Holme Lane to take him down to the industrial area in the valley bottom.

He waited impatiently for traffic to clear, pulled out, then after a couple of hundred yards swung into Holme Lane, his eyes constantly on the rising smoke, trying to work out exactly where it was coming from. He was focused so intently on this that he almost took no heed of the car stationary at the junction, waiting to pull out onto Bury Road. He saw it and part of his mind registered it, but it was only when he was fifty yards past that he screeched to a halt and realized what he had seen. Three men in a car – just the sort of thing he had been on the lookout for whilst parked up on Queen's Square earlier.

Perhaps it was the make and model of car that had thrown him off guard – a somewhat sedate, dull-looking Rover 3.5 coupé, two shades of brown, a sort of middle-aged man's motor, not one he'd necessarily expect to see three buckos in, even though he knew the car itself was a fast mover. He had expected to see them in something sleeker.

And there was also something familiar about it, but he couldn't quite place it as his brain shuffled through all this information.

He braked sharply, looking into his rear-view mirror to see the car pull out onto Bury Road and head south.

He yanked the wheel down and executed a fast three-point turn, his car rocking on its bouncy suspension.

He was going to check out the Rover, but because he wasn't

remotely certain that the fire he could see down in the valley had anything to do with the robbery, or that the Rover itself was even suspicious – and that he had left his checkpoint without permission – he decided he wouldn't trouble comms for the moment, just see how things developed.

By the time his car's nose had reached the junction, the Rover was almost out of sight. Henry skittered out with a slight misgiving at the sight of clouds of very iffy-looking exhaust smoke behind him as he floored the Cavalier in first, then second, and with a very rough gear change between that might well have sheared off some nasty cogs, he accelerated after the Rover.

It was moving quickly and by the time he came up behind it, it was approaching the set of traffic lights just outside the village of Edenfield, basically the last outpost of Lancashire Constabulary before entering Greater Manchester's area.

The brake lights came on as the car slowed for a red light.

Henry could actually now see the outline of four people on board – in his first glimpse back down the road he thought there had only been three, so maybe one of them had been bent over tying a shoe or something. The two in the back, their features indistinguishable, turned to look out of the rear window.

The car stopped for the light, giving Henry chance to catch up. As he slowed behind it he reached across for his flat cap and fitted it onto his head. Just in case there were any shenanigans here, he didn't want anyone to claim he couldn't be identified as a cop. Whoever was in the car, innocent or otherwise, had to know what he was before he even spoke to them.

The light was still on red. Henry pulled up twenty feet behind the Rover.

The men in the back were still looking at him.

He had their attention.

He pointed at them with his right forefinger and jerked it to the left: *pull in*.

Suddenly both rear doors swung open and the occupants got out, faces angled downwards, pulling balaclava masks over their faces.

Both brandished sawn-off shotguns.

'Holy crap,' Henry uttered.

Both guns arced up in his direction.

He crunched his car into reverse – blunting more cogs – and literally stood on the accelerator pedal, his back pressed hard against his seat, and the car swerved backwards, Henry with his right hand on the wheel, his torso twisted at forty-five degrees, his head jerking forwards and backwards.

The men ran fast and low, catching up with him, and then, as if synchronized, they aimed and fired. Henry heard the slightly delayed stereo of the discharge, then physically felt the impact of the blast from the shot as it hit the car, thudding into the bodywork like pebbledashing being flung against a wall.

Henry screamed, 'Shit,' kept his foot rammed on the pedal, thankful there were no other cars behind him to impede his ignominious retreat.

Message delivered, the two men ran back to the Rover and bundled themselves into the back seat, their doors slamming as the car sped off through the lights.

Henry stalled his car, swore, slammed in the clutch and twisted the ignition key with his right hand, using the forefinger of his left hand to press the transmit button on his PR and call for assistance. As the engine fired up, he went after the Rover, still speaking into his radio, trying his best to sound cool and laid-back, even though the front of his car had just been blasted by two shotguns.

He raced into Edenfield, where because of parked cars on either side the road narrowed, just about wide enough for two cars to pass, and the speed limit dropped back to thirty, not really a village to hurtle through.

Henry touched sixty.

The Rover was still in view and Henry speculated what the plans of its occupants might now be. They were being chased by a lone cop and as the border with Greater Manchester loomed, and patrols in that area were hopefully being alerted by Rawtenstall comms, Henry thought they might try and ditch the car and try to escape on foot. But then again, maybe not. Henry knew there wouldn't be many patrols to deploy over the border and the police over there would have to drop everything and converge on the chase, all of which took time.

The sergeant called Henry, who replied, 'Go 'head.'

'The Rover was reported stolen in the early hours of this morning from Failsworth, Manchester.'

Henry ingested this information. That fitted more or less with what he knew of this gang's MO. Steal two cars from Manchester, use one to commit the robbery, ditch and burn it, then jump into another stolen one which is then abandoned. He guessed that the smoke he had been about to investigate would be the car used in the robbery.

A look of grim satisfaction came onto Henry's face. It had been worth leaving the checkpoint.

He smacked the steering wheel in triumph, then succinctly brought comms up to speed with his current location and situation.

The Rover was still ahead and in sight. Once it had passed through Edenfield centre it veered right and headed towards the roundabout that formed a junction with the bypass, at the point where that road became the M66 motorway, but there was no actual slip road onto the motorway which meant that the driver's options were becoming limited.

The Rover careened onto the roundabout, narrowly avoiding other traffic, and rocked dangerously as the driver forced the car into a tight left turn straight off the roundabout and back up towards Edenfield again.

Henry stuck with it, part of his mind trying to recall why the Rover seemed familiar, and on this stretch of road he gained on the Rover, which appeared to have lost some power, or maybe the driver had missed a gear or two. At the next junction, Henry expected the car to go right, but to his surprise it skidded sharp left, towards Edenfield. As the car screeched around this corner, the rear nearside passenger hung out of the window and blasted both barrels of his shotgun at Henry.

Instinctively, Henry ducked and once again felt the splatter of lead shot against the front of his car. He pulled his foot off the accelerator, relaying his position to comms again – still trying to keep the fear and excitement out of his voice. He was told that a section patrol and a traffic car were en route, as was DI Fanshaw-Bayley from the scene of the robbery, and to keep the car in sight if possible, but not to engage the occupants in any way. Bit too late for that, Henry thought wryly.

The two-car chase shot back through Edenfield village, traffic coming towards them along the narrow road, being forced to swerve out of the way and slam on.

Henry clung on and, as the adrenaline flooded into his system, he did not once have the thought that he might be being foolhardy. Even though he had now been shot at twice, it never occurred to him to abandon the pursuit or that he might lose his life. All he wanted to do was catch criminals and this was one hell of a way to do it. Combining danger, adrenaline, excitement and screeching tyres. Things couldn't get much better and this was the beauty of a cop's life: the humdrum followed by the intense rush. If he could have thrown sex into the blend, it would have been perfect for him . . . though perhaps that could come later.

They cleared the built-up area in a haze of speed and at the traffic lights where Henry had been first shot at, the Rover bore left, forking towards Haslingden and dropping underneath the bypass towards a tiny settlement called Ewood Bridge.

Henry relayed the change of direction to comms, just as the Rover braked sharply almost at the bottom of the hill and came to a slithering stop.

Henry slammed on. He later reflected that he could have taken the opportunity to smash his car into the back of the Rover, but he didn't, and what happened, happened.

Once again the rear doors of the stolen car opened and the two still-masked men jumped out, wielding their shotguns.

Henry crunched his car into reverse, but the robbers sprinted up to him, one either side of the police car before he could put any distance between him and them. One blasted Henry's front nearside tyre which immediately deflated with a sickening lurch.

The man on Henry's side then took a further two steps up to the driver's door window and placed the muzzles of both barrels up against the glass at the level of Henry's head.

Then, Henry felt real terror for the first time.

He looked at those black side-by-side holes, like the eyes of death staring at him. Something inside him churned all his organs into a quivering mush, his heart, lungs, kidneys, the whole of the inside of his chest seemed to drain away.

Then the man swung the weapon like a pendulum and drove the barrels through the window, smashing crumbled glass all over Henry. He leaned in and forced the weapon into Henry's face.

'Your lucky day,' the man growled, his eyes burning behind the two holes in the balaclava. He reared away from Henry and ran back to the Rover with his accomplice. They bundled themselves back in and the car sped away down the hill.

Henry watched it, almost catatonic in fear.

Then his vital signs clicked back in. He breathed in and shook himself out of his trance, then exhaled very slowly and unsteadily, both hands gripping the steering wheel, pulling himself together. He answered his radio to a desperate-sounding comms, demanding his current position and situation report, which he relayed with a distinct tremor in his voice.

The two-tone brown Rover was never seen again – at least not in working order. It turned up in Salford, Greater Manchester, having been set alight on a recreation ground and burned to nothing more than a blistered shell, of no forensic use whatsoever.

It also transpired that the fire Henry had been driving to investigate on the industrial area was the getaway car from the robbery. By the time the fire brigade arrived, it too was just a blackened shell. That car had also been reported stolen in Manchester earlier that day.

Henry peered over the cracked rim of his mug of tea. The DI had taken a seat opposite, his wide frame only just supported by the plastic chair. The two men eyed each other suspiciously.

'What I don't get,' the DI said, as though it was painful to say, 'is why you were in Edenfield in the first place. If my memory serves me correct, you should've been on a checkpoint in Queens Square.'

'Ahh,' Henry said. Rumbled. This was the question he had thought he would not face – why did you leave your checkpoint?

'And remember this, PC Christie,' Fanshaw-Bayley waggled a stubby finger at him, 'you can't kid a kidder.'

'I got bored,' Henry admitted. He placed his mug down on the table. The two men were in the refreshment room on the first floor of the police station. Henry had stolen a teabag and liberated someone else's milk from the fridge to make himself the brew. He had wanted to sit down alone for ten minutes, just to pull himself together, to regroup.

He had charged into the incident without any thought, really, and it was only on reflection – and 'reflection' wasn't something the young Henry Christie did willingly – he realized he should have backed off. Maybe. Most car chases don't end up with a shotgun being stuffed up the nose and he would argue that he wasn't to know it would culminate like that.

'I got bored and went to check out any likely areas where they might dump the getaway car. I thought that if they were going to pass me at the checkpoint, they would have done so . . . so I went for a mooch.'

'Against explicit instructions.'

'If that car had driven past me at the checkpoint, the result would have been the same. I'd've gone after it.'

'There's a flaw there.'

'I know,' Henry admitted. 'The Rover wasn't the one they used as a getaway from the scene. It was the Vauxhall Ventora burned out down Holme Lane. But that car did not drive past me, which also means they had some local knowledge because they must have come off the main road and found their way to Holme Lane via the back roads – and that isn't a straight-forward journey. You need to know your way around to do that.'

Fanshaw-Bayley considered Henry. 'You think they have a local connection?'

'Probably.'

The DI nodded, then changed the subject. 'I've had all the top brass ringing me to see how you are.'

'I'm deeply moved. None of the calls seem to have found their way to me, though.'

'That's because I want any credit for catching these bad guys,' Fanshaw-Bayley said and blinked like a reptile. 'Not a jumped-up PC with attitude.'

'At least you're honest,' Henry said.

Fanshaw-Bayley smirked as though he had heard something mildly amusing. 'I'm a detective.'

Henry nodded knowingly. Some, not all, of the detectives he had so far encountered in his short career were not especially honest, other than in their quest for self-aggrandisement and plaudits. They seemed manipulative schemers only interested in themselves and were held in poor regard by other members of the constabulary. But the CID was a very powerful branch and had very influential people right up to the top of the organization who wielded a lot of clout. Henry wasn't sure how healthy that was for the force but he did know one thing – none of that made him want to be a detective any less. He was just certain that if he ever became one, he would be different. He would treat the uniform branch with respect, not disdain; he would share knowledge and information.

'Anyway, that said,' the DI continued, 'I can see a spark of something in you. I think you have a bit of work to do on your reasoning and your obvious dislike of being told what to do, but you've got a bit of an instinct in here.' He tapped his own forehead. 'So maybe one day you might make a jack . . . but you cannot go about raising your hackles to your superiors, nor can you go about *not* following orders. Get that?'

'Even if it means almost catching a violent gang?'

'Even if it means that . . . but, well done. It could have come out a lot worse, but you're still here to tell the tale. Not many of us have that sort of experience.'

'Not sure I want it again.'

'Sometimes it comes with the territory.'

Henry picked up his mug and sipped his tea, now going cold and unpalatable.

'Fancy a job?' Fanshaw-Bayley asked. 'Bit of a jolly?'

'Suppose so. What job?' he asked with caution at the sudden change of subject.

'Wait here . . . I'll get back to you.' He pushed himself up, but then leaned over Henry, who could smell garlic on his breath and see a crumb in his moustache. 'Do you know people call me "FB" for short?'

'I didn't – but it makes sense.'

'Fanshaw-Bayley being a bit of a mouthful?'

'Uh, yeah, suppose.'

'Wrong. Think about it.' He stood upright. 'Hang on here.'

Henry went to find another teabag – he had discovered somebody's secret stash at the back of a cupboard in the tiny galley kitchen – and made himself another mug, using someone else's milk also. Then he went to settle himself down on a settee in the lounge area where his intention was to savour his drink in silence, then get back out on the streets. He knew that the DI – 'FB' – had mustered a few cops and was getting them to do a house-to-house in Crawshawbooth, whilst Henry wanted to get down to the industrial area at the bottom of Holme Lane and do some of his own enquiries around there to see if anyone saw the Rover being parked there before the robbery, and then if anyone saw the actual getaway car, the Vauxhall Ventora, being dumped and torched there, and the transfer of the offenders from car to car.

Whatever plans FB had for him, Henry was determined to get as involved as possible in the hunt for this very bad set of villains ('villains' was a word he loved) because he knew that if they weren't stopped – and soon – someone was going to get in their way and get blown away. They had fired a handgun at the robbery scene, then fired a shotgun at a police officer, even though Henry realized they were really warning shots and he had been lucky that they were feeling lenient today. These guys were well down the violent-crime continuum and in the near future some poor sod, maybe a cop, would get his or her head blown off.

A fresh shimmer of dread ran through Henry's body as he re-lived the shotgun moment, his mind's eye visualizing the gun pressed against the window next to his head. It would only have taken a nervous jerk of the masked man's finger and Henry would have had no head to speak of.

He placed his mug of tea down, stood up and on very dithery legs he left the lounge, walked along the corridor and turned into the gents' toilet. He entered the single cubicle and locked the door.

Then he knelt down in front of the toilet bowl, hung his head over it and convulsed from his guts upwards.

Afterwards he washed his very pale face and returned to the lounge to continue drinking his tea.

When he next glanced up, WPC Jo Wade, the new-ish police-woman who had been working comms and the front desk earlier, came in, beaming, holding up a sheet of paper that had been ripped from the teleprinter.

Henry managed a sad half-smile in return.

She sat alongside him on the settee and declared, 'You and me are going to spend the night together.'

FIVE

Henry James Christie had been born and bred in East Lancashire and lived with his parents there until his very early teens before moving across to the Lancashire coast – Blackpool – for his father's job. He was still living there when he joined the police at nineteen.

In the 1970s the organization still had a much skewed, authoritarian view on how it treated its employees and had an unwritten policy that all new recruits should be posted as far away from their homes as possible. This could not be applied to every rookie cop, but where possible it was.

Therefore Henry's first posting was to Blackburn, thirty miles away. It made no sense, but it was a time when decisions made in the higher echelons of the force were never questioned or criticized.

It was believed it was the best thing for new officers to work in a completely strange and unfamiliar environment because there was less chance of them fraternizing or being abused by people they knew, nor could they ever be influenced by their own local knowledge.

It was completely ludicrous, of course, but it was a policy that was ruthlessly applied for many years.

So Henry – who considered himself a 'sandgrown 'un', as the denizens of Blackpool are known – found himself transported from the bright lights of the world's busiest holiday resort to dark satanic mill-land where, much to his surprise, he thoroughly enjoyed himself in the busiest town in Lancashire. What he didn't expect was to be then posted even further afield to Rossendale, which to him was then an unfamiliar area of green valleys, harsh moorland, derelict mills and unused railway lines and a population, half of which it was rumoured had never set foot outside the valley.

Whereas Henry had never set foot in it.

He still vividly recalled the morning he was told he was being posted to Rawtenstall. It was during his refs break on an early shift in Blackburn and his patrol sergeant came to sit next to him as he wolfed his full English breakfast in the station canteen. He could tell the sergeant was uncomfortable as he imparted the information that due to 'operational reasons' Henry was to be transferred with immediate effect.

'Rawtenstall?' he blurted. 'Where's that? And why . . . I've only just got here, really.'

The sergeant shrugged. Back then, young, single cops were fair game for transfers, and Henry fitted that bill. Rawtenstall was desperately short of staff for various reasons and he was just the officer to plug that gap.

After his breakfast – which stuck in his gullet – he went to find a map of the county to find out exactly where he was going, his head still in a mush from the news. Sitting in the comms room at Blackburn nick, he unfolded a map and stared unbelievingly at it until he pinpointed Rawtenstall and try as he might, he couldn't even begin to work out a route to the place, which seemed isolated, wild and a little scary. There didn't seem to be any main roads to it, although he was sure there would be.

He emerged pale-faced from comms, shell-shocked at his fate: to be cast into the wilderness where, he had been told, men were men and sheep were very cautious. And not only that, it was rumoured that because the sides of the valleys in that part of the world were so steep, the sheep had shorter legs on one side of their body than the other, just so they could balance on the gradients. They could not, however, turn to face the opposite direction or they would topple over.

Despite what the sergeant said about 'immediate effect', he had just over a month to get used to the idea, during which time he drove to Rawtenstall a few times so he could get the location fixed in his head.

In that time he also had to find new lodgings – or 'digs' – as it would be impractical to travel every day from Blackburn, especially in winter when the journey could be treacherous – plus Henry didn't like having to travel too far to work. He was given a few addresses to check out and settled on a landlady who lived in a terraced house in Rawtenstall. She reminded Henry of the brassy landlady in the film *Get Carter* who took in and then screwed the Michael Caine character. Henry harboured hopes of the same thing happening to him, being taken in by an older, experienced woman, but it never materialized. Their relationship was purely professional and just a bit chilly. He lived in a single bedroom, bathroom down the hall, breakfast and tea provided with access to the living room to watch TV. There were strict rules on hours and visits by members of the opposite sex, which Henry broke regularly.

He didn't last long there, mainly because the landlady caught him in bed one afternoon, trying to have sex as silently as possible with a policewoman he had sneaked in. He was given a month's notice.

This suited Henry because he ended up living in a rented terraced house with another bobby and his life became much more bearable and liberated, but very unstructured, with the exception of work.

Also, the shock of being posted somewhere he had never heard of soon wore off.

He was ultimately determined to leave the valley for busier police pastures but he did realize the potential of the place as a learning environment, because unlike Blackburn, where backup was never far away, in the valley an officer usually operated alone. It was here he learned how to be a cop, learned to apply law and procedure, learned how to deal with and talk to the public and started to develop his skills as a detective, his ultimate goal.

This was how he had managed to wangle a secondment as a CID aide to Blackburn, but had fallen foul of a DI who kicked him back to Rossendale, an incident that frustrated the hell out of him as he thought it might be a nail in the coffin of his career as a detective.

One thing he knew for certain was that he was starting from scratch and that he would have to remember to keep his mouth shut a bit more, not just declare UDI and do whatever he wanted.

FB was the ruler of the roost in Rossendale and Henry was bright enough to realize that getting him on his side was a good move, even if he already disliked and mistrusted him.

Henry knew that his own biggest problem was seeing things in black and white, right and wrong, and he was only really just becoming familiar with those murky shades between those ends of the continuum.

Not that that made it any easier for him to accept that Vladimir Kaminski was walking the streets when he should really be banged up facing a rape charge.

But Henry had to keep FB sweet – at least until he could fathom how to drag Kaminski back in and nail the bastard to the wall . . . judicially speaking.

In the meantime, he would just have to go with the flow and hope that nothing worse happened to Sally Lee. He also wanted to be involved in the hunt for the armed robbers who had scared him shitless – and that also meant keeping on FB's good side.

But he also knew he was constricted by doing his 'day job'. He had a specific area to police and whilst he had a lot of freedom in how he did it, he couldn't just go wandering off into Greater Manchester to make his own enquiries just because he felt like it.

Had he been a detective, things would have been different. They had much more freedom to follow things through, something else that appealed to him.

But he wasn't – yet.

One day, maybe . . . . So in the meantime he had to play the game by brown-nosing, being buoyant and positive about the dregs that FB might toss to him like a dog waiting for table scraps.

Such as this latest offering . . . which was why he was rushing from the police station to his rented house to grab a change of clothes and reflect on WPC Wade's suggestive remark about spending the night together.

The words had taken Henry aback. He had looked stupidly at her.

'What do you mean?'

She grinned teasingly, then raised her finely plucked eyebrows and said, 'On business.'

She waved the sheet of paper at him. Henry saw it was actually a message sheet ripped from the teleprinter. He made a grab for it, but she snatched it playfully away. 'Say please.'

'Please.' He held out his hand. He didn't feel like playing

games. His day, so far, had not gone well and he was feeling extremely grumpy.

She obviously considered toying with him but responded to the look in his eyes and gave him the message.

He took it and read. It was from the Kent police in Dover who had apprehended a young man about to board the Calais ferry, a lad who had been circulated as wanted for burglary in Rawtenstall.

'Jack Bowman,' Henry muttered. He knew of Bowman, one of the valley's most prolific burglars, who had been on the run for about a month.

'Mr Fanshaw-Bayley wants me and you to go down and pick him up. He's in custody, Dover nick,' Jo said energetically. 'Isn't it exciting?'

'Does he now?' Henry muttered, realizing that this prisoner escort trip must be the 'jolly' FB had referred to. Henry tried to stop his mouth from curling crookedly into a pissed-off snarl. He pretended to read the message again, but in reality he was trying to work out the logistics. The best part of a three hundred mile run down, three hundred back, probably six hours each way at best; it was mid-afternoon now so the journey would necessitate an overnight stay, probably in some shoddy bed-and-breakfast hellhole. On top of that he had a date tonight with his young lady friend, Kate. It was a newish relationship verging on serious and he didn't want to miss that. The prospect of a tedious journey from one end of the country to the other did not appeal in the slightest, even with Jo, who was evidently up for it.

'We could get down there, go out on the town,' she enthused. 'Pint or two, curry.'

'Have you ever been to Dover?' Henry asked grimly. 'It's not exactly Singapore.'

'No . . . anyway,' she burbled on, 'we need a change of clothes, and there's a car for us at group garage in Accrington. I've sorted it. And I've got some money from petty cash.'

'You've thought this through.'

Her eyes focused on his. 'Oh yeah,' she said huskily. Henry was convinced her pupils dilated with a rush of blood and despite himself, and the thought of the planned evening with his girlfriend, he too felt an inner rush that left his mouth dry. 'It's all arranged. I've even sorted the accommodation . . . separate rooms, obviously.'

'I need to speak to the DI.'

He stood up quickly and shot down the corridor to FB's office, the door which, as always, was closed. FB was not one of those bosses with an open-door policy. Henry rapped on it, then waited for the requisite countdown before FB called him in.

'You again?'

Henry flapped the teleprinter message. Not in FB's face, as he would have liked, but just in the air. 'Is this the job, boss?'

'Yes.'

'A prisoner escort?'

'It's a jolly, isn't it? And in some pretty company, too.'

'Not exactly my idea of a *job*, though,' Henry whined.

'It's a job that needs doing.'

'Can't disagree with that, but not by me. I finish my shift in half an hour and I've got plans for the evening.'

'Shelve 'em. You're a cop. Stuff like this comes with the territory.' FB waited for Henry's challenge. 'And it's a uniform job escorting prisoners.'

'Right . . . OK.'

'But there's a carrot in it for you: Jack Bowman. I've got evidence on him for three burglaries. I think he's committed about forty more.'

'I know that.'

'He's all yours,' FB said magnanimously. 'Get him back, get him to confess, test your interrogation skills . . . If nothing comes of it, just charge him with the three I can prove.'

Henry started to perk up. 'He's mine?'

'You get him, you have him. If you don't want to go, I'll find someone else willing. You could clear up a lot of crime here. Bowman's a one-man burglary machine. But if your social life . . .'

'I'm on it,' Henry snapped.

Now all he had to do was let Kate know that the job had come between them.

Henry's rented house was off a main road on a side street that led to a dead end. A very basic two-up, two-down terrace that had only recently had an inside toilet and bathroom and central heating installed. But it was adequate for two single, horny cops who did not crave great comfort, just a bed each, a TV in the lounge and a Chinese takeaway and good pub within walking distance.

Henry crashed through the front door and shot upstairs to the narrow landing where he was greeted by the wonderful sight of the very sleepy, rumpled landlady of the aforementioned pub emerging naked from his colleague's bedroom. She blinked at Henry through a very unkempt fringe of hair and smiled as his eyes opened so wide at the vision of her body, he thought they were likely to pop out on stalks.

'Hi, Henry,' she said thickly and turned into the bathroom, giving him a flash of her ample, dimpled bum.

Then she was gone.

'Lucky sod,' Henry mumbled and went into his bedroom at the back of the house. This consisted of a three-quarter-size bed with one bedside cabinet and a small wardrobe that he'd bought from a local DIY store and somehow assembled himself. The process of putting it together had taught him he wasn't cut out for do it yourself. He changed quickly into jeans and a shirt, then threw a change of underwear and socks into a soft zip-up bag, together with his toilet bag.

When he came back onto the landing, he heard the toilet flush, then the bathroom door opened and the landlady stepped out. She stood before him, naked and unashamed – and quite hairless – and after a saucy jiggle of her boobs disappeared back into the bedroom, giving Henry a second glance of her bottom, which he had one day hoped to grab. His colleague and housemate had got there first.

'I'm going to get one of those for myself one day,' he said under his breath, then went back downstairs and got into the marked police car he had helped himself to. Even though it was only a Mini Metro, there was no room to spin it round in the cobbled street and he had to reverse it all the way back onto the main road, then head back to the police station, worrying how he was going to explain it to Kate.

One thing for certain, his tale would not include the name Jo Wade.

*   *   *

Kate worked in a local insurance brokers, close enough to walk to from Rawtenstall nick, but Henry's courage evaporated on the drive back. He found a phone in an empty office, one from which he knew he could get an outside line by dialling 9, and called the brokerage.

'Valley Insurances,' a bright female voice answered: Kate Marsden, the girl Henry had met at the scene of a brutal murder. She had discovered the body of a missing girl whilst out walking her dog on the moors above Haslingden. Henry, and FB, had attended and it had been Henry's job to take the young lady's statement. She was fresh, gorgeous, and instantly took his breath and heart away.

That had been a few months ago and their relationship had deepened and was becoming long-term serious. Before meeting her Henry had played a big part in the vibrant single-cop scene in Rossendale, during which time he'd had many encounters and had often rolled into work in a morning after a night of boozing and debauchery, and could hardly keep his eyes open. Some of his dalliances had been with policewomen, but most had been with women he met on the pub/club scene in the valley, which for its size, was thriving.

Meeting Kate had curtailed these activities, mostly, but Henry knew he couldn't yet be trusted. Although he had done nothing to encourage the interest of WPC Jo Wade, he was pretty certain that a night away with her could easily lead to something silly.

Whilst the old part of him wanted that, at the same time, another newer, more mature part was beating him about the head and yelling, 'No, no, no.'

Henry's devil on one shoulder versus the angel on the other, a contest that would rule his entire life, although he did not know it at that moment.

All he did know was that he was falling in love with Kate, but yet his twenty-three-year-old testosterone still demanded to be unleashed on as many consenting females as possible.

'Hi, love, it's me,' Henry said down the phone.

'Hi, sweetie . . . and even from those four words I can tell it's bad news,' Kate said perceptively. Henry winced. *Even now she can read me like a book.* 'What is it?' she asked.

'I'm going to have to cancel tonight. Sorry,' he said feebly.

'Oh . . .'

'Er, something's come up and I have to go to Dover to pick up a prisoner. It's an overnighter. The DI says I have to. I don't want to,' he babbled unconvincingly, 'but I have to.'

'It's OK,' she said softly. 'I can't say I wasn't looking forward to tonight. It must be at least three days since we . . . y'know? Needless to say, you were on a promise.'

'I know, I know . . . I'm really sorry.'

'Who's going with you? I presume it'll take two of you?'

'Just . . . just one of the other PCs.'

'Anyone I know?' Kate had slowly started to meet a few of his work friends and colleagues.

'Er, no . . . new lad,' Henry fibbed through gritted teeth. *Why don't I just tell her?* he berated himself.

'When are you setting off?'

'About now.'

'OK . . . Henry?' Kate started cautiously. 'Will this sort of thing happen a lot? You know, if we stay together? Like I hope we will.'

'I hope not, but it sort of goes with the job.'

'Yeah, I know.' There was a heavy silence on the line. 'Are we going to stay together?' she asked.

'Don't see why not.'

'What sort of answer is that?'

'Not a good one . . . I meant, yes, we will stay together. For definite.'

He heard her sigh and he knew he should have told her there and then that he loved her. He knew it was what she wanted to hear, and what he wanted to declare . . . but that old devil on his shoulder was prodding him with a very fiery red trident.

'I'll ring you when I get to Dover.'

'OK.' She sounded wistful.

'I was wondering where you'd got to . . .'

Henry spun at the voice. WPC Wade had found him and entered the room where he was making the call. He clamped his left hand down on the receiver and looked at her leaning against the door jamb, like a vamp. She had also been home to change and was now wearing tight-fitting jeans and a low-cut blouse.

'Shh,' he mouthed silently to her, horror on his face, his head shaking frantically.

'Oops, sorry,' she pouted.

Henry gave her a death stare and flicked his fingers at her in a 'go away' gesture.

'Who was that?' Kate asked.

'No one . . . just someone . . . telling me to get my skates on. I need to pick up a car from Accrington and drop one off.'

'Mm, OK . . . anything else?'

Henry thought he could have told her about being shot at and having lost a rapist but decided that stuff could wait. 'No . . . I should be back mid-afternoon tomorrow, but then I've got to interview the prisoner . . . so can we pick up tomorrow night?'

'Yeah, suppose.' Kate's voice had lost all enthusiasm.

Feeling empty and dishonest, Henry hung up and stared at the phone for a moment before turning his head slowly back to the door where Jo was still to be seen.

'Are we good to go?'

Henry nodded, wondering if he would be coming back as a single man again. 'Bugger,' he said and rose slowly.

SIX

After a scenes of crime officer had found some shotgun pellets embedded in the bodywork of the Cavalier and dug a few out as evidence, then taken a series of photographs of the wounded car, Henry Sellotaped a plastic carrier bag over the smashed driver's door window then he and Jo jumped in and drove over to the garage at Accrington police station. Here they left the Cavalier and its shot-damaged tyre to be repaired – Henry guessing it would be mainly a case of body filler and touch-up paint but that a new tyre would have to be bought. Then, having tossed their overnight gear into the boot of their replacement car, an older ex-Task Force Vauxhall Victor, now part of the divisional pool of vehicles, they discovered it needed to be refuelled, the screenwash needed completely refilling and engine oil was just a memory for the dipstick. In other words, the usual scenario for a police car.

Those problems sorted, including making up a mileage book that hadn't seen an entry for over a week, the last reading in it almost a thousand miles less than was on the odometer, they began their journey south, with Henry at the wheel.

Progress was slow, the main motorways, the M6 and M1, being extremely busy.

They made one stop at Birmingham, then hit the London rush hour at the worst time imaginable: 6.00pm. It took an hour and a half to circumnavigate the capital before dropping down into Kent and driving into Dover just before 9pm. Henry had done all the driving, but he didn't mind because he could claim that concentrating on the road was the reason for not saying too much. Jo also did not say too much, but sat contentedly in the front passenger seat, watching the world whizz by. Henry was aware that she kept taking sneaky glances at him, but he also had a few peeks at her, too.

The first port of call was to Dover police station, just to introduce themselves, announce their arrival and make arrangements for the prisoner pick-up next morning. Once that was done they got directions to their bed and breakfast accommodation, which they found quite easily, and booked in.

As promised, the rooms were separate – but adjacent. There was no en-suite bathroom or toilet, these facilities being across the hallway. It was a fairly dank and dingy establishment and Henry was glad he would only be spending one night in it. Once they had settled in, they went out for some food and beer.

The evening was still reasonably pleasant and warm. The strong sea-smell of the English Channel invaded Henry's nostrils, but he thought it was a good aroma. They strolled down the main street, identified a Chinese restaurant that would do very nicely, but decided on a drink first and easily found a decent pub in which they bought a pint of lager each. Henry paid.

It was quiet and they found a couple of chairs by the bow window and sat opposite each other across a beaten copper-topped table.

Henry raised his glass and they chinked.

'Cheers.'

He took a long draught, his throat dry after the long drive. Jo took a long drink, too.

The beer had an instant effect.

Henry smiled. Jo smiled back. He said, 'Made it.'

'That's the first time I've seen you smile all day.'

Henry blew out his cheeks. 'Lost a good prisoner, got shot at, and I'm not altogether certain that I'll be going back to a warm reception from my girlfriend.'

'Quite a day. How are you feeling?'

Henry pouted and shrugged. 'Dunno, really. Bit stressed.'

'I'd be a wreck,' Jo said. 'Especially if someone blasted a shotgun at me. It was bad enough in comms. You must be quite brave . . . and cool. I was listening to you transmitting during the car chase. I'd've been shouting and screaming!' She lifted her beer to her mouth and looked at Henry across the top of the glass, her eyes moist and sparkling.

He shrugged modestly, incapable of denying her assessment of him.

'What did it feel like, to have a gun pointed at you?'

'Scary, actually. I could easily have wet myself.'

'But you didn't.'

'No, I didn't.' Somehow he could not bring himself to tell her about how he had vomited his fear.

'Brave,' she confirmed.

'Or stupid.'

'No, brave,' she insisted.

'Thank you.' Henry looked her in the eye, knowing this was a mating ritual.

'Have you told your girlfriend about your adventures?'

'Not yet.'

'She'll be impressed.'

'Not so sure.' He took another sip of his beer and heard his stomach rumble. It was only then he realized that the last meal he'd eaten was breakfast. 'I need some food down me.'

The Chinese was average but OK. Hot and sour soup followed by sweet and sour chicken for Henry, won-ton soup and king prawn chop suey for Jo, accompanied by more beer and a loosening of the conversation, which started innocently enough talking about themselves, asking about each other, but then started to disintegrate little by little into suggestiveness and innuendo.

After the meal they rolled back to the pub for a couple more pints before closing time.

Henry used the public payphone in the toilet corridor to call Kate, but wished he hadn't. She began pleasantly but when she clocked that Henry was talking with four pints down him and then he let slip he was accompanied by a 'she', Kate hung up leaving him staring at a dead telephone.

At which point Jo, who had just visited the ladies', sidled past and saw the expression of grief on his face.

She came up close. 'What's the matter?'

'Hung up,' he said desolately. 'She hung up.' He slammed the receiver back onto its cradle and turned to Jo who was standing just inches away, looking up at him, lips slightly parted. She had reapplied her lipstick and her lips looked very red and shiny.

'You know, what happens in Dover, stays in Dover. Yeah?' she said.

''Scuse me.' A large man pushed his way between them,

heading towards the toilets. They stepped apart to allow him through, their eyes staying firmly locked onto one another's.

'Let's get a nightcap,' Henry suggested.

'No, no, no,' she said. 'Not before this.' She moved right up to him, slid a hand behind his neck, stood on tiptoe and eased his face towards hers, their lips crushing together, sending a surge of electricity shooting through him as she virtually plastered herself to him. Henry instantly grew hard as his hands cupped her face and he worked his tongue into her mouth.

They broke apart, gasping.

'I've wanted to kiss you ever since I first saw you, Henry. Been watching you for ages, but you've never noticed me, have you?'

Henry's response stuck in his throat.

'And now I want to . . . you know?' she said huskily.

'Yeah, I know . . . let's pass on the nightcap.'

It was the screeching of the seagulls that woke Henry. He had a splitting headache and a left arm very much dead to the world as it was trapped under Jo's neck. For a moment he thought he was pinned under a boulder and he might have to saw it off. He eased it free, sat up on the edge of the narrow bed, placing a foot on the empty bottle of Asti that had appeared like magic from Jo's luggage last night (together with fresh strawberries, much to his amazement). A great deal of the wine had been lost or spilled whilst dribbling it from mouth to mouth, or when, as Henry recalled vividly, Jo had filled her mouth with it and then taken him in there too, almost making him leap to the ceiling as the amazing combination of her tongue and the wine bubbles sent a wave of painful ecstasy right through his core. He had howled with pleasure and nearly choked on a strawberry.

He massaged the blood flow back into his arm, feeling the silent crackle of painful pins and needles as sensation returned to his fingertips.

His balance wasn't quite there when he stood up and he staggered slightly, having to keep upright with the help of the wall. He found a pair of underpants that had been discarded with delight by Jo quite early on in the proceedings, and put them on, having to do a balancing jig at the same time. He didn't realize, or care, that they were on inside-out. All he wanted was to pee, drink some cold water and find some paracetamol tablets from somewhere.

He took a moment to look at Jo, still sleeping undisturbed, unable to believe they had performed such acrobatic and energetic moves in such a small area without crashing off or hurting themselves.

They had, he concluded, fucked each other's brains out.

Unable to shake his delicate head at the memory just in case it fell off, he walked heavy-footed out of the bedroom and over to the toilet across the corridor. Then he went to the separate bathroom where he had a lukewarm shower with his eyes permanently squinting because his head felt as if an axe was embedded in it.

After using a hand towel to dry himself – remembering too late that he'd left his bath towel in the bedroom – he scuttled back to find Jo still sleeping.

Just enough time, he thought, to slide in alongside her. Which he did, after kicking off his inside-out underpants. She murmured something dreamily and without seeming to awaken and without opening her eyes, she rolled on top of him and guided him deep inside her, then started to move languorously above him.

Henry hurled himself out of bed like he'd been prodded by a red-hot poker. His sex- and booze-blurred mind had assumed it was still early, but a glance and a forced focus at his digital watch on the floor beside the bed told him how very wrong he was. 'C'mon, c'mon, get moving,' he said, scrambling around naked for his underwear. 'We're late, we're late.'

Jo had fallen back to sleep and she looked drowsily at him, hardly able to open her eyelids. 'Wha . . .?'

'It's nearly ten . . . crimes! We said we'd collect him at nine.'

'It'll be all right. He's not going anywhere, is he?' She sighed, flopped back onto the bed and covered her head with a pillow.

'It won't be right,' Henry said, pulling a scrunched-up shirt out of his bag and thrusting his arms into it. He hated being late and he also hated not keeping his promises.

'We'll tell 'em we got unavoidably delayed,' Jo said from under the pillow.

'Doing what, exactly?'

She pulled the pillow down and gave Henry a sultry grin. 'You know what.'

'Yeah, I do.' He took a pace over to the bed and ripped the sheets off her, stopping suddenly as he took in her nakedness. His lower jaw sagged and his mouth popped open at the vision. For a moment he was entranced – and she knew it.

'Shit . . . you'll get me in trouble,' he said, and reached for his jeans. 'Come on, we've got a prisoner to take up north.'

'He's been ready an hour . . . and a half,' the dour station sergeant at Dover nick said as he took in the faces of the two Lancashire officers. 'We thought you'd gone home without him.'

'Big apologies,' Henry stammered, not really knowing what to say. 'It was a watch issue.' He held out his left arm and waggled his wrist. 'It stopped for some reason,' he lied.

The sergeant looked as though he was going to say something but instead his eyes simply played over the two shamefaced PCs and the corners of his mouth turned down cynically, knowingly. He was good at simple maths, easily calculating one plus one. He shook his head sadly and beckoned them through to the cell complex. They walked past a holding cage in which sat the lone figure of Jack Bowman, prolific burglar from the valley. All the paperwork was ready, as was Bowman's property, which Henry checked, signed for and took possession of. He went back to the holding cage.

'Mornin', Jack,' Henry said, starting to wake up. At last. He let his handcuffs dangle off his finger.

Bowman was a sour-eyed lad in his late teens, rake-thin like all good burglars should be, with the build of a whippet. Not very tall, with a pinched face that displayed no hint of compromise. Henry, who kept abreast of as many villains as possible, knew that Bowman was one of the numerous offspring of the Bowman clan who inhabited the Hall Carr estate in Rawtenstall. The Bowmans were a state-funded enterprise and supplemented their all too generous hand-outs by means of small-time, but large-scale, volume crime. Hence they were experts at breaking into homes and cars and were great at shoplifting, which they had off to a fine art. Jack was probably the best burglar in the valley, moving around like a shadow and entering people's homes by a number of methods depending on the circumstances. He was real nifty with a fishing rod and hook through letter boxes, and was also a great opportunist having burgled many homes by simply slipping in through open doors. He was also known for breaking and entering by the traditional route – removing panes of glass from ground-floor windows and climbing through. He was also good at shimmying up drainpipes. Sometimes, if he didn't break the glass in windows, he would replace it on leaving and occasionally victims couldn't even work out how their property had been violated – until a gust of wind blew the glass out and it smashed.

In fact, he was an all-round burglar, and was rarely caught.

Bowman stood up, saying nothing, and passed his hands clasped together through the bars of the holding cage for Henry to ratchet the cuffs onto his wrists.

'Not too tight?' Bowman looked disinterestedly at Henry. 'I'll take that as a no,' Henry said. 'All set for a long journey? Done your number one and two?'

'I'll expect a comfort break somewhere.' Bowman broke his silence.

'We'll see. Depends, doesn't it?'

'On what?'

'Attitude and behaviour, and if I think I can trust you.' Henry's face was only a foot away from Bowman's. He lowered his voice and tried to sound menacing. 'You fuck about, I'll put another pair of cuffs on you, OK? If we do stop and you try anything daft, I'll flatten you and that's a promise. OK? So just sit back and enjoy the ride and we'll stay amicable.'

Bowman kept his eyes on Henry's but the expression on his face didn't change.

Henry manoeuvred Bowman into the back of the Vauxhall so he was sitting behind the front passenger, putting a bit of a diagonal gap between prisoner and driver. There was nothing worse than a prisoner trying to strangle the driver, it made for all sorts of problems. Then he took the handcuff off Bowman's right wrist and looped it around the elbow rest on the door so that the prisoner was effectively cuffed by his left hand to the car. It wasn't the most secure of fixtures because the car wasn't built for transporting prisoners and a good, concerted yank would probably be enough to break the armrest off, but it would have to do. It would keep him in one place and if he started anything it would give Henry and Jo a bit of time to react. The alternative was to keep his hands cuffed in front of him, but that would have given him freedom to move and maybe attack the officers. It would also have meant that the non-driving escort would have to sit in the back with him and neither Henry nor Jo wanted that.

Transporting bodies in vehicles not made or adapted for the task was always a risky business, which was why Henry re-affirmed his promise to Bowman as he engaged the child lock and closed the door.

'You behave and we'll be fine, OK?'

Bowman closed his eyes disdainfully and wriggled himself comfortable.

'What do you reckon?' Jo asked Henry as they stood by the car.

'Nothing's perfect. Just keep an eye on him. There's a mirror in the sun visor on your side, so keep looking at him, watch what he's up to. It'll probably be all right. Worst he can do is run off, I suppose.'

'Or strangle you on the motorway and we can have a multi-car pile-up.'

'There is that.'

'I'm famished, by the way,' Jo said.

'Ditto.' They had missed breakfast because of their late start.

'And thirsty. I need a coffee.'

Henry nodded. 'There's a cafe across the road. You want to get a couple of bacon sarnies and brews from it? Then we'll set off.'

'It's a plan. What about boyo?' Jo nodded towards Bowman.

'Let's keep him sweet.' Henry leaned in the car and asked if he wanted anything, offering what they were having.

Bowman's expression changed for the first time – to one of shock. 'You're offering me something?'

'Bacon butty and a brew,' Henry confirmed. 'On us.'

'That would be fantastic. The food in there' – he jerked his free thumb at the police station – 'is shit.'

'OK, we eat it here, then get going.'

Jo bought the food and they had a little picnic in the back yard of the police station. The two officers stood by or leaned on the car, enjoying the revitalizing effect of the food and drink on their systems.

'Our first breakfast together, eh?' Jo remarked.

Trying not to show that he nearly choked on his food, Henry gave her a crooked smile and quickly threw a mouthful of coffee down his throat.

'Are we an item now?' she enquired.

That question, too, was asked as a mixture of bacon and bread was about to pass into Henry's throat. Once more he managed to avoid spluttering it all over her. He took a swig of coffee, looked at her and said, 'No,' quietly. He saw her face harden.

'What about last night?' she hissed dangerously.

Another question, bowled so low that it turned Henry's stomach. 'No,' he said again. 'You said . . .' he spluttered.

Jo took over. 'What happens in Dover stays in Dover?'

'Yeah, exactly,' he said, as if he had just proved a point of law.

'That was before it happened.'

'So what changed?'

'Us. You. Me. I didn't expect . . .' Her voice trailed off whimsically. 'It was wonderful, wasn't it?'

'Uh – yeah.' Henry's eyes shot back and forth like a man standing before a firing squad.

'So we've got a thing, yeah?'

'Look. This isn't the time or place to talk about this,' Henry said quietly. 'We've got a prisoner to transport three hundred miles. Let's just get that over with, shall we?'

Her glare could have frozen hell at one end of the spectrum or fired up Vesuvius for a surprise eruption at the other, and Henry had a sudden hollowness in his legs which, ironically, both also felt like lead weights. He also felt like vomiting up his newly eaten breakfast.

'OK,' she clipped, and the one word sent a tremor of apprehension through him.

But yet, he thought as he climbed into the driver's seat, what is the problem here? He tried to rationalize it with his male brain whilst reversing and then negotiating the tight yard before nosing out on the street.

He was young and single. OK, he might be seeing someone, but the bottom line was that he *was* single and in theory could see anyone he chose. That was his right as a hot-blooded male. As it was Jo's right as a single, horny female. And, he believed, she couldn't expect anything more from him than a one-off one-night stand of passion. It had been a no-strings agreement, so what did she expect? An engagement ring? These things happened. Get a grip, girl.

These thoughts swarmed through his mind as he headed towards London, intending to loop around the south-west of the city and join the M1 north.

From a logical, objective viewpoint, there was no case to answer.

He was seeing Kate, but they'd made no actual pledges to each other, so he was free and all he'd wanted from Jo was a bit of fun near the white cliffs of Dover and as nice a girl as she was, and great fun in bed, Henry knew she wasn't the girl for him.

But yet, what was really playing on his mind was his deep regret in having spent the night with her . . . and try as he might he could not quite finger the reason why he was feeling the way he did.

By the time he linked up with the M1, none of the occupants in the car had said anything. The prisoner was dozing and Jo, who had started the journey with her arms folded crossly under her bosom and her sun visor angled down so she could watch Bowman, had also fallen asleep. Henry was grateful for the peace and quiet.

Progress was slow and unspectacular on the M1, but Henry was aware that he needed to pull into a service area soon to refuel because he'd neglected to do so in Dover and the gauge was hovering in the red. He also needed to visit the loo.

Jo had surfaced from her slumbers, glancing occasionally but silently at Henry, fidgeting on her seat.

Bowman, too, was now awake. 'I need a piss, maybe take a shit, too,' he declared.

Henry saw Jo smirk.

Toilet breaks were of course another problem for a long-distance escort. These were the vulnerable moments, the logistics of taking a prisoner to a public toilet. So far the journey had been safe and self-contained, but once Henry drew onto a motorway service area, it was a whole different scenario. He had to allow Bowman to use the toilet, but how he did it was another thing.

Once they stepped into the public areas, Henry would prefer to be handcuffed to Bowman, but that made a toilet visit very unpleasant for both men. If Bowman insisted that he had to take a shit, there was no way Henry could be cuffed to him anyway. He would have to be released and Henry would have to stand guard outside the cubicle like a lemon as the prisoner performed and no doubt messed about, too. None of the scenarios appealed. The possibility of an escape was very real.

They came off at the next service area.

Henry stopped as close as he could to the building that incorporated the shops, cafe and toilets.

'OK, we do it this way,' he began. 'I go to the loo, leaving you two in the car. When I get back, you can go if you need to,' he nodded at Jo. 'Then we'll both take Mr Bowman. You wait outside the toilets and I'll keep watch on him inside . . . if it all goes to plan and you behave,' Henry said to Bowman, 'then we'll have a brew in the cafe, OK?'

The passengers nodded.

Henry went first, then came back to the car. Jo then went and returned a short while later. During her absence, Henry reiterated his warning to Bowman and reminded him of his threat to flatten him if he did a runner. He forced Bowman to acknowledge what was being said to him.

'I heard you,' he said sullenly to Henry's badgering.

'Well think on,' Henry said, glancing across the car park to see Jo on her way back.

He released the cuff encircling the elbow rest and closed it around Bowman's free wrist so that his hands were cuffed in front of him. Then, with a cop either side of him and Henry also keeping a firm grip on Bowman's upper arm, they walked into the services. Jo stayed outside the men's and Henry steered the young man in.

'Still want a shit?' Henry asked.

Bowman nodded. Henry found a vacant cubicle and reversed the prisoner into it, removing the cuffs out of sight of the other men using the facilities.

'Remember what I said,' Henry said and checked the cubicle.

'Yep.'

Henry backed out and Bowman closed the door, making Henry frown as he heard the latch slide into place. His prisoner was now behind a locked door, albeit a fairly flimsy one with a gap at the bottom and the top, although it was the gaps on the walls inside that bothered Henry. Bowman was built with a skeleton as flexible as a house mouse, able to squeeze through the tightest of gaps, and Henry knew he was easily capable of slipping under the lower gap or climbing over the higher one and making a break for freedom.

He just didn't trust him.

With this in mind, Henry stepped right back across the toilets to the wall opposite so that, with not too much effort, or bending or going on tiptoes, he could see Bowman's feet, even if what he was doing did attract a lot of peculiar stares from other men in the loo.

The prisoner's feet stayed where they were, firmly planted down in front of the toilet with his jeans dropped around his ankles, so although it seemed he wasn't going to try anything, Henry stayed vigilant. Losing a prisoner was not on his agenda, not something he could ever live down.

Henry angled his head and dipped his knees to look under the door.

Bowman's feet were not there.

Henry gasped, shot across the short distance that separated him from the toilet door and crashed the whole weight of his body against it. It didn't give, so he took a step back, lifted his right foot and flat-footed the door at the locking bolt. One very hard kick sent the door crashing back on its hinges, breaking the slim bolt and revealing the toilet cubicle. And the fact that Bowman was still there sitting on the toilet, having pulled up his jeans and then raised his feet a few inches off the floor just to make Henry believe he'd gone. He smirked at Henry, the second person to smirk at him in a matter of minutes, and making Henry start to feel paranoid, as though he was the butt of other people's silent jokes.

'What the fuck d'you think you're playing at, shit head?' Henry growled.

'Don't know what you mean.' Bowman laughed in Henry's face.

Henry grabbed his jacket front, lifted him off the toilet seat and rammed him backwards against the cistern and back wall of the cubicle. 'I'll treat you right and nice, Mr Bowman, but don't you fuck with me in return. I'm not in any mood for it, OK?'

'Why? That policewoman you shagged last night givin' you a hard time?' Bowman's smirk remained stuck on his face, not remotely intimidated by Henry's show of strength. 'I got ears, I heard what she said. Good fuck, was she?'

Without a word Henry spun Bowman around, able to lift, turn and manipulate his light body easily, and handcuffed him again, this time with his hands behind his back. He clicked the ratchets tight on his wrists, so they dug sharply into his skin. Then he grabbed the lad's jacket in his right fist, stepped back out of the cubicle and virtually ran him out of the toilets, Bowman's feet tiptoeing to keep his balance. He pushed him out into the main concourse, past a startled Jo and quite a few members of the public.

Jo dropped into step at Henry's shoulder, unquestioning and accepting immediately that something had gone on in the toilets.

Henry frog-marched Bowman out onto the car park and forced him into the back seat of the police car, leaving his hands still tied behind his back, chucking him sprawling across the seat, then slamming the door on him. Bowman laid out on his back and started to pound the car window with the bottom of his feet and scream obscenities.

Yanking the door open again and doing his best to avoid the kicking feet, Henry grappled with him, grabbed his jacket again and heaved him upright, held him tight and spoke into his ear.

He was not even breathing heavily when he growled, 'Easy or hard? Easy is as has been, hard is me sat in the back seat with you for the rest of the journey with you in a head lock which I'll tighten as and when necessary. Your choice, little boy.'

Bowman, gasping from the adrenaline rush and exertion, stared furiously ahead, nostrils flaring.

'We can be friends or we can be enemies. I personally don't give a rat's arse, cos when you get back, you'll be locked in a cell and I'll be going home.'

Henry waited for an answer.

All the while, Jo watched on in open-mouthed amazement.

'I want a fag,' Bowman said.

'Not the answer I was looking for. Behave or not behave – that is the question.'

'Behave,' he muttered grudgingly.

'Lie down on your face,' Henry said and pushed him across the seat. Henry then released his right hand from the cuffs, lifted him around and secured him back to the elbow rest on the car door.

'Fag?' Bowman said hopefully. 'In my property?'

A couple of minutes later Henry had rolled the back window down and Bowman was smoking, happily exhaling the smoke out of the window.

Henry still hadn't explained a thing to Jo. He straightened up and looked at her. 'Brew? We'll have it out here instead of in the cafe.'

'Yeah, suppose so,' she said, baffled. 'When exactly are you going to tell me what's going on? What happened in there?'.

'He lifted his feet up,' Henry said, having now regained full control of his emotions.

'He what?' Her face screwed up with incredulity.

'He lifted his feet up and he shouldn't have done and he knows he shouldn't have done, but now we're both simpatico, as you might say.'

'Eh?'

'Just go with it and keep an eye on the little twat while I go get us some brews. Tea? Coffee? Sugar? Milk?'

SEVEN

Somewhere on the M6 between junctions seventeen and eighteen they hit a traffic-stopping tailback. Because there was no radio of any description in the car, police or otherwise, they were cocooned in a tiny bubble of incommunicado, no way to contact the outside world and no way of telling if the hold-up was because of an accident or just a phantom traffic jam, a phenomenon that was becoming increasingly common on British motorways as the volume of traffic continued to rise.

Whatever the cause, they were stuck in the middle of three thick lanes of motor vehicles nose-to-tail inching slowly forwards, but mostly static.

Henry had been at the wheel for almost four hours and was beginning to feel drained. His eyes were gritty and as he sat there only three feet away from the car in front, his chin dipped forwards, but he jerked himself back awake, shook his head and rubbed his sandpaper-like eyes.

Alongside him, Jo, having done her best to stay awake, was now gone, her head lolled forwards, her chin implanted on her chest.

Henry glanced into the rear-view mirror at Bowman. He sat with his head tilted back, eyes closed, apparently dozing.

Since leaving the motorway services Henry had attempted to get Bowman to talk about himself, his offences and why he was in Dover about to board a ferry for France.

His questions remained unanswered by a sullen prisoner.

Henry had given up, content to wait for his time in the interview room, and silence reigned in the car, punctuated only by sidelong glances shot from Jo to him that, whilst noiseless, said many, many uncomfortable things . . . up until the point at which sleep overpowered her.

'Shit,' Henry breathed and rolled his window down a few inches to get some gulps of fresh air, which was not actually fresh at all, was mostly exhaust fumes. He wound the window back up, infuriated.

The traffic had come to a complete standstill. Henry thought it must be an accident rather than just volume of cars.

His mind drifted back to his personal predicament.

He was coming to a very prickly conclusion.

The fact was, and although he knew it was cheesy, when he thought of Kate, his mouth dried up and his heart raced; then when he actually, physically saw her and came into contact with her, something overcame him that he had trouble describing, something overwhelming.

But why?

She was a straightforward girl, as beautiful as anything, but with a little, slightly crooked nose and lovely teeth, lips to die for and a body he didn't seem to be able to get enough of – even six months down the line. He couldn't wait to bed her at every opportunity – and she him. So it was a mutual lust and attraction, although for the life of him he couldn't even begin to work out what she saw in him: flaky, unreliable, immature, often stupid. A daft lad who didn't know on which side his bread was buttered.

His forehead furrowed deeply.

It wasn't just the sex, though – as wonderful as it was. It was her whole being, her aura, her personality; it seemed to lasso him and drag him in. Her bounce, her forthrightness, her simplicity and lack of guile.

He groaned and closed his eyes, sighed deeply, as confused as hell. Why was it all so complicated and why did he still want to sleep with any female who would have him?

'Can I open this window a touch?' Bowman asked politely. Henry glanced over his shoulder. 'Inch or two? Bit of fresh air. It's stifling in here.'

'Just a crack,' Henry said, 'that's all.'

Jo stirred and looked sleepily at him, reminding him guiltily of seeing her naked first thing this morning in a grotty bedroom in a Dover B&B. He avoided her eyes and Bowman opened his window. At first it opened slowly, just an inch as he had requested.

Then there was a blur of movement as he wound the window down quickly, as far as he could. It would only open halfway for child-safety reasons, but if a child wanted to get out of the car and was big and savvy, even if the child locks were on he could reach out and opening the door by grabbing the outer handle – which is exactly what Bowman did.

The window opened halfway. He twisted and reached through with his right arm, flipped up the handle, and the door was open. In a flurry he was gone, legging it across the motorway, vaulting over the crash barrier and disappearing into a field before either Henry or Jo could react.

All Henry could see was the pair of handcuffs dangling uselessly from the elbow rest, the door open, the prisoner gone.

And all he could feel was a terrible sense of dread and stupidity.

Silence.

Detective Inspector Fanshaw-Bayley's eyes played mercilessly over the two forlorn figures parading in front of him in his office. Both had been required to change back into uniform.

More silence.

It was like a deadly, psychological weapon.

FB was seated behind his desk, saying nothing. Henry and Jo were standing opposite, heads bowed in shame, waiting for the storm that would surely come. The fourth in a series of off-the-scale bollockings that the two had endured. One from a sergeant, one from a uniformed inspector, one from the sub-divisional chief inspector. They had been brow-beaten to death.

FB spoke at last. 'So let me get this right . . . You allowed . . . *allowed* . . . a prisoner to escape from your lawful custody? Somehow, this prisoner, who you had handcuffed to a car door, managed to get his hand out of the cuff, open a window – which you said he could do, PC Christie – reach through and open the door and escape across a busy motorway. Hm. And on top of that, neither one of you even bothered to chase him. Is that about the long and short of it?'

'It would have been too dangerous to chase . . .' Henry began, but was stopped by FB's instantly raised hand.

'Don't want to hear crap . . . Is that the long and short of it, is what I asked?'

'Pretty much, sir,' Henry mumbled, demoralized.

A clacking sound came from FB's mouth as his tongue moved around, like he tasted something bitter in there.

More silence then. Just the sound of FB's breathing.

'So how did it happen?' he asked.

Neither offender had an answer to that.

But FB did. 'Gross negligence is how.' Henry opened his mouth to protest. FB held up a warning finger. 'Gross negligence,' he restated, twisting the skewer. 'A complete disregard for procedure. How, tell me, how come you were both sitting in the front of the car? Did you think this was a fucking day trip to Blackpool? Some bloody social outing?'

FB's rising rage was visible in the way his large body was starting to tremble and audible in the intensifying tone of his voice.

'Surely to God, one of you should have been sitting alongside the prisoner to ensure something like this didn't happen? Would that not have been the sensible thing to do?'

'Yes, boss,' Henry said. FB's eyes glowered chillingly at him.

'Judgement,' FB said, almost whimsically. 'Severe lack of judgement and professionalism.' His head sagged despairingly, then rose again, his eyes once more locking onto Henry. 'And you, being the senior officer, shall shoulder all of the blame – do I make myself clear? You' – he snapped, his head jerking towards Jo, who visibly jumped, 'get out.'

'Sorry, sir?' She was unable to believe her ears.

'Get out,' he said slowly. 'One very big lesson learned, missy.'

'Yes sir, sorry sir,' she squeaked, glanced compassionately at Henry, then turned and fled from the DI's office.

Leaving Henry and FB together.

FB leaned back in his chair, exhaled long and slow, his eyes constantly playing over Henry contemptuously.

'A lot of people of very high rank are going to be queuing up to shout very loudly at you, PC Christie.'

'I know. It's already started.'

'How does it feel?'

'Horrible.'

'Good – it should. This is fucking basic stuff. You should've been on the ball with this lad . . . I mean, Christ . . . he was trying to get out of the country. Stands to reason he didn't want to come back here, doesn't it? If he got a chance he was going to do a runner, wasn't he? Did you need that spelling out? Prisoners run away if they can.'

'Yes, sir.'

'So how did it happen?'

'I mustn't have fastened the cuff tight enough and he managed to squeeze his left hand out of it . . . left some skin on the metal . . . must have done it when he knew we weren't looking.'

'Or were snoozing.'

'No one snoozed, sir. I just got complacent. Nobody's fault but mine.'

'Very bold, PC Christie.'

'Like you said, sir, down to me. WPC Wade doesn't know anything better . . . She's still new in the job. I should've made her sit alongside him, but I didn't and now . . .'

'You will be disciplined.'

'Fair enough.'

'Now go, before I really lose my rag.'

Ten minutes later Henry was standing in front of a bar in a pub. That was the length of time it had taken him to throw his clip-on tie, epaulettes, handcuffs, staff and tunic into his locker, leave the police station – avoiding the sniggers of everyone else, because everyone knew it had been necessary to recirculate Bowman as wanted – trudge to his car and get to the pub near his house on Bacup Road.

It irked him intensely that two other people were ahead of him to be served . . . but only a short time later it was his turn.

The lady behind the bar was the one he had seen emerging naked from his housemate's bedroom the day before, but even that image did not brighten up his thoughts.

'Usual, Henry?' she asked. A smile played on her lips as she, too, undoubtedly, relived the brief incident.

'Please.'

He watched the golden liquid fill the glass, then the fizzy head overflow as it was handed to him.

'Are you all right, lovey?' she asked, concerned by the look on his face.

He smiled thinly and nodded. 'Yeah, thanks.' He took the beer and headed for a seat at the back. It was still quite early, the place had only just opened for the evening trade after the mid-afternoon break, and although Henry had been in a queue to be served, only a handful of customers were in. In an hour the pub would be packed, but for the moment he was pretty much alone, just himself, his drink and his bleak thoughts.

Losing a prisoner from the back of a car was almost the ultimate sin and Henry knew it should not have happened. He'd been careless and it had come around to slap him on the backside and now he was going to get punished. The discipline would be inconsequential. He could hack being paraded in front of a few grizzled senior officers and bawled out, an entry made into his personal file and maybe a small fine. He would take that on the chin. It was what he deserved.

What was far worse in his mind was the dent to his reputation and the knock-on effect it would have, not just from colleagues (he'd already been sniggered at), but in career advancement. You didn't let a prisoner go one week, then the week after expect to get on CID. They had longer memories than that and Henry expected that FB would have his cards marked now for cocking up such a simple job. Henry seemed to be single-handedly screwing up his own chances.

His lager tasted good. It sent a chill all the way across his chest. He took a long draught, then another, and then it was gone. And then he was back at the bar, ordering another.

'Well?' the landlady demanded, placing down his new pint on the bar top. She was called Steph.

Not understanding, Henry said dimly, 'Well what?'

She sighed as if he was beyond help. 'Did you like what you saw?' She raised her finely plucked eyebrows.

'Oh yes,' he replied, now understanding: did he like seeing her naked? Taking hold of his pint he returned to his seat, his mood for some reason darkening even more and a sensation of recklessness coming over him. He sat down and looked back towards the bar. Steph was still watching him, her arms folded and her head tilted approvingly, a smile quivering on her lipsticked lips.

Henry knew she was no stranger to the beds of police officers but had so far managed to evade his. A tightening of his stomach muscles made him wonder if that omission would be rectified tonight. He sipped his beer thoughtfully, knowing that this pint – the second – would be his tipping point. Two was always the magic number, beer-wise. Any more and he knew that whatever resolve he had would completely evaporate and he would probably leap into the abyss.

With just two down him he could drive safely, make clear judgements and control his reactions to everything. One more and he lost his senses. For a big young man, he did not hold his liquor well.

He sipped his pint. Carefully. It didn't help that he was drinking on an empty stomach and the alcohol entered his bloodstream quickly so that after the third pint, his evening began to unravel.

It was pretty much a blur from that point on.

The pub filled up gradually. Amongst the customers were people he knew from work as well as some locals. The third pint morphed into a fourth at which point he knew he had to get some food down him. This was provided by the landlady who gave him a chicken curry, half rice/half chips, on the house. He wolfed it down and suddenly felt completely sober again, thinking that the alcohol had been soaked up by the naan bread.

It hadn't.

He checked the time and was surprised to see it had already reached nine-thirty.

There was something on his mind, something important, but he couldn't quite work out what it was, even though he was sure his brain was now clear.

He looked at his empty dish which was suddenly whisked away from him by the landlady and his empty pint glass replenished by the fifth pint of the night and a whisky chaser, neither of which he had ordered. He lifted the golden spirit and sank it in one, then took hold of his beer which he stared at quizzically. He tried to work out what number it was, but he'd lost count and didn't care, really. He took a long pull of it and realized how well it mixed with the whisky. A perfect combination – lager, curry and Scotch.

The evening chugged on in a series of images and unremembered conversations.

Jo Wade appeared around about ten o'clock and sat beside

him. He seemed to think he had a deep and meaningful conversation with her but later could not remember one word of it, other than it seemed to be dour and full of recrimination. He did recall pushing a wisp of her hair back from her face and next thing he was kissing her . . . really snogging, tongues in mouths and some serious, but hidden, groping.

Again, he wasn't certain how long this went on for.

He recalled seeing her at the bar, talking to the landlady, both of them staring across at him, obviously discussing him. Jo returned with another pint and chaser.

A few more people from work drifted in. He had a laugh with them, a couple of them patted his shoulder but he couldn't work out why. His mind started a slow spin.

The next thing he remembered was pounding music, cigarette smoke, disco lights and the fact that he was dancing with Jo, although dancing was not the best description of Henry's unco-ordinated dance-floor moves. It took a while for him to work out where he was, although he did not know how he got there. He was in the nightclub, the Royale, in the basement of the Royal Hotel in the centre of Waterfoot, the tiny town situated between Rawtenstall and Bacup. It was another regular haunt of cops on the prowl, somewhere Henry had spent too much time in the last few years.

Jo was dancing up close to him. Her moves, in stark contrast to his, were slinky, sexy and in time to the music.

Henry tried a few of his Mick Jagger moves to a Bee Gees song and incorporated one or two John Travolta touches and was pleased to see Jo laughing at him. They lurched off the tiny, crowded dance floor and found a murky alcove where the kissing and groping restarted. This did not last too long as Jo dragged Henry out of the club, surfacing into the cool night air and falling into a taxi. A couple of minutes later it pulled up at the bottom of Henry's street. Jo paid the driver and the two of them stumbled arm in arm up the cobbled street to Henry's house, crashing through the door and scrambling up the stairs to his bedroom. They fell across his bed in a heap, a tangle of limbs and desperately started to rip each other's clothes off, Henry suddenly aware he was still in half uniform under his civvie jacket: blue shirt, trousers and black shoes. He had a sudden vision of a drunken dancing cop in the night club and what a complete tool he must have looked.

Within moments Jo was straddling him, bouncing up and down, whilst Henry, still as ungraceful as he had been at dancing, tried his very best to keep time for a while until he realized that he was not enjoying himself.

With amazing clarity he stopped mid-thrust and looked up at this lovely young woman who was screwing him, someone he'd only known in passing really, hadn't even had a proper conversation with because the drunken ones didn't count.

For a beat, Jo wasn't aware that Henry had stopped moving, so engrossed in the activity was she, with her head thrown back, biting her lips.

Then she did – and stopped in mid-air before sliding down the length of Henry's penis, picking up the wrong message, believing that his expression was one of affection, not horror.

'Hi, babe,' she whispered, kissed him on the mouth, around his face and neck and chest, taking a nipple between her perfectly white teeth and biting hard whilst moving very slowly now.

'No,' he said. 'No.'

She glanced up from his chest, dragging the nipple up in her teeth as though she was going to rip it from his chest. Then she let it go with a wet 'plop' and said, 'You no like?'

'No.' He eased himself out of her and pushed her gently to one side.

'What's the matter?'

'Not right,' he said thickly. 'Got to go.'

'Go where?'

'Go . . . just go,' he said and fell off the bed into the pile of discarded clothes. He picked himself up stupidly and staggered out of the bedroom into the bathroom where he sank to his knees in front of the toilet and threw up copiously as his world looped unsteadily around him. He lifted his head and stared at the door handle, watching it rise mysteriously, then fall back into place as he attempted to focus.

He was sick once more, emptying his stomach of all its contents, then he pushed himself up using the toilet bowl as leverage, only to lose his grip. One hand slithered down and splashed into the mix of vomit and water in the bowl.

He kept his hand in there and flushed the toilet, rinsing his fingers in the gushing water before rising and staggering to the sink. He turned on the hot tap and waited for the water to heat up, then washed his hands and splashed his face, swaying slightly off balance all the time, occasionally having to grab the edge of the basin to keep upright.

Taking a deep breath he propelled himself away from the sink, out through the bathroom door, across the hall and back into his bedroom.

Jo was out of it. She was curled up in a tight, naked ball, breathing heavily as she slept under a thin sheet.

Henry stood unsteadily and regarded her, the room rotating slowly. Then he sat on the edge of the bed and held his head in his hands for a while before crawling across the floor to a chair over the back of which he'd left a pair of jeans and a T-shirt. He knew he couldn't stand up to get dressed. It was beyond his present capabilities, so he pulled on the clothes whilst sitting on the floor. This was not the easiest of tasks but, eventually fully dressed, he clambered to his feet, using the corner of the bed as purchase, not realizing his T-shirt was not only on back to front, but also inside-out.

The next few minutes were spent trying to put his feet into a pair of trainers.

He hit the door jamb on the way out and slammed against the wall opposite. At the top of the stairs he gripped the handrail tightly and looked at the steep, narrow steps, realizing that he could not safely walk down them. He lowered himself carefully onto his bottom, going for the safe option, one step at a time.

Whilst still working this out, the door to his housemate's bedroom creaked open and Henry blinked. For the second night in a row, the landlady stepped out naked. She spotted Henry, who stared fuzzily at her. She came to the banister and leaned over, allowing her breasts to sway a couple of feet away from his face. Their graceful movement hypnotized him for a moment.

His right hand dithered, wanting to reach out and touch them.

'Henry Christie,' she cooed. 'What's going on?'

'Uh . . . dunno . . . gotta do summat,' he slurred.

This time she deliberately made her breasts hover above him by leaning a little further forward. His jaw sagged. She giggled.

'What about us?' she asked.

Henry, who could hardly keep his head from lolling like a nodding dog on the back shelf of a car, muttered something incomprehensible, pushed himself off the top step and shot down the stairs like he was riding a toboggan. He hit the hallway with a heavy thump and crumbled before sitting up, groaning.

'Hell fire, you idiot!' the landlady shrieked.

'I'm all right.' He took a few breaths, then forced himself up to his feet and headed to the front door, exiting with a crash.

Outside, the night was cool. Henry stood in the middle of the street and said, 'Right,' and set off down the uneven cobbles to the main road. He had left his car in the pub car park. He knew he had to get to it, needed to drive it and, very urgently, see Kate.

In his extremely inebriated state, this all seemed eminently logical to him.

EIGHT

At three in the morning the roads of Rossendale were virtually bereft of other vehicles, including prowling or parked-up cop cars. This was a fortunate statistic for Henry as he raced through the valley at the wheel of his beat-up ten-year old Morris Marina coupé with the exhaust blowing, concentrating hard – as only a drunk driver could – and getting it completely wrong almost every foot of the way.

He truly believed he was driving just under the speed limit for whichever stretch of the highway he was travelling along. Twenty-eight in a thirty zone, thirty-nine in a forty. In truth he exceeded the limit all the way, but his dreamy drunken state slowed everything down for him. Once or twice he did try to read the speedo but found it hard to focus, though he was certain the needle hovered around the correct speed.

He was also certain he drove correctly and accurately, positioning his car perfectly in the straights and in the corners, but he did wonder what the bang was at one point when he – unwittingly – drifted wide on a bend and skimmed the kerb. He ricocheted off and the steering wheel was ripped out of his grasp, but the incident registered only vaguely.

That he completed his fairly short journey without demolishing roadside furniture or powering headfirst into a lamppost and killing himself was little short of a miracle.

But such is often the case with drunk drivers.

Unless they got stopped, either by a police patrol or something harder than their car, they usually managed to complete their journey in one piece and either experienced guilt-ridden reflection or the opposite and wondered what all the fuss was about.

However, Henry made it unscathed, didn't kill anyone or damage anything, pulling up outside Kate's house in a leafy avenue in Helmshore, a village on the eastern edge of Haslingden. He thought he had parked magnificently, not realizing he had put three wheels on the grass verge.

Moments later he was pounding desperately on the front door with tears streaming down his face, sobbing uncontrollably as he hammered away.

Sequentially, the house lights came on.

Kate lived with her parents, Bert and Elsie, in a big detached house and her mother and father slept in the front, bay-windowed bedroom. That was the first light that came on, followed by a twitch of the curtains and a white face at the window. Kate's mum looked down fearfully, knowing that an early hours knock rarely brought good news. She moved out of the way and allowed her husband to look down at the pathetic figure below, who he recognized instantly.

'What the hell's he doing?' he said.

Bert Marsden had met Henry on a few occasions and had no particular affection for him. Intuitively he fixed him as a fickle young man with questionable social skills, no charm whatsoever, and clearly nowhere near good enough for his one and only daughter. She deserved someone better. A banker or an accountant, he had suggested reasonably to Kate, rather than a rough-edged, overconfident and rude cop with probably no chance of any career advancement and only after one thing: his daughter's body.

'He'll never make a detective as long as he's got a hole where the sun don't shine,' he guffawed when Kate had revealed Henry's aspirations to him. 'And I know people,' he said, sticking a finger in his own chest. 'Not remotely impressed,' he added, lips curled with condescension.

Henry staggered back from the door and looked up at the figures in the window.

Bert opened one and leaned out. 'What do you want? Do you know what time it is?'

'Kate, Kate, I wanna see Kate,' Henry babbled. Unfortunately looking upwards and tilting his head back caused him to lose his balance.

He teetered backwards even further, uncoordinated, and the back of his knees hit the lip of a large terracotta flower pot and he tipped over spectacularly, ending up splayed out on the lawn like a huge beached starfish.

'He's pissed,' Bert said. 'Would you believe it, he's bloody pissed.'

Kate's room was at the back of the house. Her light, followed by the landing light, came on. She had been roused by the knocking and general commotion and, pulling her dressing gown around tightly, she came into her parents' bedroom, still drowsy with sleep.

'What's going on, Dad?'

Mr Marsden spun aggressively. 'What's going on? There's a bloody drunken imbecile at the front door, that's what.'

'Dear, it's Henry,' Kate's mother interceded. Unlike her husband, she had a bit of a soft spot for him.

'Henry? Let me see.'

Kate pushed past her mother and nudged her father out of the way in order to lean out of the window to see Henry still flat on his back on the lawn. The overturned plant pot explained the scenario.

'Henry?'

He raised his head and pathetically said, 'Yes.'

With a mutter and shake of her head, Kate moved back into the bedroom and rushed past her parents.

'I told you he was no good,' her father called smugly, as if all his dreams had come true and Henry was acting in the way he knew was the real Henry.

'Dad,' Kate shot back despairingly, 'he might've hurt himself.'

'We can but hope,' he muttered.

The three nightwear-clad members of the family trooped downstairs to the front door. Kate let herself out to tend to Henry, who was attempting to sit up, but somehow his hands kept slipping from under him on the damp grass, and he thudded back to earth.

Kate swooped down next to him.

'Henry, are you all right?'

'Kate, is that you?'

'Yes, it's me, Henry.' She leaned over and wafted away the reek of alcohol on his breath and also glanced at his car, parked at an acute angle on the grass verge. 'Have you driven here?'

'I . . . I don't know . . . have I?'

'Oh God,' she moaned. 'Come on, let's get you up, come on
. . .' She took an arm and pulled him upright, then limb by limb

up onto his feet, catching him as he lost balance again and almost went over. 'What are you doing here?'

'I dunno . . . I just thought,' he said. 'Something . . . I thought . . .'

Kate realized that nothing coherent was going to leave Henry's mouth. She took a firm grip of his bicep and steered him up to the house where her father waited at the door scowling, as though she was bringing in a dead rat, and her mother watched wide-eyed.

Henry greeted them in an avuncular way, warmly and with the misplaced courtesy of a drunk.

'You're not bringing *that* in here, are you?' Kate's father demanded.

She stopped Henry, but whilst his feet came to a standstill, the top half of his body swayed dangerously. 'Yes I am,' she said firmly and the older man backed off. 'He's my boyfriend.' Her right hand delved into Henry's jeans pocket and found his car keys which she handed with aplomb to her father. 'He's had a spot of bother parking. Can you just straighten up his car for him? It's a bit skew-whiff.'

'I'm in my pyjamas.'

'And?'

Henry wavered precariously. Kate caught him and propelled him past her parents. He grinned lopsidedly at them and said, 'Hi, Mum and Dad, mister and missus . . . thingy . . .'

Kate kept him going, down the hallway and up the stairs. Getting him up them was a gruelling event in itself and, almost exhausted by heaving and manoeuvring him, Kate eventually managed to drag him into the main bathroom.

He stood stupidly in front of her, his head lolling, his mouth snarling a terrifying grin as though he had no control of his facial features and had been injected with a muscle relaxant. In some ways, he had.

'Kaaaaate,' he said.

'Let's get you in the shower,' she said, business-like.

'Right – good idea.'

He suddenly leaned forwards and planted a messy wet kiss on her cheek. 'I think I'm a bit drunk.'

'Really?' She nodded and pushed him away.

He tried to focus on her, but her face, rather like the door handle he'd tried to stare at earlier, kept rising upwards in a hazy cloud.

'I really, really, really, love ya,' he said. 'I mean, sherioushly love yeh.'

Then his stomach heaved.

Kate saw it coming, whirled him around and forced him down onto his knees by the toilet and, more or less, caught all the vomit.

'I love you too,' she said quietly, 'you daft big lug.' She rubbed his back tenderly as he threw up once more, then farted. Kate giggled.

It wasn't a great sleep. Some of it was the darkest he had ever been in. A swirling black hole, unsettled and uncomfortable, and he shifted about on the bed remorselessly, sometimes blabbing, other times just moaning until eventually, as the alcohol was broken down by his overworked liver, sleep came proper.

His eyes flickered open as his head started to pound densely and then a searing pain volleyed up behind his eyeballs as though someone was performing an ice-pick lobotomy on the frontal lobe of his brain.

He held the soft part of his hands against his eyes then gradually peeled them away to check out exactly where he was. For a moment, he was unsure, then his memory came back – and he groaned with shame. Henry was never one to claim he could not remember what had happened when drunk. He knew more or less what had happened up to the point where he had been led, staggering, out of the bathroom into Kate's bedroom . . . it was only then that things got unclear.

He knew he was now in Kate's bed. Naked. He lifted the duvet and looked down at his body, slim, muscled, tanned from a recent week in Majorca, but as he wafted the cover he could tell he hadn't had the shower that had been mentioned. The body odour was not great.

He allowed the duvet to fall back into place and then lay unmoving, terrified that if he lifted his head, the back of his skull would fall off.

When the bedroom door opened he kept staring at the ceiling

until the person who had entered the room came into his arc of vision.

Kate loomed over him.

'Morning,' she said quietly, 'or should I say, afternoon?'

'You're joking.'

'No – it's twelve-thirty. PM.'

'Oh God – work!'

'Don't worry, fixed it. I got Terry to report you sick. Bad tummy.' Terry was one of Henry's partners on the crime car.

'Thanks,' he said. 'What about you? Shouldn't you be at work?'

'I'm sick, too. Bad tummy,' she fibbed.

'You shouldn't have.'

Kate perched on the edge of the bed and touched Henry's face with cool fingertips.

'Sorry,' he said weakly.

'My dad, bless him, is outraged.'

'So he should be. What an arse. Me, not him.'

Kate looked at him. 'What was it all about?'

Henry snorted a laugh. 'Sudden, overwhelming realization, I guess.'

'Magnified a hundred times by drink, *I* guess.'

'There's always that,' he conceded.

She leaned over and kissed him, then drew away with her lovely nose screwed up. 'You whiff,' she said. 'I was going to dunk you in the shower but it seemed like too much hard work, so I bundled you into bed instead.'

'And stripped me naked.'

'I liked that bit.'

'I might have done, too, but the memory's a bit blank from the toilet fart onwards.'

'Do you want that shower now? I think you need it. Then some food and drink down you?'

'Yeah, yeah.'

Henry had not spent much time in Kate's parents' house. Occasional evenings watching TV and that was about it. Because he could keenly sense her dad's disapproval of him, he didn't ever feel comfortable or welcome, so most of his private courting of Kate took place back at his rented house or in the car, or in pubs in the Rossendale area. He had certainly never spent the night – or any time – in her bed and had never been in the shower.

Which was amazing. The most powerful, hottest shower he had ever stood under, putting the weedy electrical trickle thing in his own bathroom to shame.

He stood under it for a long time, revelling in the force of the jets drilling against his skin, whilst at the same time cringing inwardly at his recall of the night before.

The click of the shower door opening spun him around.

Kate stepped in, naked. The two of them instantly grabbed each other, kissing passionately under the water jets, their bodies tight up against each other, Henry hard against her belly, the sensation of her skin and small, soft breasts crushed against his chest driving him crazy.

He broke from the embrace. 'Is this wise?' he asked.

'Probably not,' she gasped throatily, taking him in her hands. 'Not at all.'

'Bad couple of days,' Henry said.

They were having a late lunch at the Duke of Wellington pub on Grane Road. After the shower and a bout of the most wonderful love-making he had ever experienced in his short life, he had dashed back to his rented house in the re-parked Marina for a change of clothing, relieved to find that Jo had disappeared without a trace and nor was there any sign of the naked landlady (or did I dream that, he wondered). Then he flew back to pick up Kate and head out for lunch, although to find somewhere serving food beyond 2pm was quite hard. Much to the annoyance of staff of the Wellington, Henry and Kate turned up at 1.55pm.

'One rapist allowed to go free, having my car peppered by a shotgun and then losing a prisoner on the M6. I was just pissed off and cross with myself, had a pint, then another, then lost all track of time and completely forgot to call you . . . and I'm sorry. It all went to rats.'

'We could've got drunk together if you had. That would've been good.'

'Mm, we haven't really done that yet, have we?'

'There's lots of things we haven't done yet.' She gave him a meaningful look.

'Big tick in the box today, though,' he smirked.

'I never knew a shower could be so invigorating.'

He smiled at the memory and placed a chunk of steak and ale pie into his mouth. The meat was hot and succulent, having the desired effect of totally re-energizing him. He chewed it thoughtfully, pondering how best to broach the next subject. There was no way he would reveal his encounters with Jo, because he wasn't nuts enough to believe that Kate would be understanding on that score. That was something to keep under wraps, or bury six feet under. But he knew he did have some things to tell Kate.

He placed down his cutlery and looked at her.

'I came to a very big realization,' he explained. 'About the way I feel about you.' His spoke hesitantly, not least because he was unused to delving into his heart and unearthing tender words and phrases. Up to meeting Kate he would not have described any of his encounters with ladies as anything but lust- and sex-driven, often alcohol-fuelled binges, rarely accompanied by anything approaching love.

Kate, without guile or manipulation, was changing all that.

'Really?' She arched her eyebrows. 'And what would that be?'

Henry shrugged, embarrassed. 'I love you, I mean really love you.'

'Oh.'

'That it? Oh?' Henry saw her chest rise and fall slowly, her sparkling eyes playing over his face. 'I know I'm a dimwit and stupid, but I'm intelligent enough to know that I'm crazy in love with you. You don't have to come back to me immediately on it. I know it's a big statement to take in, so you can have a think about it and if you don't feel the same, then that's OK . . . clearly I'll be gutted and all that, but there's no pressure, honest . . .'

She placed her forefinger over his lips. 'You're babbling,' she said.

'I'm babbling,' he agreed.

They held each other's gaze for a long moment and Kate said, 'I love you too, Henry Christie.'

He exhaled long and hard and wiped the sweat of terror from his brow. 'Thank the lord for that.'

*   *   *

'So – bad couple of days?' Kate said.

They were back at her parents' house and, for the first time, had made love in Kate's soft and deep three-quarter-width bed, and despite her reassurances that they wouldn't be back until after six, it had been a slightly nerve-wracking experience and Henry always had one ear listening out just in case the front door went and he was forced to do a runner via the bedroom window.

Kate snuggled up under his arm, a fingertip tracing across his chest, circling his nipples.

'Yeah, pretty crappy,' he said. 'Going to end up carpeted.'

'They don't know how lucky they are to have you.'

'You're right, they don't. I could do with getting away from here – somehow.'

'Blackburn?'

'Further afield.'

'Darwen?' she giggled.

'Back to the coast.' He glanced slyly at her.

'Blackpool?'

'Yeah . . . might be a good idea from a career point of view. I've cooked my goose in this neck of the woods, I think. Blackpool looks a great place to work and my kith and kin are out there.'

Kate became silent, a silence that Henry could physically feel.

'Do you mean that?' she asked worriedly.

'Don't know . . . just musing, I suppose.'

'What about me?'

'Well, I mean, I'd obviously take you.'

Kate propped herself up on one elbow. 'And how would that happen?'

Henry pouted and shrugged. 'As a leg iron?' he suggested.

'Eh?'

'Look . . . tell you what . . . why don't we get married?'

Kate sighed with irritation. 'Henry, if that was a proposal it was pretty dumb.' Her voice was heavy with disappointment. 'It was more like a business arrangement or something.' She flopped onto the bed, exasperated.

And Henry got the message. He threw the sheet off, stood by the bed, took Kate by the hand, urging her to stand up until both of them stood facing each other, completely naked.

'OK,' he said . . . and then saw the look of utter dread. He had intended to go down on one knee and propose, but even he realized that doing it naked and dangly was probably not the most romantic of scenarios. 'Tell you what.' He drew her close to him. 'Let me put that proposal on hold for a while until, say, circumstances are more appropriate. Let's just make love again instead.'

'All right,' she agreed and kissed his chest, then began to lower herself, kissing his stomach until she was the one kneeling in front of him.

An hour later, Henry dressed himself whilst sitting on the edge of the bed. It was almost five in the afternoon, too close to the expected arrival time of mummy and daddy to be dawdling naked around the house.

Kate was also dressing.

'So what are you going to do?'

'About what, sweetie?' he responded.

'Work. The here and now of it.'

He pulled a sock on, slowly and thoughtfully, whilst she wrestled with a pair of tights. 'Make amends,' he said; then decisively. 'Catch the little bastard I allowed to escape, catch those bloody armed robbers and, if I can, nail a rapist too.' He put his other sock on.

NINE

A lthough Henry's next tour of duty did not begin until 8am the following day, he went in early, rolling into the nick just after 7.15. He wanted to sort out his return from sickness form first, which he did. He then checked the duty states, a huge sheet of paper compiled by hand by an inspector detailing every officer and their shifts in the valley for that day and the week ahead. He saw Jo was on an early shift which started at six, and she was presently out on patrol. Henry wanted to speak to her later and try to extricate himself as delicately as possible from any entanglement with her. It wasn't something he was relishing, but it had to be tackled.

After leafing through his in-tray, in which two Crown Court committal files had been returned by the prosecutions department for some follow-up work, he booked out a PR and then went up to the first floor to do some digging.

Even though the armed robberies that had been committed by the Manchester gang in Rossendale were very serious crimes – particularly for an area perceived to be such a sleepy backwater (which of course was one of the reasons it had been targeted by the gang) – and all were increasing incrementally in violence, a dedicated incident room and police operation had not yet been set up to investigate. In the main it was just local detectives and uniforms with some help from the Regional Crime Squad, but with no one working full time on the case. That said, Henry suspected that the RCS might be doing more than they admitted to, because arresting the robbers would be a great scalp for them.

Even so, a few detectives from the first-floor CID office had overspilled into the small lecture room and bagged one corner of it so they could spread out a bit, and this is where Henry went. He wanted to sift through whatever they had, which was not much really, A flip chart, a few sheets of paper stuck onto the wall and not a lot else – something Henry found almost incredible. The valley had been subjected to a series of violent attacks and no one deemed it particularly important to devote a team of officers, full time, to sort it. Henry knew that the detectives who were looking into the robberies also had to balance that with the rest of their tasks.

Not good enough, he thought. Things would change when some poor bloody shopkeeper got his head blasted off. Even though shots had been fired at the latest job, and Henry's police car blasted with shotgun pellets, even this didn't seem to galvanize the CID into action.

Standing in the commandeered corner of the lecture room surveying the pitiful amount of work on display, Henry muttered, 'Need a rocket up their backsides,' to no one in particular.

'Who does?'

Henry turned and thought, 'For a tubby guy, he moves like a ninja.'

FB was standing there, having entered the room via the door at the opposite end. He had done so silently, tiptoeing in to keep his heel protectors from clicking.

'I thought you were off sick?' FB demanded.

'I was, now I'm back.'

'Was the bollocking too much for you?' FB asked cynically. 'Did I make you cry – blub, blub?'

'No,' Henry sneered. 'I got pissed and had a hangover so I decided to take the day off.' This was not far from the truth, although the sick note said upset stomach.

'Going off sick is for wussies,' FB said, 'hangover or otherwise. Anyway, what are you doing in here?'

'Just familiarizing myself with the background to these robberies.' Henry wafted a hand at the flip charts.

'And have you learned anything you don't already know?'

Henry cast a cynical glance at the corner of the room. 'Hardly,' he admitted. 'How come there isn't a full squad on this?'

'There will be after the most recent job and your shotgun incident.'

Henry brightened up slightly.

'I've got a team of eight jacks on it for two weeks, starting today – taking over this room.'

'Can I . . .?' Henry began to venture.

'No,' FB said firmly, anticipating the question.

'Detectives only?'

'Something like that . . .'

'But they tried to shoot me!'

FB guffawed. 'And that gives you a right to come on the squad? Don't think so . . . and, anyway, how would it look to other uniform PCs if you were drafted in? Someone who lets prisoners go? How would that reflect on me? Besides which, you're not the only PC who wants to get on CID. There are more deserving guys than you and if I wanted a uniform on the squad, which I don't, I'd be picking one of them first.'

Henry held up his hands in surrender. 'Point taken. Sir.'

He withdrew from the room and stomped back downstairs, picked up his car keys and jumped into the Ford Escort that had been brought over from the car pool as a temporary replacement for the wounded Cavalier. He set out on patrol alone, his partner in the pursuit of crime that day not coming on duty until ten, so they worked staggered shifts to provide more cover.

Turning out of the station yard, he suddenly slammed on his brakes and reversed back into the space, then went back into the nick and up to the Collator's Office, which was open. The Collator himself, a very long-in-the-tooth detective constable called Charlie Martin, was sitting drinking his first coffee of the day and lighting up probably his fourth cigarette.

The Collator was basically a collector, analyser and disseminator of intelligence about criminals and their activities. The information came from a number of sources, mostly from bobbies on the beat who were encouraged to fill in information slips about anything and everyone they saw or spoke to during their tour of duty. Much of it was dross and simply went on file, some of it was gold – and often snaffled by the CID – and some of it ended up on the Collator's bulletin, a local intelligence newsletter, published a couple of times a week. It wasn't a very scientific process.

DC Charlie Martin, Henry knew, was a great source of information. He had a prodigious memory, filled with twenty-five years of detective work, and he knew a lot about criminals, dates, places, associations, family trees, sometimes family secrets. Charlie had been the Collator in Rossendale for five years and

Henry thought he was brilliant at it. Round peg, round hole and all that.

His minus point was that he smoked pungent-smelling, self-rolled cigarettes, and his office always reeked of tobacco smoke, but it was something Henry was prepared to tolerate. Charlie quite liked Henry and regularly drip-fed him information about local villains. In turn, Henry regularly submitted intelligence slips to him.

He glanced up as Henry came into the office just as his thin, weed-like cigarette caught light with a flame that died down to a smoulder. He inhaled a lungful that almost finished the cigarette in one, then exhaled with a long breath of pleasure, the smoke spiralling up towards the suspended ceiling where it hung like a storm cloud.

'Henry my boy, how the hell are you? Still allowing prisoners to roam free?' he cackled, then coughed, his chest reverberating worryingly. Noting Henry's facial response, Charlie said, 'Better get used to the jibes, Henry, at least until somebody else does something more stupid, which they will. Only then can you guarantee you'll be yesterday's news.'

Henry shrugged, took a seat.

'So what can I do you for?' the old detective asked.

'I want to recapture Jack Bowman, obviously; I also want to lock up Vladimir Kaminski and throw away the key; I also want a shot at this armed gang who took a pot shot at me or two. Not necessarily in that order.'

Charlie's next drag finished the roll-up. He held the smoke in his lungs as he extinguished the cigarette with the tip of his thumb and forefinger, then placed the butt in a tobacco tin containing his loose tobacco and other butts. Henry knew they would be recycled and cannibalized in the future, such was the way of self-rollers. He blew out and said, 'You want me to help you?'

'Yup.'

'Firstly I won't tread on the DI's toes. He's my boss and he wants the glory of nailing that gang and I've no doubt he'll get it and it would be unwise to rattle his cage. My advice on that front is just to help out if you can. Not that I can cast much light on the gang anyway. We've got a list of suspects a mile long from Manchester, so I guess we'll try to run a surveillance job on them, or just round up the usual suspects and sweat 'em.'

Henry listened, nodding.

'As regards Kaminski, it's another toe-treading job.'

'How do you mean?'

'The best way to get to Kaminski is to kick his shins on a Friday night and get him riled up. Then you'll have him bang to rights.'

'Why?' Henry's eyes narrowed.

'Because . . .' Charlie's voice dropped to a secretive whisper, 'if you haven't sussed it already . . .' He gave Henry an encouraging gesture – a 'come on, think about it' one – but Henry just looked blank. 'Do I have to spell it out?'

'Sorry . . .'

'Between you, me and the gatepost, he's one of the DI's informants and as such the DI does not like him being meddled with.' He made a cutting gesture with his hands as if to say, 'Enough said.'

A groan emanated from Henry. 'The bigger bloody picture.' He slapped his own forehead. 'That's what it all meant . . . but hang on, Charlie, he's FB's informant at the cost of him being a rapist?'

The Collator did not reply, just gave Henry a knowing look.

'That stinks.'

'Maybe, but by the same token, Miss Sally Lee is also a very tricky manipulator.'

'She was raped. I'm certain about it.'

'No doubt she was, H, but she's almost too much trouble to be worth it. I'm sure FB'd nail Kaminski's balls to the flagpole if he had raped a complete stranger . . . but it's a domestic thing.'

'You really mean that?'

'That's how it is, Henry.'

Henry kept his teeth jammed together, unable to believe the pervading attitude, but knowing that Charlie spoke the truth. Henry had a sudden lurching feeling that he was completely out of step with contemporary police, and maybe public, thinking on domestic abuse. That it was more trouble than it was worth to rescue – usually – women from a life of hell. Henry dropped it onto the back burner for the moment and said, 'What about

Jack Bowman, then? Can I have all the Intel you have on him because I showed my arse in Burton's window and now I want to make amends?'

'You can have everything we have on file.'

'Is there anything you can tell me that's not on file?'

'Probably not . . . although . . . I don't think this is in, but did you know that Bowman is Sally Lee's stepbrother, or something like that?'

'I don't remember reading that in Bowman's file,' Henry said, surprised.

'Well, not everything gets in police files, you know.'

He weighed up sneaking into the morning CID briefing but decided against it, not wishing to invoke FB's ire. After spending twenty minutes leafing through the files on Bowman, Kaminski (in which obviously there was no mention of him being an informant) and the armed robberies, Henry turned out for a mooch around the towns he was covering that morning – Rawtenstall, Waterfoot and Haslingden, known collectively as Rossendale West – whilst deciding on his plan of action and where he should start.

The problem with being a patrol officer, albeit on the crime car where there was a certain amount of freedom, was that it was impossible to spend all one's time just doing one thing because, as a local resource, other things always needed attention. There was no way Henry could just say to comms, 'Don't call me, I'll call you,' because he had to respond to the radio.

This was frustrating, but simply how it was.

So when he drove out just after eight that morning, with the intention of putting his game plan together, he wasn't surprised to be deployed to a burglary at an address on Bury Road, Rawtenstall. Someone had entered an old lady's house during the night and stolen property whilst she was asleep.

Henry was at the house within three minutes, dealing with a frightened, virtually housebound old woman who had – fortunately – slept through the break-in. Had she woken to find a burglar in her house, there was every chance the shock would have killed her.

She was distraught enough to find the broken kitchen window

and that her fridge had been raided, her purse and its contents stolen and other bits and bats of property gone, including a solid-silver framed photograph of herself and her long-dead husband on their wedding day in 1938, a year before he went to war and never came back. Further evidence of the break-in was the calling-card turd left by the offender on the kitchen floor, a nasty habit quite a few burglars had. Sometimes it was from nerves, but with some it was from a desire to defile other people's property.

'It's the photograph that really gets to me, besides the burglar being a dirty little bastard,' the old lady, Mrs Ethel Fudge, said tearfully. Henry was brewing a cup of tea for her. He brought it through to the living room and placed it on a side table next to her armchair. She was sitting in the chair, her walking frame positioned in front of her knees. 'The money doesn't bother me, or the food, or the photograph frame itself . . . I mean they can have all that lot . . . it's just my photograph, me and Kevin on our wedding day. It's the only one I have of us.'

Henry sat on the very old leather sofa and watched a tear come out of her eye and felt a surge of anger at the offender of this crime. He knew that in all probability the photo itself would have already been taken out of the frame, ripped up and chucked away; the frame itself would get sold on for a pittance, a few pounds to fund a drug habit, no doubt.

'I won't make any promises, Mrs Fudge, but I'll do my very best to find out who committed this crime and recover the frame and picture.'

She gave Henry a wan, disbelieving smile. 'Thanks, but I won't hold my breath.' She sighed heavily.

Henry said, 'Give me a good description of the frame, please.' He took out his pocket notebook.

After clearing up the burglar's mess, Henry felt muted on leaving the house as he told the lady that a scenes of crime officer would be calling later that morning and that he, Henry, would sort out a glazier to attend her house to repair the broken window. His first port of call would be to a couple of second-hand shops in town to alert them about the picture frame, though he doubted if this would be much use. The proprietors were known to deal in stolen property, but Henry could only try his best. Maybe put the shits up them or appeal to their better nature, just in case the frame was offered to them.

He went and knocked on a few of the neighbours' houses, but didn't turn up any witnesses, then searched the back alley, looked in dustbins and over walls to see if he could spot if the purse had been thrown away after being emptied, but he found nothing. He spent about an hour at the scene in total, probably longer than his bosses would have liked, but he knew there was much more to attending a domestic burglary than just writing down and circulating details. Having a stranger enter your house was traumatic to most people. To an eighty-two-year-old woman it was devastating and possibly life-threatening, which is why he spent some extra time with her, reassuring her and listening to her fears, and promising a result and a revisit.

As he radioed in he was given two more burglaries to attend, one at a sports club and the other at a town-centre clothing shop. It was way past eleven by the time he had visited and sorted them out.

Next stop was the police station, where he needed to write up and submit the crime details.

He also knew he had to get his head around the Crown Court files in his tray. They had 'urgent' stickers on them. On the way into the nick he did a last circuit of the town and noticed that one of the second-hand shops he intended to visit was open, so he pulled onto the double yellow lines outside and went in the shop, leaving his hazard warning lights flashing and hoping that the town-centre traffic warden would recognize the car as a police vehicle and not stick a ticket on it.

It was like entering an Aladdin's cave. Virtually everything was on display in Fat Jack's Emporium, from settees to bikes, jewellery to kids' toys. Most of what was visible was legitimate, but Fat Jack, the proprietor, was known to do a nice trade in fencing stolen goods and a lot of people who provided him with such had stolen them to order – his order. He had a vibrant trade in video-cassette players and counterfeit films on video, together with car radio/cassette players, most of which found their way out of town.

Henry made a point of visiting Fat Jack – real name Dominic Tighe and who was not particularly large and whose nickname was impossible to explain – on a regular basis. He wandered through the goods on display, a winding trail from door to counter, behind which was Tighe, leaning over and reading the *Daily Mirror*, cigarette in one hand and a cracked mug of tea within reach of the other.

He didn't look up at Henry even though he had seen him enter the shop. Tighe always liked to show some disrespect for the law, even though when he came face to face with a cop, particularly a detective, he usually crumbled into false obsequiousness, which often worked in his favour. He had learned that police officers liked people fawning to them because it boosted their ego. If, however, he found himself under arrest he became a completely different character: a bastard.

'Morning, PC Christie.'

Henry stood opposite, arms folded.

'Can I do for you?'

'I want to go through to the back and search your property for stolen goods,' Henry lied.

Henry could almost sense Tighe's body blanching at the prospect. The man's head rose slowly, a glint of uncertainty in his eyes. 'With respect, you'll be needing a warrant for that.'

'Good job I've got one, then,' Henry said. He reached into his back pocket and pulled out a folded sheet of A4 paper. Tighe's eyes focused on it as Henry unfolded it carefully, but his expression changed to one of utter contempt as he realized that the paper was just a badly folded Chinese takeaway menu.

'Got you there, Fat Jack,' Henry beamed mischievously.

'Not fucking funny,' Tighe said in a slightly high-pitched voice. He had to cough twice to get it back to his normal pitch.

'Your reaction was, though . . . which makes me think.' Henry nodded to the store-room door at the rear of the shop.

'If you'd asked nicely and hadn't tossed me around, I would've gladly given you permission, without need of a warrant, to look in the back. Not now, though.'

'Ho, ho, as if,' Henry said, enjoying the exchange. He loved antagonizing criminals, truly believed it was one of the jobs a cop had to do. Wind them up, rile them, always make them feel uncomfortable, at every opportunity. Having succeeded in that noble endeavour with this miscreant he said, 'An old lady's house was burgled last night, not much taken of value except a silver photo frame, eight by six, with an old wedding photo in it. I want it back,' he said firmly.

'Bit vague, innit?' Tighe said.

'Someone offers you a silver photo frame – how vague is that? And don't scare off whoever it is. Take the frame and call me. I want it back – that's the main thing. It's got great sentimental value. And, of course, I want the name of the villain, too.'

'You want me to fork out my money – my money – and then give you the frame?'

'Yes, I do,' Henry affirmed.

The two men had a little stare-off battle of wills for a moment until Tighe relented. 'OK.'

'And that little gesture will save you a lot of aggro – for a week or two, anyway.'

'Suppose it doesn't turn up?'

'Then you'll get aggro – and a real search warrant, not a Chinese takeaway menu.'

Henry bade him farewell and left the shop, emerging onto the street to see the heartless town-centre traffic warden standing and looking at Henry's car, flicking open his ticket wallet like it was a *Star Trek* communicator.

Henry rushed across. The warden was known for his ruthless streak and had hacked off a few local cops by ticketing illegally parked police cars, much to the delight of the local press which supported his actions to the hilt.

'Cop car, cop business,' Henry said haughtily.

'I know. Unfortunately I've already started to write out a ticket and once that process has begun, it is impossible to reverse.'

Henry looked askance. He could clearly see that pen had not been put to paper.

'No you haven't,' he said.

The traffic warden gave him a cruel look, extended his arm so his cuff slid back, exaggerated the gesture of putting his ball-point pen to the tip of his tongue, then began to write.

Henry stared at him in disbelief.

It was extremely easy to accumulate paperwork as a uniformed cop, but Henry prided himself that he never allowed himself to get snowed under.

The crimes he had attended that morning had to be written up and circulated, so he did that task on his return to the station. Then he handed his car keys over to his crime car partner who had come on at ten and asked if he would mind taking over whilst Henry got to grips with the Crown Court files he needed to work on. His colleague happily took over from him and Henry nipped out to a nearby butty shop and bought himself a couple of crispy bacon sandwiches and then, with a mug of tea in hand (made with his own teabags and milk), he found himself a quiet corner of the report-writing room and got to work.

There was nothing majorly complicated that needed attention. Henry was good at paperwork but every so often queries were generated from the prosecution solicitors or barristers who would be taking the files to court, and all he really needed to do that morning was make a few phone calls to chase up a witness and rewrite a section of one of the summaries. He got on with it, whilst at the same time wondering how to track down the little shit who'd escaped from his custody, kick Vladimir Kaminski's shins and nail a gang of armed robbers – all before dinner.

WPC Jo Wade loved being a young single female cop – at least for the time being. It was a great existence, being part of a shift of officers where camaraderie was great, the work was fun and serious at the same time, and being part of a social scene that was exciting and carefree. At first she thought she had been posted to the end of the earth when she was told she was going to the valley, but in a matter of weeks she had settled into the lifestyle.

The work was wonderful. She treated it professionally and compassionately. She loved helping people, solving problems and also arresting a few miscreants along the way. She had been seriously gutted about the escaping prisoner and she felt guilt – but immense relief – that Henry was taking the blame for the debacle. She was not yet out of the two-year probationary period that all constables had to go through and something like that could have cost her her job. Her services could be terminated without any reason given.

Which is one of the reasons why she had been extra nice to Henry for the second time, but for the life of her, she could not

recall how the night before last had ended. She recalled staggering back to Henry's house from the night club, getting naked
and screwing, but beyond that – nothing.

Next thing she was waking up alone with no sign of Henry
anywhere and no idea when he had disappeared. She thought
he'd gone to work but only later found out that he'd reported in
sick.

She knew Henry was back on duty and at some stage she
intended to hook up with him for a chat. One thing she was
certain of was that she liked what she'd had and wanted more
of him, girlfriend or otherwise.

So far that morning she hadn't managed to bump into him.
She'd heard his deployments to various burglaries over the radio
but she too had been busy with other things; somehow she
intended to track him down before she finished at two. She knew
he finished at four, so what could be better, she pondered, than
him coming round to her flat after he'd finished for some more
intimacy and a takeaway?

The prospect put a big smile on her face as she drove her
patrol car around Rawtenstall that morning and decided to pop
into a Spar convenience store on Burnley Road for a chat with
the Asian owner. He was always having racial problems and the
shop had become one of Jo's regular brew stops.

She parked behind the shop, out of sight, walked around to
the front entrance.

Her mind was full of the prospect of Henry Christie and she
paid little heed to the Ford Granada parked on the tiny run-on
car park outside the shop, one dark figure on board. She had no
inkling whatsoever that she was stepping into the middle of a
fully-fledged armed robbery in progress.

The telephone on the writing table rang. For a second Henry
considered ignoring it but he was waiting for a witness to call
him back and had told her to ask for this extension. He scooped
up the phone.

'Henry . . . Dave in comms,' came the voice of the station
duty PC.

'Hi.'

'Just had a call from Dom Tighe at Fat Jack's,' the PC began, and even as he was saying these words Henry was rising to his feet, grabbing his PR and jacket and hat, the phone still clasped to his ear. 'Said you'd been in this morning re some stolen property . . . apparently some guy's just been in and tried to sell him a silver photo frame . . .'

Juggling clothes and phone, Henry said, 'Did he say who?'

'No – didn't know the guy.'

'Likely story . . . How long ago?'

'Last ten minutes.'

'On my way,' Henry said and slammed the phone down and thought, 'Shit!' He didn't have a car. He rushed through the corridors to the sergeant's office where all the patrol car keys were hung. The morning patrol sergeant was sitting at his desk, delving into his sandwich box whilst scanning a newspaper. He lifted his head and watched open-mouthed as Henry barged in and snaffled the only set of keys on the rack.

'Oi!' the sergeant yelled, revealing a mouthful of beef-paste sandwich.

'Needs must,' Henry said, disappearing with the keys, which were for the sergeant's car. He ran along the main corridor and crashed out through the double doors into the rear yard.

He ran to one of the covered parking bays and climbed into the liveried Austin Metro which he skidded out of the yard and then hurled through the streets, heading towards Fat Jack's, screeching to a halt outside the shop on the double-yellows where he took a second to arrange his clothing and appointments a little more comfortably.

As he opened the door, the cool voice of the station duty PC, underpinned by a tone of urgency, came over the PR.

'Patrols to attend Anwar's Spar shop, Burnley Road. Report of armed robbery and officer down, repeat – *officer down* – having been shot.'

Without hesitation, Henry responded.

There were three of them in the shop when Jo Wade stepped through the front door. Her pleasant thoughts were smashed to smithereens as she crossed the threshold and saw the scene in front of her.

Three armed men, their faces ski-masked.

One of them was behind the counter, emptying the contents of the cigarette shelves and till into a small hessian sack. The shop owner stood terrified to one side, arms raised.

Two other robbers armed with shotguns were aiming them at the two customers who had been backed up against the bread shelves.

As Jo stepped in, she froze.

And it was over in an instant.

The gang were high on speed, operating like wild men. The one closest to Jo as she came into the shop whirled towards her, saw the uniform, fired.

The blast from the double barrels slammed into her lower stomach, doubling her over, driving her against the wall. She slithered slowly down onto her backside, total shock and disbelief on her face as she looked down at the huge hole that had been punched in her guts. No words came out of her twisted mouth.

Within seconds, the gang had gone, all three of them leaping across Jo's outstretched legs, one of them actually stepping on her thigh and almost tripping over.

Henry gunned the Metro – in as much as a 998cc engine could be gunned – swerving along the streets, honking the pathetic little horn (there was no two-tone on a bog-standard section patrol car) but at least it had a blue light fitted and screwed to the roof that didn't slide off as the car's speed increased.

He was at the scene in two minutes, first cop to arrive.

It puzzled him slightly he couldn't see Jo's police car, but guessed it was parked out back. Henry mounted the kerb and leapt out of the car, bursting through the shop door, finding Jo on the floor, surrounded by four scared people.

He pushed through and squatted next to her, fighting his own rising panic.

Her terror-filled eyes looked pleadingly at him.

'Henry,' she whispered, 'I was just thinking about you.'

He called comms to chase up the ambulance and further assistance, giving a cool situation report in spite of the feelings boiling within him. Then, holding a clean tea towel over the horrendous gaping wound in her stomach, Henry slid beside her and eased his left arm around her shoulder, gently moving up against her, aware she was trembling and shaking and going into deep shock.

'Henry, I'm really cold and it hurts so much.'

'I'll warm you up, sweetie. And it's not as bad as it looks. You'll be OK.' He moved a lock of her hair away from her face.

She exhaled long and with difficulty, wincing dreadfully as a searing pain creased her body. She grabbed Henry's hand, the one holding the cloth over the wound, digging her nails in deep.

'It's OK, it's OK,' he whispered into her ear. 'Just hold on as tight as you need to. The ambulance is coming.'

He was aware of the onlookers, the people who had been caught up in the robbery, standing around, probably feeling useless. But suddenly he felt as though he was in a disconnected, distorted bubble of unreality.

'Henry, it really hurts.'

'I know . . . just hold onto me, hold on . . . the ambulance is almost here . . . they'll get you sorted.'

She convulsed with pain. 'Oh God.'

Henry held her slightly tighter, aware of a wetness underneath him: the spreading pool of Jo's blood.

'It's OK, OK, love.'

'Henry . . . is that you?'

'Yeah, yeah . . . it's me.'

'I was just thinking about you.'

'I know, I was just thinking about you, too.'

In the distance he heard the ambulance sirens for the first time.

'Not long now, not long.'

Jo coughed and bubbles of blood spittled out of her mouth.

Henry groaned inwardly. That was bad.

The sirens were close now.

She died in his arms as the first ambulance man ran into the shop.

TEN

The pounding on the front door eventually penetrated through the hiss of the shower and the hum of the electric motor, beating through the force field that seemed to be encasing Henry Christie's head in a grey haze.

Henry's ears came on stream as the knocking persisted, wouldn't go away.

'Just get lost,' he said, and lifted his face into the burning hot, but fairly weak jets, wishing they would wash away his all-pervading bleakness.

But the knocking continued. Whoever it was knew Henry was in and would not be deterred by a no-response. It was a cop's knock. Reluctantly he turned off the water and stepped out of the bath in which the shower was located and began to dry himself. He put on tracksuit bottoms and T-shirt and padded down the tight steps to the front door, still rubbing his short-cropped hair with a hand towel as he opened up.

'Thought you'd drowned.' It was DI Fanshaw-Bayley, FB. Henry's nostrils dilated as he regarded his DI. 'Can I come in?'

Henry sighed, stepped aside and allowed FB's chubby form to roll past him into the narrow hallway to the kitchen at the back of the rented house.

'You making a brew?' FB said, easing himself onto a chair next to the fold-leaf kitchen table.

Henry said nothing, but filled the kettle and dropped two tea bags into two mugs. The kettle started to heat up noisily. Henry leaned against the sink.

'How are you feeling?'

'Guess.'

'You did well, Henry . . . The people in the shop who saw you said you were there for her.'

Henry shook his head and looked away sharply, his lips tight lines as he fought to control anger and grief.

'The chief constable's out and about – although we did

have to give him directions to get to the valley. He's been to
see Jo's parents in Lancaster. He wants to see you at some
stage today.'

'I'll give that a miss.'

'Don't think so.'

'Tell him I'm not fit and I'm likely to rip his face off.'

The kettle boiled. Henry made the tea and handed one to FB.
Henry took a sip of his. It burned his lips. He had his back to
FB now, staring out of the kitchen window into the back yard.
'I couldn't stop her dying,' he said bitterly.

'No one could have, not even if she'd been in hospital one
minute after being shot.'

Henry exhaled with fury, raging at himself. He rounded on
FB like a tiger. 'This,' he stammered, 'this needn't have happened.'

'It couldn't have been prevented,' FB said defensively.

Henry's face set. 'You know what I was thinking this morning
in the lecture room? When I was looking at the pathetic police
operation to catch these bastards?'

'They might not even be the same crew,' FB cut in.

'What?' Henry's voice rose incredulously. 'Getaway car
torched not a million miles away from the one the other day?
Another stolen car ready and waiting for them to jump into and
then that one torched in Manchester? Pull the other one, boss.
It's the same team and you know it. And what the hell have we
done about it? Just let 'em get more and more violent and then
– surprise! This happens. An innocent girl gets gunned down like
vermin. It should never have come to this. We should've been
onto these bastards from the first job, not let it build up. We are
to blame for this.'

'We don't get into the blame game here.'

'Unless it suits,' Henry blasted. He could see FB's chins
wobbling and his face glowing with anger.

'The only people to blame are the ones with guns, PC Christie.'
A formal, defensive statement. 'Stop carrying the weight of the
world on your shoulders.'

Henry didn't seem to have heard. 'I'll tell you what I was
thinking . . .'

FB stood up. 'I don't want to know what you were thinking,
Henry, understood?' His head tilted back challengingly. 'And I

don't want you to even think about blabbing anything to anyone about your not required thoughts on the matter.'

'You mean the chief constable? You don't want me to tell him what a half-arsed response the CID were making to apprehend a brutal gang of armed robbers that should have had a team of twelve detectives on their tail from the word go? Is that why you're here? To warn me off?' Henry was painfully aware he was treading a very thin line by addressing a senior officer in this manner, particularly one who had a dangerous streak a mile wide in him and was known to bear grudges. But at least Henry knew that if it came to explanations he could claim being out of his mind at the grief of witnessing the death of a colleague. He was actually grieving, but he wasn't out of his mind.

He was simply furious, wanted to lash out.

'Henry, you can tell the chief constable whatever you bloody well want – if you decide to see him. But remember one thing, he's an ex-detective. Being a jack is in his blood. And he'll understand our response to the problem of an armed gang.' FB smiled cruelly.

Henry swallowed something about the size of a brick.

Throwing his Teddy out of the cot was not a good idea.

'And no,' FB said calmly, 'I did not come for that reason.'

'Why then?' Henry asked quietly. 'A shoulder to cry on?'

FB regarded the constable critically, his fat jaw rotating as he sized Henry up and down.

'To tell you that a proper operation is now up and running to catch these cop-murdering bastards . . . and that before Jo was shot, I was in the process of setting up a bigger operation anyway and you know that.'

Henry fired him a look of disbelief. Stable doors and horses bolting came to his mind.

'Just ask around if you don't believe me. I was on the blower all morning pulling a team together. The bastards just caught us on the hop and Jo walked into something we couldn't have foreseen.'

'And now they're unlikely to come back here in a hurry,' Henry observed.

'Agree,' FB nodded. 'They'll go to ground in Manchester, which makes it very hard for us to follow up. But I do think they'll be back and we need to be ready for them in that case, which we will be.'

Henry said, 'So you've come to tell me that?'

'Yes, and something else. If you're up for it, I want you on the murder squad, but only if you're emotionally stable enough.'

'Doing what? Brewing up for the detective constables? The numpty woodentop?'

'No.' FB half-smiled. 'Well that, obviously, goes without saying,' he teased. 'You certainly are a woodentop, as they say in the Met.'

Henry shook his head and folded his arms, waited cynically.

'Clearly this will be a murder investigation now,' FB announced.

'Clearly.'

FB snapped his mouth shut at the interruption and reconsidered Henry. 'You know, you really do need to learn to keep it shut, Henry. Big gob achieves nowt.'

Henry pretended to pull a zipper across his lips.

'You mentioned you thought there might be a local connection . . . not the most original thought, admittedly,' FB said, just in case Henry might have believed he was the only cop thinking things through. 'I want you to look into that.'

'What about everything else I have on my plate?'

'We've all got shit on our plates,' FB snarled. 'Man up, deal with it.'

Henry wound his neck in, rather like a tortoise.

'You're drafted onto the murder squad as of now. Whatever you've got pending, deal with it or pass it on, but you won't be given anything else. You're on the squad, I've sorted it with your crime car boss, so now you can make a valid contribution to finding these bastards who rob, murder and terrorize. How does that sound?'

'Plain clothes?'

'Whatever's appropriate.'

'Who will I be working with?'

'You'll be all alone.'

'OK.'

'And the other thing I want you to spend time doing is mooching in Manchester.'

'Mooching?'

'Eyes and ears. In the vicinity of where the second getaway cars are abandoned. See what you can pick up, yeah?'

'Alone again?'

'Naturally.'

The first thing Henry had to deal with was making a witness statement. He did this after FB had gone, driving back to the station at Rawtenstall – which was now crawling with cops. A few people stopped, spoke and commiserated with him. Henry was pleasant but he wanted to get the statement written whilst the incident was still clear in his head. He snaffled a few CID 9's and 9a's, the witness statement forms, and did a quick exit, driving back to his house where he pulled out the kitchen table and got writing.

He'd done it in less than an hour, all the while wondering if the man who had killed Jo was the same one who'd fired at him. A man with an itchy finger and a death wish. He made a mental note to read the statements taken from the customers at the shop and see if whatever description they made, vague though it would be because there wasn't a lot to describe – a masked man with a gun – matched his own memories of the masked man.

After that he knew that his next port of call that evening should really be to see Kate and spend some time with her, connecting with his emotions.

The more he thought about doing that, the more his lip curled.

What he needed was a drink. Several. And the fact that his local hostelry was in walking distance sealed the pact. He changed into jeans and a jacket, strolled down and ordered his first pint of the night from Steph, the landlady who he had not yet seen naked that day.

He fell into bed at 1am after staying for a lock-in after the pub closed at 11. The lock-in had turned into a mini-celebration-cum-wake of Jo Wade's life, carried out by the usual in-crowd of cops who often gathered in the pub. By the time the doors were closed, Henry had finished his fourth pint and moved onto whisky. The landlady provided a steaming tureen of chicken curry, a huge bowl of boiled rice and a stack of naan breads. The cops set upon the feast like hyenas on an injured warthog.

They raised their glasses to Jo and then turned as one to Henry and silently toasted him in an unrehearsed, spontaneous gesture which made him blink back a tear and start to blub a little – until someone bought him another Bell's whisky.

He made his excuses after that and headed for the toilets at the back of the pub, bouncing off the walls as he stumbled drunkenly to them.

It seemed to take an inordinate length of time to urinate and he had to steady himself a few times and prop his forehead on the toilet wall to prevent himself from staggering sideways.

When he emerged, zipping himself up, the landlady was waiting for him.

'Can I assist you in your grief?' Her eyes sparkled enticingly and once again Henry was bedazzled by the prospect of jumping into bed with another female. Such was the simplicity of the life of a single cop in the valley, if he or she wished it to be that way. Henry was finding it hard to break the habit.

Steph took a firm hold of his jacket, then jerked him roughly towards her until their faces were only inches apart. Her eyes stared deeply into his, then she dragged him that last inch and their lips mashed together for a long, slow, drunken kiss. When they disengaged, Henry found himself literally breathless. 'Have you ever had a landlady?' she asked throatily.

'It's on my to-do list,' he said in the moment before she yanked him back into a clinch and walked him back against the wall with a crash. He went with the flow, although there was that black cloud somewhere in his mind telling him to do a sharp exit. Not just that when he made love to any lady, he much preferred to have a clear head because he enjoyed it all the more. A bit tipsy was OK, but being stone-drunk was not always that pleasurable. The other section of the cloud concerned Kate and his declaration to her and his half-baked marriage proposal not many hours ago.

Yet here he was, locked in an embrace with a woman at least a dozen years older than he was, pathetically fighting off the urge to drag her to bed.

He extricated himself clumsily. 'No, this isn't right,' he said and pushed her gently away.

But her eyes were on fire, radiating sexual desire. 'If you're bothered about Gerry,' Gerry being Henry's housemate, 'don't be. He's away on a driving course.' She told him something he didn't know. He might have been his housemate but they certainly didn't live in each other's pockets.

She fought back at that, pulling him towards her, unwilling to take no for an answer. One hand slithered around his neck, another grabbed the front of his jeans which, despite Henry's mixed emotions and alcoholic state, bulged. He gasped and she forced her tongue into his ear. He emitted a whimper of submission as this organ worked in and out and she murmured, 'Let me screw you senseless, Henry.'

It was an offer he failed to refuse. She led him easily up the back stairs into her boudoir and carried out her promise.

Afterwards, Henry scooped up his clothes – they had been flung around the room as Steph had undressed him, half reminding him of a dog digging madly for a bone – and got dressed in the en-suite shower room, although he couldn't be bothered putting on his underpants or socks. He stuffed them into his jacket pocket. The landlady was asleep, having exhausted herself. He gave her a drunken wave, then stumbled back into the pub where the wake for Jo was still strongly underway, with a cop behind the bar serving the drinks and placing the money in an honesty box on the bar top. This is what usually happened at a lock-in.

They gave Henry a victorious cheer as he made his way through the bar, acknowledging the accolade with a shy bow and a royal wave. He let himself out through the locked doors, closing them behind him and, weaving like a stereotypical drunk, walked back to his house and bed, where he fell instantly asleep.

He woke at seven, feeling horrible, crawled on his hands and knees to the bathroom, slid over the side of the bath like a creeping blob from a sci-fi movie and fired up the shower. He sat underneath it until he woke up.

After this he downed three paracetamols, donned his running gear and set off for a three-mile trot to clear his head, even if his brain felt as though it had come free from its moorings inside his skull.

On his return he showered again, then fried up egg and bacon, made a strong filter coffee and devoured this amazing tasting breakfast. Then, dressed in jeans, shirt and a leather jacket, he drove into work, almost fit to face the world.

Henry had claimed that he thought the armed robbers, now murderers too, must be using a local connection to identify their targets. It was unlikely that they would simply roll into town and rob the first place they came across. It would have to be planned. His claim, though, was purely conjecture on his part. They could just as easily be reccying premises themselves, but the thing about crime investigation was that hypotheses were put forward and then followed up, either to be discarded as fanciful thinking, or shown to have some value.

Henry saw it as his job to work out if there was a local connection or not.

If not, so be it. Shrug the shoulders, move on.

But he had to give it a go . . . plus, there was just something at the back of his mind niggling away.

As he drove into work he wondered how best to go about his task and decided that his first job would be to check if any of the targeted businesses had CCTV cameras installed and, if so, which of the detectives who had been looking into the attacks had reviewed the tapes, what had been seen and was it of any value to Henry's bit of the puzzle.

The station was bustling again. The rear yard was overflowing with cars Henry did not recognize, indicating an influx of personnel from all points of the county. He made his way up to the first floor and discovered that the lecture room had been transformed into an incident room, now crowded with sitting and standing detectives and uniform officers, awaiting a briefing. Henry loved the anticipatory buzz of it, and a shimmer ran through him. He nodded at a few people he knew, including a couple of detectives from Blackburn, then took up a position at the back wall and waited for action.

A couple of minutes later, FB bustled in, followed by the chief constable, and the two of stood in front of the dry-wipe board and flip-chart easel at the front of the room.

A hush descended, the chief took a breath and, as Henry guessed, he gave an emotional and motivational rallying call to the squad about the need for professionalism, diligence and persistence to catch the offenders who had so brutally taken one of their colleagues. A large photograph of Jo, blown up from her personal record, was pinned to the wall. Once that was done, he handed over to FB, who began the briefing proper.

When this finished, Henry made himself scarce for a while to avoid any possibility of contact with the chief. He didn't fancy talking to the guy about what had happened.

Then, when he thought the chief had gone, he went to see the detective who had been allocated the job of exhibits officer, a sensible first port of call, Henry would have thought, but the meeting only really made Henry realize just how amateurish the set-up was.

The officer was an experienced detective, drafted in from Blackburn, where Henry had met him a few times during his recent ill-fated secondment.

He frowned deeply at Henry as the request was made.

'I need to look at the video footage from the tapes seized from any of the shops that have been hit,' Henry explained. 'So . . . can I have the tapes, please?'

'What tapes?'

'The CCTV footage from the shops?' Henry's voice had a rising inflection of disbelief in it.

'Like I said – what tapes?'

'You mean no one's seized any tapes from the shops?' Henry now tried to keep his voice on a conversational level, trying not to show his utter horror.

'Well – I've only just started this job yesterday, but so far I haven't seen any tapes,' the DC said. 'Perhaps you could go and seize them. Might be a good idea.'

Henry had envisaged being given an armful of videotapes containing hours of mostly useless footage, but just to confirm how slapdash the whole thing had been so far, he left with an armful of nothing.

'You need to generate an action and make sure the allocator has seen it, then no one duplicates what you're doing,' the DC called after him.

'I will,' Henry said over his shoulder.

'Hey – aren't you the one who nearly clocked DI Chase?' he

called after Henry, mentioning the name of the DI in Blackburn Henry had so nearly decked.

'No,' Henry denied the accusation, even though it was true.

'Ah well, shame . . . the guy needs a seeing to.'

Further enquiries revealed that no one, so far, had had the nous to get the tapes from the shops. This was an important little lesson for Henry, which he filed away in his mind: sometimes even the most obvious, simple things get overlooked, and he was astounded that no one book or document existed, a process map, almost, of how serious investigations should be conducted, what to consider, what to do . . . but it seemed that investigations were just done on the hoof, based on experience and gut feeling. Some sort of murder investigation manual would be a great idea, he thought. Maybe one day . . .

He snaffled a set of keys from the sergeant's office again and went on the hunt for some evidence.

He revisited all the shops that had been robbed, including the latest one which was still a murder crime scene. But his hoard was pitiful. The use of security cameras was patchy across the board and only three of the shops had them. One shop had only one tape that was constantly rewound and then reused when it reached the end and the other two had a couple of tapes each but were not automatically set up to record and he learned that the VCRs were often completely forgotten about until someone in the shop just happened to remember to switch them on.

All in all, Henry thought, crap. Big Brother was hardly watching anything in 1982.

He had envisaged having to sit through dozens of tapes that had systematically and chronologically recorded footage of daily life in the shops, but he came away from his visits with only five tapes that had been reused numerous times. He had expected to be sat for days on end in a darkened room, drinking coffee, sifting through hours of boring footage but the reality was it would be just a few hours and if he could find a good quality tape player he would be able to skim quickly through the tapes on fast-forward and save some time.

He returned to the station, labelled the tapes and booked them into the evidence system, then logged them back out to himself.

Next task was to sit somewhere comfortable to watch them – and he had an idea on that score.

In passing, he quickly checked his tray. The two committal files were still on top, their return dates seeming to flash ominously at him. With yesterday's incident he obviously hadn't completed them as intended and had no desire to pick them up today, either.

Underneath the two thick files was a new one, slipped in by a sergeant.

It was Jack Bowman's, stapled to the front of which was the 'wanted/escaped from custody' circulation and another note pinned to that from FB which simply read, 'Please expedite.'

Henry slid it out and had a quick glance through it. When he had gone to Dover all he had been in possession of was Bowman's original arrest warrant, but this file contained details of the three house burglaries offences Bowman was wanted for, and made mention he was suspected of about forty others. Henry scanned through them and wasn't surprised to see they were all of a similar nature. Bowman had broken, mainly, into terraced houses, usually through the back door, or by breaking a ground-floor window; sometimes he had shimmied up drainpipes and used glass cutters on windows, showing he was a very dextrous burglar indeed. He had stolen cash and easily portable trinkets and jewellery and often broke in whilst the occupants were asleep, and sometimes he had excreted in hallways or on landings – something Henry wasn't aware of.

And, Henry noted, with a little surge of excitement, most of the victims were old-age pensioners.

Very similar, in fact, to the burglary he had attended the previous day at Mrs Fudge's house.

Some of the MOs were identical, even the type of property stolen.

A silver photograph frame was something that Jack Bowman would happily steal and then try to sell.

'Little bastard's back in town,' Henry mused.

He stacked the videocassettes on top of his tray and left the station on foot. He intended to make two stops.

First he popped into the insurance brokers on Bank Street. Sitting primly at a desk behind the counter was Kate, whose face rose as he entered. She smiled her customer-focused smile for just a brief moment, but then her expression iced over when she realized it was Henry and that she hadn't heard from him in almost two days.

He leaned on the counter, flashing his boyish half-grin, which didn't seem to have the desired effect. She got up menacingly from her chair, making him quiver with a fear he had never felt before. Why did this woman – this mere slip of a girl, really – do this to him?

As she approached him he changed his own facial expression to one of great sadness, blinking like a little lamb.

It had no effect on Kate.

She jerked up to him and under her breath she said harshly, 'I haven't seen or heard from you in God knows how long and then you turn up acting like a bloody schoolboy, Henry.'

'You're cross,' he said, trying to sound puzzled.

'I'm bloody fuming . . . What is it, shag 'em and leave 'em? That will not happen to me, Henry James Christie.' Her eyes were like devil's orbs. Henry almost expected to see a trident in her hand and red horns growing from her forehead as she morphed into a devil ready to do battle with the cowardly devil on his shoulder.

'I . . . I . . . er . . .' he stammered.

'I . . . I . . . er . . . – what the hell does that mean?' she mimicked him cruelly.

'I'm sorry,' he ventured meekly.

'You virtually ask me to marry you and then nothing! Zilch! What was that – just to get your leg over?'

'No, no, no,' he protested.

'Did you mean it, or was it just a ploy to get a blow job?'

Kate's voice rose on the last three words and the two other ladies who worked in the office at separate desks, who had been watching and trying to earwig the conversation, looked at each other with shocked, wide open eyes.

'Both,' he admitted.

Kate eyeballed him steadily.

'I . . . had a bit of a busy day yesterday,' he said, still trying to elicit sympathy.

Kate softened. 'I know, and you should have contacted me,

we should have seen each other.' She sighed and nodded towards a consultation room on the public side of the counter where customers were taken to finalize deals. 'In there,' she ordered him.

She came out from behind the counter and hustled him into the room, almost propelling him through the door. She stepped in behind him and closed the door softly and turned the butterfly lock and leaned on the door.

'Trapped,' she said.

'Spider and the fly.'

'I need to be kissed, Henry.' Her voice had become husky – and not a little threatening. 'C'mere.'

'Well that was a first – and on duty,' he muttered whilst walking jauntily up Bank Street. He blew out his cheeks and made another discreet check of his flies, with a little skip and a hop as he went.

He was still grinning as he entered Fat Jack's and negotiated his way through the display goods to the counter where, once more, he found Dominic Tighe, aka Fat Jack, studying a newspaper, cigarette in one hand, brew in the other. He didn't look up.

Henry stood there quietly, arms folded. He could feel his jugular pulsing.

'Well I did my bit,' Tighe said, turning the pages of his newspaper.

'So where is it?'

'He ran with it.'

'What happened?'

'Guy came in, tried to sell me a silver photograph frame.' Still he didn't look up.

A beat of silence. 'And?'

'I must've given some vibes that made him nervous.'

'And?'

'He snatched it back and legged it.'

'Name?'

'Jack Bowman – but I didn't tell you that.'

ELEVEN

Henry scurried back to the station intending to root out Bowman's file to remind himself of the burglar's last known address, because he was going to pay it a visit. Not that he expected to find the escapee there, but he would never know until he knocked, or kicked the door in, and he knew he had enough reasonable suspicion to do that if he had to. Or at least he could manufacture some if necessary.

As he took the videocassettes off his tray and re-stacked them on the table, FB swung into the office on the door jamb. 'Where have you been?' he demanded.

'Making enquiries,' Henry responded, picking up a tape to show he wasn't lying, and waggling it at FB. 'Why?'

'We need more monkeys, that's why.'

'Eh?'

'Muscle – we need some muscle. I want to go and hit an address in Salford with the Regional Crime Squad, but I need some cannon fodder.'

'What address? Why?'

'Upstairs now,' FB said and swung back out of the office.

Ten minutes later Henry was sitting in the back of a personnel carrier with four other constables, a PC driving with Fanshaw-Bayley and another detective crushed together alongside the driver on the bench seat.

Henry cynically understood the psychology of it. The superior detectives up front, as uncomfortable as it was, and the dumb-ass riff-raff plebs in the back.

He smiled and didn't care. He had a sledgehammer propped up between his thighs and he was going to smash down a door. One of life's little pleasures.

A detective from the RCS joined them at Salford police station, together with a uniformed inspector from Greater Manchester Police who came along for the ride to ensure no funny business happened. The inspector took a list of the names of everyone present in the carrier and issued a briefing about behaviour. GMP was accommodating this raid because of its urgent nature and the fact it was a follow-up to the shooting of a colleague. Normally GMP would have insisted on being fully in control, but acquiesced to the circumstances on this occasion because it was a hot, dynamic operation.

The RCS detective squeezed onto the front seat with FB and the other jack and the inspector sat in the back of the van with the five constables, four of them in uniform, Henry still in plain clothes. The inspector leaned forward and directed the driver to the outskirts of the estate where the raid was to take place and gave a commentary about life in Salford.

'This isn't like one of your poxy little estates in Lancs,' he boasted proudly. 'Everyone here hates the cops and if they get chance, they'll have you. There's knives and guns galore and not many people afraid to use them on the police. So watch out.'

'What's the plan, then?' Henry piped up, as a plan of how they were going to hit this particular address seemed sadly lacking.

'I'll knock on the front door for you,' the inspector said. 'A few of you need to be behind me. If I get a reply, I'll step aside and in you go. If not, bring on the sledgehammers.'

A pretty thin plan, Henry thought, knowing it should be much, much better than this, operating on a wing and a prayer, hoping for the best. Disorganized and dangerous, he thought, but exciting nonetheless. He would happily go with the flow.

'He lives on the top floor of a four-storey block of council houses,' the inspector said, referring to the target. 'It might be as well if a couple of guys were round the back, just in case he tries to jump for it. It has been known.'

FB, who had been listening to the inspector with his arm draped over the seat, looked at Henry. 'You and me,' he said. 'Plain clothes would be better than a couple of uniforms hanging about, spooking folk.' To the inspector he said, 'Drop us off a short distance from the address and we'll make our way on foot. Give us a few minutes to get into position, then hit the place.'

Henry tried to hide his disappointment. He wouldn't be smashing down a door after all.

They drove to the perimeter of the council estate where FB

and Henry dropped out of the carrier and began to walk after getting directions from the local man.

The estate didn't look too bad, Henry thought. Actually not much to choose between here and something similar in Blackburn, despite the smug claims of the inspector. It was a big, densely populated estate dominated by four four-storey blocks of flats, one at each corner, giving it a German prisoner-of-war-camp feel. Henry half expected to see guards brandishing machine guns.

Henry and FB shuffled along, neither under any illusion that the residents who spotted them would think they were anything but cops, or at least someone from the authorities. It didn't help that they had de-bussed from a police van, but at least they'd done it off the estate.

'So who exactly is he?' Henry asked. 'Other than his name, he wasn't adequately described.'

FB was already puffing, walking not being his favourite mode of travel. 'He,' he gasped, 'is Manchester's best armed robber over the last ten years. John Longridge, forty-five years old, a string of previous convictions since he was seventeen for pointing guns at people and relieving them of their hard-gotten gains. Been sent down four times and got out just over six months ago, just about the time the robberies on our patch started. That said, he's more a planner than a doer these days.'

'Is there anything to actually link him to our jobs?'

'Nope . . . but even if he isn't involved, he'll know someone who is.'

'So . . . just a speculative arrest?'

FB merely raised his overgrown eyebrows at what was clearly a rhetorical question.

The two men turned into a high-walled ginnel that led onto the estate and opened out behind the block of flats they were interested in.

'We're going to do a proper Lancashire job on him,' FB said bigheadedly. 'Sweat the fucker. He'll know something, or we'll stitch him up with something. Either way, good.'

Henry groaned mentally, and they emerged from the alley and looked up at the flats. As the directions promised, they were at the back of the block in which John Longridge's top-floor flat was to be found. The main entrance was at the front and led to a concrete stairwell and a lift that rarely worked.

FB checked his watch. 'Five minutes, spot on,' he said, catching his breath. They looked up and saw that each flat had a small balcony and that from the top it was a good sixty-foot drop to the ground. Longridge's flat was one of these back ones. 'They should be knocking just about now.'

Henry surveyed the block. Built in the 1970s, not much more than ten years ago, it was already showing very obvious signs of decay, crumbling concrete and exposed brickwork where exterior plaster had fallen away as the rain had penetrated shoddy workmanship.

He was also aware of the almost complete lack of communication here. He and FB were equipped with Lancashire Constabulary radios, but these were limited to three or four channels, none of which synched with the channel used by the police in Salford. Nor did the Lancs radios have the range to be used here in Salford, which meant that he and FB had absolutely no clue whatsoever what was going on at the front or inside the block of flats, or even if this was the correct block, though Henry believed it was.

This inter-force communication was a big problem, something that annoyed Henry. It was bad enough in-force with a radio system peppered with black spots, but working alongside another force was almost a joke, something that needed some serious strategic thinking.

'Should be knocking,' FB said again . . . hopefully.

'But we have no idea if they are, or not,' Henry said.

'True. Not good, eh?'

'Abysmal.'

Henry scanned the balconies.

Suddenly a male figure appeared on the left-hand balcony on the top floor. A young man, skin-headed, dressed in a black zip-up windjammer and black jeans, pulling a black balaclava hood over his head, giving the two cops below only a fleeting glimpse of his face.

'Lift off,' Henry said.

The man straddled the balcony rail, grabbed hold of an outer soil pipe and without hesitation acrobatically swung down, his feet dangling in mid-air for a moment before he dropped onto the balcony below. And disappeared.

Henry and FB stared, open-mouthed. Then Henry said, 'He's back.'

The man had reappeared and carried out the same manoeuvre again, but this time shimmied down the soil pipe before swinging onto the next balcony below on the second floor and went out of sight.

'It's not Longridge. Too young,' FB said, guessing from the stature of the figure.

Once more the man reappeared and this time looked down at Henry and FB below, both of whom gave him a tiny wave.

'The doors must be locked,' Henry said. 'I bet people are always appearing on their balconies.'

Then the man did the same again, with great agility, dropping onto the next balcony, reaching the first floor.

'Last one,' Henry said. 'Let's hope that door's locked too.'

Henry got a better look at the man this time. He was thick set and very strong looking, his build reminding him of someone he couldn't quite place.

Then, way above on the fourth floor, two of Henry's colleagues leaned over the rail, looking down, gesticulating and shouting.

Henry gesticulated back, pointing to the first-floor balcony, just as the escaping man reappeared at the rail, maybe twelve feet above Henry and FB, then as though he hadn't even seen them, he vaulted over it, crashing to the ground, but allowing his knees to buckle and then to roll like he was landing from a parachute drop and although the air was audibly driven out of his body by the impact he was instantly up and running, heading towards the innards of the estate without a backwards glance.

For a moment Henry and FB were dumbfounded, half-expecting him to have broken both legs.

The guy was fast and agile. But Henry was faster.

He had perhaps five yards on Henry, who powered after him with a roar of, 'Police stop!'

Within a couple of seconds, rugby-playing, squash-playing, five-a-side footballer and jogger Henry was on him, reaching out with his fingertips, but the man veered sideways at the last instant.

He sprinted across a road and ran into the high-walled ginnel that Henry and FB had just walked through.

Henry went after him.

At about the twenty-yard point, the alley went right and if someone running down it didn't turn, they would crash straight into the brick wall either accidentally or deliberately.

The man Henry was pursuing crashed into it deliberately and Henry knew why.

He came to a bone-jarring stop and instantly spun threateningly to face Henry, having realized that only one of the cops was right on his tail and he had managed to lure him into a very dangerous situation.

One on one.

In a tight alleyway.

Suddenly he was armed with a flick knife that appeared from nowhere in his right hand. He lunged at Henry who, still propelled by his express-train momentum, was as good as running onto the blade and, of course, was wearing no form of body protection whatsoever.

Henry saw the blade flash out, even heard the click as it locked into place, and his whole world slowed right down.

He knew that if he ran into the man, the blade would be driven up under his ribcage into his heart and shred that internal organ and he would bleed to death very quickly. He knew he had to do something, or die in a Manchester alleyway.

Somehow he sidestepped and contorted like a bull-fighter as the man thrust the knife up at him. Henry saw it glint by him as he turned ninety degrees and the knife whizzed up, inches away, the man staggering forwards as the blade flashed in mid-air and missed its connection with a human torso.

Henry found himself side on to the man.

Instinctively he brought up his elbow and smashed it into the centre of the man's face, as hard as possible, bone crunching bone.

The man staggered backwards, but then turned and drove the knife at Henry again.

Henry contorted again, deflected the blow with his left hand whilst his right went for the man's throat, the cleft between his thumb and forefinger going straight into the man's very visible

Adam's apple and forcing him back against the alley wall. Henry's left hand sought to grip the knife hand which remained just out of reach as he pinned him back.

He managed to get hold of the thick wrist and smash the hand against the wall, twice. The knife clattered away and Henry held him in place for a moment as if the two of them were freeze-framed in a violent Argentinian tango, virtually forehead to forehead.

Henry thought he had him.

But the truth was, Henry wasn't really a fighter, certainly not in the street sense of the word. He was a grappler, an over-powerer. He could punch, but he wasn't dirty, and in most of the police-related brawls he'd had, he had beaten people by the speed at which he could flick 'em round, trip 'em up, pin 'em down and get the cuffs on.

He would never think of head-butting someone. Or kneeing them in the balls.

But clearly the hooded man who he was now clinging on to did not think along those lines. He was a dirty street brawler.

Because he kneed Henry so hard in the testicles he was certain that his balls had been smashed up into his lower abdomen with an instant pain so incredible that spread like wildfire up from his groin and seemed to grip his heart. It was an upward blow delivered with a hard, muscular thigh and Henry's breath whooshed out of him like a ton weight had been dropped on his chest.

And if that wasn't enough to make Henry let go, the head butt was.

The man's head didn't even rear back. One moment after the knee in the balls, and in the same movement, the man's head smacked down onto the bridge of Henry's nose, blinding him with pain that echoed around his cranium as blood gushed down his nose like a waterfall.

Henry sagged to his knees, releasing the man and as his head hung and he shook it, spraying blood like a wet dog shaking itself dry, the man side-footed the side of Henry's face with the sole of his shoe, sending him sprawling.

The man then straddled him and bent low, hauling him up by his jacket. Henry's vision swam as he tried to focus on the man's wild eyes, but all he could see was the red slit of the man's mouth.

'I've already killed one,' he growled. 'You're next, cop.'

Henry's mouth had filled with blood. He spat it into the man's eyes, getting the reaction he wanted: disgust.

Instinctively, the man threw him away and wiped at his face.

Henry, making a huge effort, fighting the pain and disorientation, went for the man again, bringing him down by taking his legs from under him, but all the man did was kick Henry away and line himself up to kick him once more.

'Oi!'

The man's head jerked up to look beyond Henry, giving the floored cop a glimpse of his neck.

FB was pounding down the alleyway like a boulder in an avalanche.

The man tore himself away from Henry, scrambled to his feet and ran, leaving Henry grasping air.

FB came to a halt behind Henry, gagging for breath, bent over with his hands on his knees. 'Why'd you let him go?' he wheezed.

Riven with pain extending from his balls to his brain, Henry turned and sat on his backside, wiping his face with the bottom of his shirt.

'I don't know, boss . . . why did I?'

John Longridge was successfully arrested at his flat and none of the cops who entered had any idea that another man had shot out of the balcony window and scaled down the block like Spiderman.

What they did find as Longridge opened the door for them, where he delayed them for a while, was that he had apparently been sitting alone, watching a Clint Eastwood video. It was only when one of the cops spotted two beer glasses and that the balcony door was open that they put these fairly basic clues together and concluded that he had not been alone. That was the point at which a couple of them rushed out onto the balcony and started shouting and pointing down at Henry and FB waiting below, who in turn shouted and pointed back. Longridge was arrested without any undue kerfuffle, coming quietly and smugly, denying that anyone else had been in his flat with him when the police knocked. He was taken back to Rawtenstall in the back of the personnel carrier, surrounded by a contingent of cops.

But Henry had lost interest. At least for the time being.

His balls hurt continually, throbbing deeply, and he wasn't certain if his nose had been broken or not. He had heard and felt a crunch as the man's forehead had connected, but he knew that noses were peculiar things, mostly gristle. Maybe it was, maybe it wasn't but he spent a lot of the journey back to Lancashire with his head tilted back, or hung between his legs, with scrunched-up tissue stuffed into each nostril.

It was a very uncomfortable journey and he was glad when they pulled into Rawtenstall nick. He just wanted to get home to bed and stuff himself with whisky and paracetamols. The thought of going to hospital never even entered his head.

Just before six, Longridge was booked into custody and dumped into a cell.

FB caught up with Henry before he left.

'I'm going to let him stew overnight,' he said, 'soften him up a bit. Have a dig at him in the morning.'

'OK,' Henry said, his voice muffled by the kitchen towel he was holding over his face.

'You going to be OK?'

Henry nodded. 'You know we let Jo's killer go, don't you?'

'You did, not me. You had hold of him,' FB pointed out.

'OK, fair enough – I let him go. And he sounded and looked and sounded like the guy who threatened me with the shotgun.'

FB grinned. 'We'll get him. Don't worry.'

'I think he wants to kill again. We need to catch him sooner rather than later.'

'We will.' FB sounded confident.

'What do you reckon to Longridge?'

'He's probably nothing to do with the robberies, but he'll know who did them. I'm going to make him think he's going to get stitched up for them – and Jo's murder – unless he starts blabbing. Do you want to be in on the interviews?'

'Me?'

'No, your bloody mother.'

'Yes, boss, I do.'

'Right then – back here at eight tomorrow, cleaned up, ready to rock.'

'It's me.'

'Who's me?'

'The bloke you performed a sexual act on in the insurance brokers, and no, I won't buy my car insurance from them. I'm not susceptible to bribery. Corruption maybe, but not bribery.'

Kate giggled.

'I take it you like living dangerously?'

'Up to a point . . . Why do you sound like you've got cotton-wool balls stuck up your nose?'

'Because I have. I got nutted today.'

'Oh God, are you all right?'

'Got nutted in more ways than one, actually.'

'Oh?'

'I have a swollen sack,' Henry admitted.

Kate laughed this time.

Henry was using the phone in the report-writing room. He hadn't yet gone home and was still covered in blood and his testicles hurt like hell. He couldn't sit comfortably. The security tapes he had taken from the shops that had been robbed were stacked on the table in front of him.

'Look,' he said, 'I need to do some work tonight, but we could sort of do it together if you're up for it.'

'Like what?'

'Watching security tapes,' he posed hopefully. 'I was wondering . . . I mean, I've got a VCR at the house, but it's not a great one . . . so . . .'

'Can you use my dad's?' Is that where you were meandering to?'

'Spot on. Might be a bit boring, though. Hours of tedium.'

'Well, I've actually got some good news on that score,' Kate said. 'Mum and Dad are out tonight – all night. Going to see a show in Manchester and staying over. I've got the house to myself.'

'Party time!' Henry said gleefully.

*   *   *

He drove to his place first and got cleaned up there, throwing his T-shirt away, but scrubbing the dried blood off his leather jacket, which was too expensive to chuck. He had a shower, then inspected himself in the shaving mirror. He touched his nose gingerly, then waggled it. It was painful but he didn't think it was broken, although it was strangely swollen and the bag under his right eye was a nice shade of purple.

He then held the mirror down to his genitals.

His balls, too, were swollen and the same shade of purple as his eye. He didn't dare touch them, they were so delicately and excruciatingly painful. He just hoped there would be no lasting damage.

Twenty minutes later he arrived at Kate's with an armful of videotapes, a small bouquet of flowers he'd bought from ASDA, a bottle of white wine and a couple of cans of beer for himself, plus some chocolate: a surfeit of comfort food.

Kate was aghast at the sight of his face but he warned her to steel herself for when she eventually clapped eyes on his testicles.

At her insistence and to assuage her piqued curiosity, Henry got that bit of the evening over with in the kitchen. He was reluctant but she made it happen and he stood before her with his jeans halfway down his thighs and his underpants rolled down so she could see the sorry looking state of things.

'Oh my God!' she uttered, recoiling and bringing her hands up to her face to cover her mirth. 'They really are the colour of plums.'

'If you think it's funny, I'm off,' Henry said, affronted and a little offended.

'No, no, no,' she gasped breathlessly, trying to contain hysterics. 'Do you want me to massage them?'

Henry haughtily, but carefully, pulled his underpants and jeans back up. 'No,' he said. 'I don't want you to do anything. Just be careful around them and, y'know, a bit of sympathy wouldn't come amiss.'

'You're right,' she said, gaining some self-control. 'Your face is a proper mess too.' He allowed her to touch him gently on his cheek, but it was very painful and he drew quickly away with a sharp hiss. 'Sorry,' she said. She went onto tiptoe and kissed him on the lips. 'Tea's nearly ready.'

It was an amiable meal. She was a good cook. Afterwards they retired to the living room in which a huge TV and VCR were located. They watched some early evening TV, including an episode of *Tales of the Gold Monkey*, which was Henry's favourite. Then, beer and wine in hand, they started to watch the video footage from the shops.

It was very tiresome viewing, even though it was pleasant for Henry to sit on a large settee with Kate snuggled up close and his arm around her shoulders. Something he could get accustomed to.

'What're you looking for?'

'Don't know,' he admitted. 'Just a hunch.'

'From the master detective,' Kate laughed.

'One day,' he promised.

He worked through a couple of tapes from one shop and saw nothing, skimming through six hours' worth in about one hour using the fast-forward facility.

He was beginning to think it was a waste of time and he would be better watching TV instead.

It was only on the fifth tape that he saw something of interest.

This was a tape from the second shop that had been robbed, a convenience store near Rawtenstall town centre, run by an Asian man.

Henry had inserted the tape into the player without checking how far forward it was, thinking he was at the start and, of course, the tape counter reset itself to zero as he started to watch. His legs were outstretched over an upholstered pouf and Kate, similarly stretched, was tucked in beside him, becoming sleepy. Henry was now completely bored by the task, a state of mind not assisted by the location of Kate's left hand which lay on his jeans, just slightly above the danger/injury zone and despite his injury, he was responding to the proximity of her hand and warm body.

He groaned as she squeezed him delicately through his jeans.

He hurried the tape on, not really paying as much attention to it as he should have done. He moved it on even faster, but was then slightly puzzled when he heard the VCR click and whirr, the noise it made when a tape ended – and the tape started to rewind automatically.

'That was a short one,' he observed.

'Good. Can we go to bed? Early night?'

'It'd be rude not to,' Henry assented. He was eagerly looking forward to a full night with Kate, something that had happened only occasionally and only ever at his house which wasn't the most comfortable of places, because it was usually quite chilly and had little in the way of creature comforts. His only disappointment was the state of his balls. 'You sure Mummy and Daddy won't be back tonight?'

'I assure you.'

The tape finished rewinding and stopped with a click.

'Let's go for it then. I'll just put the tape back into its box.'

Kate rolled away. Henry sat up, gasping as a pulse of pain shot up through him. He paused a moment then dropped forward onto his hands and knees and crawled over to the TV, peering at the controls of the VCR for the tape eject button but then noticing that the tape counter was showing a minus figure of forty-four minutes, not the zero, or thereabouts, he would have expected to see.

He hummed.

'What's the matter?'

'This tape didn't go in at the beginning. I'd best just skim through it.'

'OK, love.'

'I'll be up in a moment or two if you want to go,' he said, thinking he sounded just like a married man.

'OK, I will.' She rolled up onto her feet and left the room.

Henry zeroed the tape counter then pressed play on the VCR itself then went backwards onto the settee and settled back to use the remote control to skim through the images of what, he realized, was a bloody boring shop.

The camera was positioned behind the counter, high up and to one side, giving a great view of what was going on behind the counter and a half-decent shot of customers actually at the counter. It was quite limited in its scope, but it served its purpose, he thought.

He fast-forwarded the tape. A few customers came, bought goods, chatted to the owner, and left.

Then one in particular caught his eye. Henry thumbed the stop button and rewound the tape slightly. He stopped it and pressed play.

A customer at the counter, speaking to the shop owner. Points to cigarettes stacked on the shelves on the back wall. The owner turns and selects what the customer has asked for, and his back is turned to the customer. Who leans across the counter.

Henry could see that if the customer is quick enough, there are some items on the counter – chocolate bars and sweets – that could easily be stolen and pocketed before the store owner turns back. Henry expected this to happen. But it doesn't.

The customer simply leans over and looks both ways behind the counter and for a second or two his eyes focus on the till. Then, as the shopkeeper turns back from the shelves, the customer acts all innocent and leans on the counter with his elbows as he is handed a packet of cigarettes which he pays for and stays as his money is put into the till. He says a few more words to the shop owner and just before he actually leaves the store he does the thing that makes Henry's heart leap and makes him forget the pain in his head and balls.

The customer glances up at the lens of the security camera.

And Henry's hand curls into a fist of triumph.

He rewound the tape, found the point where the customer steps into view, and then watched the transaction twice more, once at normal speed, once slowed right down. Frame by frame. He paused it when the man looked up at the lens.

The picture wavered, lines skittered across it.

But Henry smiled – and then he frowned as something else about this man struck him and his pleasure turned back to searing pain.

TWELVE

Henry was up at six the following morning after a night of cuddling only, then a big, long sleep. He took his time in 'Dad's' shower, used 'Dad's' shampoo and soap liberally, but washed his private parts carefully as they were still extremely tender. He nipped home first to get a change of clothing, and was in work for about seven.

The station was quiet and the early shift had all come in for the 7am brew in the parade room – an unofficial policing tradition practised, pretty much, across the force.

Henry nodded to them but didn't stay to take their questions. This was Jo's scale, as shifts were called, and he could sense their overwhelming sadness. He didn't want to get drawn into it today because he needed to get moving with all the stuff that was flipping around in his battered head.

But he did help himself to a mug of tea from the stainless-steel teapot, brewed from loose tea and poured out through a sieve into a mug. It tasted wonderful at that time in the morning. Something energizing about an early morning cuppa in a cop shop. Henry loved it.

He took the brew through to the sergeant's office and collected Jack Bowman's wanted file, then walked up to the Collator's office on the first floor. Charlie Martin wasn't in yet so Henry had the office to himself for a while. As a matter of course the office was accessible twenty-four hours a day because most Intel was collected by hand and stored in files and there wasn't a great deal on the Police National Computer and it was often needed in the middle of the night when the station duty officer might find himself searching for something to help out a bobby on the beat who had stop/checked someone and needed more detail. Henry spent a lot of his time sifting through stuff in the Collator's office, building up his knowledge of local crims, their families and associates.

He placed his brew down, rifled through a cabinet and hauled out Vladimir Kaminski's file. It was actually fairly thin, but it gave Henry some pointers. Kaminski had only ever been prosecuted in Lancashire twice and only for a public order offence and a minor assault, even though the Intel suggested he was suspected of some more serious assaults for which he was never charged. Even impaling some poor lad's hand to a spear-like railing didn't get him into court.

These were referred to in the file and Henry now knew why he had never faced a bench of magistrates. He was FB's informant and as such got preferential treatment and freedom he didn't really deserve. FB probably thought he was playing Kaminski, but Henry now half-suspected it was actually the other way around. It was just that FB didn't know he was the one being duped.

When offenders were arrested for certain offences that were classified as crimes, the arresting officer was obliged to record certain details relating to the offender. Fingerprints were taken, descriptive and antecedent forms were completed and it was usual that copies of these forms were kept on local files for intelligence purposes. The originals were submitted to LANCRO – the Lancashire Criminal Record Office – at headquarters.

Which was the case for Kaminski.

It was a slim file – and again, Henry suspected that FB edited it regularly – but because he had been convicted of assault, it contained copies of his mug shot, descriptives and antecedents.

Henry sat down at the Collator's desk, tea in hand. He began to read and sip.

The descriptive forms recorded the height, weight and, obviously, a detailed description of the subject, including any distinguishing marks or features, such as tattoos or scars. Henry's lips quivered whilst reading about Kaminski's tattoos. If the officer recording the details was professional and patient enough, he or she sometimes included an additional sheet of paper on which the tattoos that were sometimes difficult to describe would be sketched out. 'LOVE' and 'HATE' on the knuckles was easy enough to comprehend, as was 'ACAB' on a forearm – 'All Coppers Are Bastards' – or the name of a loved one on a bicep. Henry himself had drawn many a complicated tattoo and submitted the drawings with the forms. And the officer who had completed the descriptive forms for Kaminski had drawn several of his tattoos, one of which interested Henry greatly.

He sketched his own copy of it.

Next Henry read Kaminski's antecedent history. This basically skimmed through his upbringing, jobs he'd had (none) and his family details, parents and siblings.

Once again the officer completing them had been very detailed and Henry noted Kaminski's family origin (actually Polish/Russian) and where they now lived. He wrote out the name of one family member in particular.

After this he replaced the file and picked up the telephone and dialled an internal number for the PNC bureau at HQ and spoke to one of the operators, who happened to be someone he knew well. Then he sat back and pondered for a few moments – and suddenly remembered what had been nagging away at his brain.

'Shit!' he said and slapped his forehead.

By this time it was eight o'clock.

Henry knew the murder squad was due in for an 8.30am briefing and the station had started to get busy, detectives drifting in, a lot of milling about going on, kettles being boiled, the aroma of bought-in bacon sandwiches and toast wafting through the corridors. He also knew that he and FB were scheduled to interview John Longridge at nine, so he was a bit torn.

There were things he wanted to do but he also did not want to miss the chance of getting up-close to a villain as big as Longridge, a rare treat for any cop. He wanted to know what the guy had to say, but doubted he was directly involved in any of the robberies as such, or Jo's murder. But Henry wasn't going to be fooled into taking that as read. He would keep an open mind.

The lecture room was full of bodies and Henry took up a position right at the back, behind everyone, and waited for the briefing which was going to be conducted by a detective superintendent from headquarters who Henry had only vaguely heard of. This puzzled him slightly, as he was expecting FB to be running the show.

The superintendent came in. FB, trailing behind, looked annoyed and grim-faced. Not happy.

The superintendent stepped up to the lectern, which he rapped sharply with his knuckles, bringing everyone to attention. He then proceeded to reveal to Henry just why FB looked like a gorilla had just crapped in his car.

FB had been replaced as head of the investigation.

It was now being run by the detective super from HQ.

Henry watched FB's face as the interloper announced he was now in charge of things. FB was standing just behind the man's left shoulder, scuffing his toe caps miserably on the floor, looking very, very miffed, twirling a pen continuously. Mostly he looked at the floor, but at one point he glanced up and locked eyes briefly with Henry, then broke visual contact, a moment that said a lot to Henry.

Henry allowed himself a flicker of a smirk, but at the same time wondered why FB had been dumped. Henry thought he had been doing a decent enough job. At least there was a prisoner in the cells and even if it was a speculative arrest, there was something to work with.

This was the first time in his police service that Henry had come face to face with such a supposedly high-ranking criminal. His usual prisoners were juveniles, because that demographic – young males between the ages of twelve and seventeen – were responsible for the bulk of crime committed. He had purposely targeted them and over the past year had arrested over one hundred kids and cleared up about four hundred burglaries and other thefts. It was a considered choice because he had seen that although kids committed most of the crime, they were often avoided because they were a pain to deal with, but he believed that his approach was also a good apprentice-ship for a detective.

Most detectives dealt with older offenders and when he became a jack that's what he would do. Eventually he wanted to be engaging with the likes of John Longridge, and get onto the Regional Crime Squad and ultimately, he hoped, he would become a detective who dealt exclusively with murders. At the moment Lancashire did not have such specialists, but Henry knew it was the way forward and would happen one day.

Anyway . . . that was his vague career plan. But for the moment he would concentrate on kids and take whatever else came his way and try to get over the first hurdle, which was to actually get on CID, an aspiration that seemed to have taken a nosedive for the moment.

So, having become embroiled in Jo Wade's murder and the linked armed robberies and been given the chance to take part in the interview with Longridge, Henry was not going to miss the opportunity.

He would look upon it as a learning process, see how a seasoned detective like FB approached the interview and even though Henry was no psychologist, he was fascinated by what made people like Longridge tick.

Longridge was brought out of his cell by the station duty PC, who also doubled as a gaoler, and taken to the interview room just off the charge office.

Henry and FB followed.

Henry was carrying the paperwork and FB told him he wanted him to take contemporaneous notes of the interview, which FB would later edit – but not to record, FB chuckled as he said it, when the prisoner gets beaten up.

The interview room was cramped and not entirely fit for purpose because it also doubled as the police surgeon's room, with an examination table in one corner that took up far too much space.

Longridge sat alone on one side of the interview table, Henry and FB on the other. He had his arms folded. He was unshaven, reeked of body odour. He looked strong and broad and fit, obviously worked out regularly. His eyes drifted contemptuously from one officer to the other, showing no fear, just hate. He was still dressed in the clothes he had been arrested in.

Prior to going into the interview, FB confided to Henry that nothing of evidential value had been found in Longridge's flat in Manchester but he was working on other possible addresses and premises for him.

'Sleep OK?' FB asked as he settled his bulk into the plastic chair.

Longridge sniffed up and ignored the question.

'I'm DI Bayley,' FB said, opting for the abbreviated version of his name to keep things easy. 'This is PC Christie.'

Longridge glanced at him. Henry gave him a nod which the

prisoner also ignored. He wasn't going to be the most affable of
people, Henry sussed.

'You're not obliged to say anything unless you wish to do so
but what you say may be written down and given in evidence,'
FB cautioned him as per the Judges' Rules, the guidelines to
which the police operated in 1982 concerning the detention and
questioning of suspects. Longridge simply looked bored. Henry
scribbled away.

'I'm investigating the brutal murder of a policewoman by a
gang of armed robbers, Mr Longridge,' FB declared quite
dramatically, then paused for a reaction. Longridge stared all the
way though FB, his eyelids half-closed. Nothing came back from
him. FB went on, 'We believe you are either part of this gang
or are responsible for planning the robberies or you take a cut
from them.'

Longridge's mouth twitched. But he did not speak, which was
good from Henry's point of view because he was writing like
mad and wished he had shorthand.

'The policewoman was shot to death by one of the gang, which
makes every single one of them responsible for her murder, not
just the one who pulled the trigger of the sawn-off shotgun.'

Longridge remained impassive, unimpressed.

FB placed a hand on Henry's right wrist, the gesture meaning,
do not write anything at this point. He leaned forward.

'Let me make this clear, John,' FB said, just above a whisper.
'I know you are one of the most prolific armed robbers in the
north of England. I also know you plan armed robberies . . .
and one thing I do not like is bad guys coming across the
border from Manchester into my peaceful little patch, causing
mayhem, killing cops and sticking two fingers up at us. I don't
like it, which is why I'm going to prove that you are a member
of that gang and might even be the one who pulled the trigger
and killed an innocent girl. I'm going to do it dirty, yeah? I'm
going to fabricate evidence and I'm going to stitch you up. If
I have to.'

Henry was transfixed by the pulse on the side of Longridge's
neck, which quickened. He also felt his own heart rate increase
at FB's threats.

'You'll have a fuckin' job,' the prisoner said.

'I know. But I'm good at it,' FB assured him.

'I had nothing to do with it.'

FB leaned further forward. 'I don't fucking care.' Then he leaned back and he and Longridge had a staring competition. Longridge lost and Henry knew FB had the balance of power.

'What was your part in it?' FB asked, and tapped Henry's wrist: start again.

Longridge remained silent, which didn't surprise Henry. Most prisoners did, even the kids he dealt with. It was like prising open oysters sometimes. No one talked or confessed willingly.

'Tell you what, let's start simple. Who was the guy in your flat when the cops called yesterday?'

'There was nobody else in.'

'Wrong answer. Who was he?'

'And to be frank, I'm glad the bitch cop is dead . . .'

The thing about FB, Henry thought later, was that he might have been round and overweight, but when he moved, he moved like a striking cobra and he somehow channelled the power of his body mass all the way through to his fist.

Before Longridge finished his sentence, FB had risen, drawn back his fist and smashed it into the prisoner's face. A superbly delivered blow, catching the side of his head, twisting it round and knocking him backwards off his chair.

FB was up and around at him, dragging him up by his shirt front.

Henry watched in open-mouthed awe – and not a little fear – as FB spoke into Longridge's face, spittle coming from his mouth. 'I don't give a fuck who you are, or what you think you are, Johnny Longridge. To me, you're just a piece of shit on my shoe, a nothing, but that was a decent girl who lost her life and you are nothing in comparison to her – nothing!'

He dragged a stunned Longridge back up, picked up his chair and repositioned both of them back down.

He patted Longridge's cheek and said, 'Now we know where we stand, don't we? Who was in your flat?'

'I don't know,' he answered. 'Nobody.'

Even as he spoke, Henry could see the side of his face swelling redly.

'When the cops knocked, somebody appeared on your balcony

and shimmied down the outside of the flats. I watched him, you idiot. Who was it?'

Longridge cupped the side of his face, rotating his jaw delicately, glaring at FB. 'I can't tell you.'

'Can't or won't?'

'Whichever. You choose.'

'Why not?'

'Because whatever you think I am, a blagger or a fence or whatever, I ain't stupid. I don't deal in names, not of these people, anyway. They're fuckin' nuts. They're off their heads and they went out to kill. If it hadn't been a cop, it would've been some other poor sod. They're just glad it was a cop that walked in. Made their day. No guilt there. So knock the living shit out of me if you want, I'm saying nothing.'

Henry had been writing his words down, more or less as spoken, and he put a full stop to the speech.

'If I tell you, I'm dead. They're in business, these guys, and they don't take kindly to people grassing on them.'

'I thought you were the big "I am" in Manchester,' FB said with unhidden contempt and disbelief.

'Even the mighty fall,' Longridge admitted.

'Where were you on Tuesday morning?' FB said. That was the day of the robbery.

'Home. Flat.'

'Who with?'

'All alone – having a wank, watching porn.' His eyes hooded over as he looked at FB. Henry looked up from his scribing and in that expression he saw the depth of the man's criminality and corruption. 'And just one thing, Mr big-shot Detective, if you touch me again, I'll come for you. You might be the ruler in this place' – he gestured with his fingers – 'but not when you step into the outside world.' Then he looked at Henry. 'You can write that down if you want, son, but I'll deny it and there's no way I'm going to sign anything.' His gaze returned slowly to FB, who looked far from intimidated.

'Look forward to it,' he said. 'Interview terminated.'

Henry silently gathered his paperwork together, then they led Longridge back to the cells. At his cell door, he turned on FB.

'You gonna beat me up in the cells, fat man?'

There was no doubt that Longridge was the bigger, but fitter man.

In reply, FB punched him very, very hard and accurately in the solar plexus. The wind whooshed out of Longridge as he doubled over. FB propelled him hard into the cell. He staggered backwards and as his knees hit the bench, they gave way and he sat down involuntarily with a thump. His face angled up at FB, bearing a twisted, menacing look.

FB stepped into the cell, saying, 'Make yourself scarce,' to Henry.

'You OK, boss?'

Breathless, FB lowered himself into the seat next to Henry in the canteen. Henry had made two brews, both with pilfered teabags, milk and sugar. He pushed one of the mugs across to FB, who took it gratefully and had a sip.

'I'm OK.' He said the words, but really he wasn't.

Henry considered him, not entirely sure of what to make of him as a man. As a cop, he knew FB was a ruthless pursuer of criminals, though not necessarily of truth. Henry had a feeling that whilst justice might get done, it was at the expense of truth.

He could see FB was seething and he suspected that Longridge had suffered that morning not just because a policewoman had been killed but also because FB's nose had been put out of joint and his ego severely bruised by being replaced as head of a murder investigation he'd thought was his. Henry could see that the kudos that went with heading a successful investigation to catch a cold-blooded gang and the murderer of a policewoman could well lay the foundation of a glittering career as a detective. Being usurped by a headquarters boffin must have rankled.

'You want to talk?'

FB gave a scornful laugh. 'About what?'

'About what just happened and why.'

'You a counsellor now?'

'No, but I'm someone who witnessed an unprovoked assault that has possibly put me in a vulnerable position.'

FB shook his head. 'He won't say anything.'

'How do you know?'

'Because it's all part of the game. He has got some connection to this shite and we'll never be able to prove it because he's too far up the food chain, but he's involved, I'm certain. And he knows that I know. So don't worry, PC Christie. He only got a slap, anyway – and I thought he was going to assault me, so I got the first thump in. At least that's what a judge'll hear if it comes to that.' FB smiled conspiratorially. 'Won't he?'

Henry said nothing to that. 'What happened in the cell?'

'We came to an understanding, and that's all you need to know.'

Henry sipped his tea. 'And it had nothing to do with you being sidelined from the murder enquiry?'

'Oh yeah, that as well. A lot. Bastards.'

'Must suck.'

'Hey, don't get me wrong, I think murders should be run by superintendents, but the guy who's taken charge is a fast-track arsehole who wouldn't know a murder scene from a fuckin' landscape portrait. It's just grist to his career mill.'

'Just like it would be yours,' Henry ventured cheekily.

'Difference is, Henry, I want to make a difference. Yeah I want to be a high-ranking career detective, but I want to bring bad men to book, not show off bird shit on my uniform. So, at the moment, they can all just fuck off.'

Henry nodded. He could see the difference. Just.

Then he sat back smugly. 'How would you feel if I could prove a connection between Longridge and the gang?' Then, as a rider he added, 'Possibly.'

FB looked at him curiously.

'And say,' Henry went on, 'I could prove that mystical local connection, too? And suppose I knew who Spiderman was – and that Peter Parker is a fully paid-up member of the gang.'

'Hold on, who's Peter Parker when he's at home?'

'Spiderman's real name.'

FB screwed up his features. 'Go on, I'm listening.'

'I think I know who the other guy was in Longridge's flat, but, but, but,' Henry gabbled, 'it doesn't actually, really prove anything, except to ID the climber and show that he has a local connection.'

'What you're saying is, the one who you allowed to escape?'

'And who told me he'd already killed one cop.'

*   *   *

FB dragged Henry into his office. 'Why didn't you tell me this before?' he bleated.

'Didn't have time.'

FB sighed heavily but also looked thoughtful. His flabby jawline tightened as he worked something through, then his expression changed to one of realization, as a penny dropped.

'Bastard,' he hissed.

And Henry knew exactly what FB had just concluded – that Vladimir Kaminski was the one playing *him*, not vice versa as it should have been.

'Run me through it again, just so we're singing off the same hymn sheet.'

'When I locked Kaminski up for raping Sally Lee, I couldn't help but notice his tattoos. His skin's packed with them, but I saw one in particular when I was releasing him back – to reoffend . . .' Henry paused for effect. FB gave him a pissed-off, 'get on with it', look. 'I followed him down the corridor and saw one in particular on the back of his neck – a serpent wrapped around an automatic rifle. Just a crap, macho thing, I thought. So, I thought no more of it.' He shrugged.

'OK,' FB said.

'But then as I drove Sally back home, I saw Vladimir on Bacup Road . . . and I've only just remembered this, it's only just clicked. I watched him in my rear-view mirror. He crossed the road to a car that pulled in opposite the bus station. Didn't think anything of it at the time, even later really, but now I'm certain it was a two-tone brown Rover 3.5. It's been nagging me . . . but I only saw it fleetingly in the mirror . . .

'Next thing all hell breaks loose, the post office in Crawshawbooth is getting hammered and then I'm chasing a two-tone . . .'

'Brown Rover 3.5,' FB finished for him.

'It was only after it all finished that I thought there was something familiar about the car, but it only just dawned on me this morning as I was looking through the files and sifting it all through my brain . . .'

'OK, enough of the thought process,' FB interrupted rudely. 'So you're saying you thought you saw Vlad talking to someone in the getaway car.'

'I think it was the same car. Hands-up, y'know, I can't be one hundred per cent, but it was a Rover, and the right colour. Just saw it fleetingly but I'll bet Vlad parked it up for the gang.'

'OK, go on.'

'I've also spent a lot of time going through the very few and very shit-quality security tapes from the targeted shops. Something no one else seems to have got a grip of.'

FB looked slightly shamefaced at this. 'And?'

Henry held up one of the tapes that he'd had the foresight to bring with him into the office. He knew FB had a VCR and portable TV in his office.

'May I shove this in?'

'Be my guest.'

The equipment was on a small table in the corner of the room. Henry switched the machines on and inserted the tape, which started to run automatically.

'This is from the second shop, up on Haslingden Road, a week before it was robbed.' Henry stood aside to let FB see the screen. 'An off licence . . . and again, I know this doesn't actually prove anything but watch this.'

It was the customer at the counter. The shopkeeper turning to get cigarettes. The customer leaning over the counter, checking, the shopkeeper handing over the cigarettes.

Then the customer glancing up at the camera.

That customer being Vladimir Kaminski.

Henry paused the screen, which froze unsteadily, Kaminski's face still angled up.

'I think he's been the one choosing and sizing up the targets for the gang.'

FB remained stone silent. The pulse behind his double chin made it wobble and throb. His watery eyes were focused on the screen.

'That said, it doesn't prove anything,' Henry admitted. 'Just a guy buying fags. But it may have something to do with why he ran from me that morning at Sally's. He didn't want to get locked up because he knew the gang were due to strike that morning and he'd probably sorted out where to place the Rover, the second getaway car. He needed to be out and about – and I guess he must have sold you some bullshit, to make sure he walked.'

'No, it doesn't prove anything,' FB whispered, his whirring brain-cogs almost audible. 'Circumstantial and fleeting glimpses of a car that might've been the getaway car; him in the shop a week before it was robbed.' He looked at Henry. 'What was all this tattoo shit you started to say? Is it relevant?'

'I've got throbbing bollocks and a sore face,' Henry said, 'and my brain hurts.'

'I know all that.'

'And I know who did it.' Henry had also brought a folder with him which he opened and removed some sheets of paper from, placing them on FB's desk. He slid them across the polished surface. 'Vladimir Kaminski . . .'

'You're saying Vlad was, is, Spiderman?' FB butted in again. 'The guy from Longridge's flat? Surely not.'

Henry tutted and regarded FB with impatience. 'If I could just finish . . . When I was on the ground, all alone, facing an escaping and very violent masked felon, armed with a flick knife, I saw his neck at the moment he looked up when you decided to come and help me. I saw his throat and he had a tatt across his Adam's apple – the exact same one that Vladimir has tattooed across the back of *his* neck. A snake wrapped around a rifle.' FB stayed silent this time. 'So, I did a bit of digging this morning and found that Vlad has a younger brother called Constantine who has a criminal record for assault and robbery according to PNC and who lives in Manchester . . . but with no current address shown. I spoke to a PNC operator this morning who put his file up and confirmed the tattoo from the descriptives on the computer . . . and, apparently, this tattoo is the insignia of a criminal gang based in Gdansk, around the shipyards there. A particularly violent bunch, by all accounts.'

'A Polish gang? Then why . . .?'

'Why are the Kaminskis over here?' Henry raised his eyebrows, then shrugged. 'I don't know. They're both quite young so maybe they were brought over here by desperate parents to get their kids away from organized crime . . . dunno, just guessing. There are lots of Polish people in this neck of the woods and Russians, too. According to Constantine's antecedents, which are also on the PNC, the family came over here about four years ago, but there's nothing more than that, and I don't need to know. All I know is that they're here, they're involved in violent crime and I'm sure they're connected to the crew that's terrorizing us and I think Vlad is doing the local legwork.'

'Shit,' FB said. 'You've been an early bird, Henry.'

'How do you want to play it, boss?'

FB rubbed his face. 'Close to the chest. For starters, let's go and arrest Vlad the Impaler.'

THIRTEEN

The estate was quiet as Henry drove FB up into it in one of the unmarked CID cars – a 'Danny' as they were called for some reason no one could adequately explain. To Henry it was a shit heap of a Metro, badly looked after and hardly roadworthy. They combed the avenues and alleyways first, just in case Kaminski was out for a stroll, but they saw no one of interest.

'Let's give Sally a knock,' FB said.

Henry nodded and headed towards her house. He thought about parking up some distance away but decided against a sneaky approach. If Kaminski was at the house, he wouldn't necessarily be aware of the reason why cops were knocking at the front door and seeing FB might possibly work to their advantage and lull him into a false sense of security, although Henry doubted this.

He parked directly outside.

'If he's there, two things are likely to happen. He'll try to run and/or he'll kick off,' Henry predicted.

'Good reasons to kick the shite out of him then,' FB said.

FB had been seething silently on the short car journey. Henry guessed it was at the way Kaminski had played him. Just as FB didn't suffer fools gladly, neither did he appreciate being treated as one. Henry further guessed he was plotting a cold revenge on his informant.

They knocked hard.

There was some movement from within, but it was impossible to see what was going on as the door in the window had been panelled over and the letterbox nailed shut since Henry had last visited.

Eventually it opened.

The sight that greeted the two cops made them both react with horror.

It was Sally Lee, dressed in her usual attire, low-cut T-shirt exposing a large proportion of her breasts and her shell-suit bottoms.

That wasn't the problem.

The problem was her battered face.

Her eyes were swollen, the purple colour reminding Henry of the deep shade often found in chapels of rest. Her right one was virtually closed, just a pus-lined slit, nothing more; her left was a touch wider and it was clear this was the one she was looking through. Her right cheek was also swollen and Henry thought her cheekbone could be cracked. Her lips had been smashed, too. The injuries were similar to the ones she had previously, but they were now much, much worse.

A wave of rage washed through Henry because as well as being angry at the person who had inflicted these injuries – Kaminski – he was also very pissed off at himself, FB, and the cops in general for letting this happen to her again. Whatever her reputation, she did not deserve this.

Henry also saw bruising on her neck in the oval shape of thumb prints around her windpipe.

He could not be certain of what expression she had on her face underneath the veneer of those wounds, but guessed at contempt and resignation.

'What do you want?' Her voice grated huskily, but Henry knew it wasn't sexy-husky. It was that way because she had been half-throttled. He glanced at FB, who was staring at Sally and Henry was wondering if he, too, realized he'd let her down in a very big way.

'Is Vlad in?' FB said, shaking himself out of his reverie.

'No.' She peered at Henry through her good eye.

'Did he do this to you?' Henry indicated her face.

'Who the hell d'you think did?' she rasped accusingly, still looking at him. 'Looks like he's had a go at you, too.'

'Not quite,' Henry said, suddenly aware of his own bruised face, caused by another member of the Kaminski clan. 'Can we come in?'

She hesitated, then stepped aside, mumbling, 'I don't know why.'

Henry bit his tongue and walked through behind FB. They went into the living room, both cops checking it carefully. There was no sign of Vlad, or Sally's baby.

'Where is he?' FB demanded.

Sally shrugged. 'Don't know, don't care.' She picked up a packet of cigarettes that were stuffed between the cushions of the baby-clothes-cluttered settee and opened the packet to shuffle out a throwaway lighter and a ciggie, which she lit. She put the packet onto the mantelpiece. 'Anyway, what do you want him for?'

'We need a chat,' FB said.

'Well, he in't here.'

'Where can we find him?' FB demanded.

'No idea.'

'If we get him, he won't be coming home this time,' Henry said.

Sally turned to him, flaring. This time he could clearly tell her expression was one of disbelief. 'Like last time?'

'No . . . no . . .' Henry's voice petered out inadequately.

From the kitchen came the whistle of a steam kettle boiling. 'I'm making meself a brew. Want one?'

'No,' FB said flatly, glaring at Henry.

Sally looked at Henry. 'No . . . it's OK.'

'Up to you.' She left them in the living room.

FB swooped across to Henry. 'He won't be coming home?' he whispered hoarsely. 'Why say that?'

'I'll tell you why, boss,' Henry's voice quavered. 'Because even if we can't make anything stick on him for these robberies, I'm going to protect her like I should've done in the first place. She doesn't deserve this.'

'Oh, what's this? *Love Story*? Get a grip!'

'I'm doing what I'm supposed to be doing. Protecting life, y'know – or has all that disappeared in the mists of time? I thought that was the oath we all took when we joined up!' Henry snorted, turned and clomped belligerently out of the room and into the kitchen where Sally was pouring boiling water from an old-fashioned kettle onto a teabag in a big cracked, stained mug. Henry clocked that there were two mugs out. Sally noticed his eyes flicker down at them.

'Sure you don't want one?' she said quickly.

Henry said no, then, 'Where's junior?'

'Aaron? Upstairs asleep, thank God.'

She poured milk into the tea. Henry said, 'Don't protect him, Sally,' getting the feeling that Kaminski was probably in the house at this moment, hence the two mugs. 'If he's here, just give me the nod,' he said quietly. 'We'll take him away and you'll be safe. I promise you this time.'

Sally shook her head and squeezed the teabag against the side of the mug with a teaspoon. 'He's not here.'

'Where is he?'

'Like I said, I don't know. He just crashes here, rather than lives, y'know?' She lifted the teabag out of the mug with the spoon, turned slightly to put her foot on the pedal of the kitchen bin, which flipped up. As she flicked the squashed teabag into the already overstuffed bin, Henry glanced down for an instant as the bag slopped on top of the rest of the rubbish. The lid then clattered back into place and Sally moved over to the fridge to put the carton of milk back in. She bent down with a groan and a hiss of escaping air through her damaged lips.

'He's hit more than your face, hasn't he?'

She squinted sideways at him as she stood upright and pulled up the hem of her T-shirt, exposing her pasty white stomach. She kept the T-shirt pulled up just below the line of her breasts and teetered around full circle, showing Henry her back and the sides of her ribcage, which bore the marks of wounds caused by punching and kicking and teeth marks from being bitten. Then, facing Henry again, she lowered the T-shirt.

'Kicked the shit out of me for making a complaint against him,' she said, matter-of-fact. She picked up her tea and walked past him into the living room.

As shocked as he was, he took a stride over to the pedal bin and lifted the lid with his fingertips and saw that his eyes hadn't deceived him. He took the teabag out and dropped it into the sink then carefully, one by one, took out the pieces of the torn-up photograph he had seen on top of the other rubbish. He took them back into the living room, where Sally had taken a seat in an armchair.

Henry held out the palm of his hand on which were displayed the bits of the ripped photo. He said quietly, 'Vladimir's not here, but your stepbrother is, isn't he? Or whatever relation he is. Jack Bowman.'

Sally looked from Henry's hand to his face. He recognized the expression this time, one which said, 'Oh shit.' He angled his hand towards FB, who was watching without understanding. Henry then slid the pieces into his pocket. 'Upstairs?' he asked.

Sally nodded.

'Which room?'

'Back bedroom,' she whispered.

Henry looked at FB. 'My shout, I think.' He turned and strode into the hallway, then stopped at the foot of the stairs. He decided to creep up, although he could see it would be hard to mask any approach because the stairs were uncarpeted and looked ill-fitting and creaky.

He went up slowly, placing his feet on the outer edge of the steps where the footing was firmer and less likely to move. Then he was on the landing. He had been in a lot of similar houses in the last few years, expected to be in many more in years to come. There was a box room and bedroom at the back, further along was a bathroom/toilet and then the main bedroom at the front of the house. Classic council house. He stood, listening.

The box room door was open, the room cluttered with baby things, toys, clothes. The door to the back bedroom was closed. One step and Henry could touch it. His fingertips slid around the orb that was the handle and then gripped it, turning it slowly. His intention was to burst through and catch Jack Bowman, who he imagined would be sitting in there, presumably next to the cot, keeping still and silent, hoping the baby would not start to scream, waiting for the nasty horrible cops to leave.

There was a scuffing noise behind the door, inside the room.

Henry pushed the door but found it would not open, even though it was unlocked. Something was jammed behind it.

Henry cursed, then put his shoulder to it, forcing it and seeing the baby's cot. But it wasn't too difficult to open, so he carefully put his weight to it, pushed and entered, edging sideways through the gap he'd created, seeing the baby still asleep in the cot. Then he poked his head through and looked properly into the room – and saw Jack Bowman, prisoner on the run. He was sitting on the ledge of an open bedroom window, his feet dangling out.

'Got you,' Henry snarled, forcing his way through the gap, but he had spoken way too early. Bowman glanced over his

shoulder, confirmed it was a cop and not his sister coming through
the door. Henry shouted, 'You stop right there, pal.'

But Bowman said, 'Like fuck,' and launched himself out of
the window, disappeared out of sight.

'Jeez,' Henry said and dashed to the window, half-expecting
to see Bowman in a crumpled heap in the back garden, at least
one leg broken.

But that was too much to hope for.

He was small, wiry, lithe and light. He hit the ground perfectly,
did a forward roll to cushion the drop and dissipate the energy
and as Henry's face came to the window, Bowman was back on
his feet. He stopped and turned and gave Henry an exaggerated
and passionate double 'V' sign with both hands and shouted,
'Wanker,' then sprinted across the debris-strewn garden, vaulted
over the broken back fence and was gone.

With a distorted look, Henry balled his fists furiously – and
behind him, little baby Aaron started to scream.

Henry went back down where FB and Sally waited for him,
expectantly.

'Jumped out the bloody window,' Henry said, explaining the
lack of a prisoner in his grip. 'And your kid's screaming for its
mummy.'

Sally smiled, wincing as the pain of doing so hurt her face.

FB simply regarded Henry as if he was a buffoon.

'Where's the picture frame?' Henry asked Sally. He could tell
she was about to protest and demand, 'Which picture frame?'
but Henry stopped that by saying quickly, 'And don't say you
don't know, Sal. The picture frame your bro took from the old
woman's house he burgled the other day. I want it back and I
want it now and if you don't give it to me straight away, I'll rip
this house apart and who knows what the hell else I'll discover.'

'You can't.'

'Can.'

She shot a glance at FB, who said, 'He can and he will, love.'

'Dining room,' she admitted mutely.

'Thank you,' Henry said. He went down the hall into the dining
room and found the silver picture frame on the fireplace, now
displaying a photograph of Sally and baby Aaron, smiling proudly.
Henry walked back to the living room, dismantling the frame to

extract the photo, which he handed back to Sally, coldly saying, 'Be thankful I haven't torn up *your* memory.'

Despite a drive around and knocking on a few likely doors and speaking to a few likely characters, the two cops could not unearth Vladimir Kaminski, who had gone to ground, as had the escapee Jack Bowman. Henry and FB returned empty handed to Rawtenstall police station and went their separate ways for the time being.

Henry went back into the report-writing room to finish his Crown Court files whilst he had chance. He intended to go hunting for Kaminski and Bowman later. They were a bit like lions, only came out at sunset.

At the desk he placed the thick files down but before opening them he reached into his jacket and came out with the torn-up photograph that he had saved from Sally Lee's kitchen bin.

He let the jagged pieces fall onto the desk, then began to reassemble them like a jigsaw until he had an almost complete photograph again.

It was a black-and-white photograph, faded, of a man and a woman on their wedding day.

When Henry had automatically glanced down when Sally Lee had dropped the teabag into the kitchen bin he had glimpsed a torn piece of the photograph and that had been of a woman's face and in that instant he had immediately recognized it as a very much younger version of the old woman whose house had been burgled. Mrs Fudge.

At least he had recovered the picture frame, the one Jack Bowman had unsuccessfully attempted to sell at Fat Jack's second-hand shop. That was now in the police 'other property' store (as opposed to found property) and Henry was going to return it to the old lady sooner rather than later.

The photograph troubled him, for emotional and sentimental reasons.

It was all well and good getting the silver frame back, but what the old lady really wanted was the photograph, the only one in existence of her wedding day. The one that Sally and her brother had callously torn to shreds and replaced in the frame with one of their own.

The one now in scraps in front of Henry. He certainly didn't have the skills to reassemble it decently. He sighed heavily as he looked at it, seeing the ecstatic faces of two young people in love on the best day of their lives. She was extremely pretty and he very handsome and it reminded Henry of the old photos of his parents on their wedding day. Except his parents were still alive, still married, and Mrs Fudge had lost her husband not long after the wedding, when he went to war and never came back.

'Hey!' FB leaned unexpectedly into the room, interrupting Henry's thoughts.

'Boss.'

'Forgot to say – well spotted re the photo . . . maybe we should've dragged Sally in for handling stolen goods or harbouring a wanted crim?'

Henry screwed up his face. 'Nah – too much like hard work for not much result.'

'Ahh,' FB said knowingly, 'I see you're beginning to look at the bigger picture. You don't need to lock everyone up every time.'

'Mm,' Henry muttered dubiously.

'Anyway, well done, PC Christie . . . What's this?' FB looked over Henry's shoulder.

'Wondering if it's salvageable or not. It'd be nice to get it back to the old lady in one piece, somehow.'

FB slapped Henry's back. 'Best of luck with that, soft-arse,' he said and was gone.

'You're so compassionate,' Henry mumbled, his brow creased. Then he had a thought, gathered the pieces of the photograph together and scooped them into an envelope, and left the police station.

As much as Sally Lee had tried to hide the fact that Jack Bowman was hiding up in her back bedroom and was happy to handle stolen property, Henry was still concerned about her welfare. On his return to the nick after his little errand, he sought out the woman police sergeant who ran the Juvenile Bureau, had a quick chat and got an unlisted phone number from her.

After that he snaffled another set of car keys – this time for the patrol inspector's Maestro – without permission and set off back up to the estate to see Sally once more.

He parked outside and knocked. She answered sullenly, her child slung over her shoulder. She was clearly not impressed to have Henry on her threshold.

'You again? Neither of 'em's here.'

'It's you I've come to see,' he said. She one-eyed him suspiciously. 'You going to let me in?'

Reluctantly she let go of the front door and trudged back into the living room and laid the sleeping child out on the settee, tucked in and safe by a cushion.

'What do you want?' She found her cigarettes again, pushed down between the cushions of the settee, tapped one out and lit it, blowing smoke up to the ceiling.

'I want to know how long you're going to take this for?' he said.

'Take what?' she asked, but knew exactly what he was talking about.

'The abuse. The beatings. The rapes.'

'Henry – you're effin' dim, aren't you? I'll take it till I'm dead, I suppose. You twats won't do anything, I don't have anywhere to go, I've no friggin' money and I've got that!' She jabbed the nicotine-stained first and second fingers of her right hand, between which she held a crumpled cigarette, at the sleeping child. 'I'm trapped,' she said slowly, then arched her eyebrows for him to understand. 'Anyway, we've been through this.'

'I want to help you. I want to arrest Vladimir and charge him with your rape and the assaults . . . and screw the system that says I can't . . . but you have to help me to help yourself. I'll get him off the street into custody and keep him there, but it's you that will make it happen as much as me.'

Sally sat down next to the baby, still smoking. She said nothing, but Henry could see her thought process in action by the look on her face.

'I'm not prepared to do it, though, unless you promise you'll see it through. If you don't, then it'll all be pointless, you'll stay trapped and you'll get hammered every time he feels like hitting out.'

Her mouth tightened. She wiped her eyes.

Henry had been speechifying whilst standing up. He sat on the edge of the chair opposite, looking at Sally.

'I know it'll be hard. I *know* that. But it's the only way to break free from him, or you can just let yourself be caught in this vicious circle and one day, the only way it'll be broken is when you die . . . maybe.' His eyes played over her face, wondering if his harsh words were having any effect.

She took another drag, blew the smoke up high. 'How would it work?' she asked quietly.

A shimmer of hope skipped through Henry. 'I took the liberty of contacting a women's refuge on your behalf.' She shot him a look of horror. He held up a hand. 'No obligation, Sally, but there's a room for you and your baby if you want.'

'Sounds shit.'

'It is basic, yeah. Bit like being in a motel, but each room has a bed, cot, settee and a telly and a private bathroom. So yeah, basic, but you'll be safe there and you'll be out of here. Just short term, yeah? I'll get you settled in there tonight, then I'll come and see you in the morning, take a good statement and then arrest Vlad as soon as possible after that. Then he's off the streets and when he's on remand, you come back here and plot your future. How about it?'

'What about your boss? That little fat bastard?'

'I'll handle him,' Henry said with a confidence he didn't feel. He was making a lot of 'can-do' claims to Sally, when he knew for certain he would have to do some of it under the radar that was FB's nose.

Sally thought it through silently, savouring her cigarette. Eventually she drew the smouldering tobacco back as far as the filter, crushed it in an overflowing ashtray on the settee arm, and stood up.

'What do I need?'

'What you can pack into a suitcase for a couple of nights for you and the baby. I can come and collect anything else you might need later. I take it you have a suitcase?'

She nodded. 'I'll get my shit.'

Henry smiled encouragingly. 'They'll look after you, I promise.'

'I'll need to take some whisky with me.'

'That's fine.'

'Watch the kid,' Sally instructed him and left the room.

The child did not move, other than the tiny rise and fall of the chest.

Henry used his PR to call up the woman sergeant in the Juvenile Bureau and confirmed that the 'offer' had been taken up. The WPS acknowledged this and said she would call ahead with an ETA. They spoke cryptically just in case FB was listening or if someone was scanning the police airwaves illegally.

'Half an hour,' Henry told her.

There was a thump-thump-thump as Sally came back down the stairs dragging an overloaded suitcase behind her, step by step. She put a duffel coat on. She picked up the baby and wrapped him in a blanket, looked around and picked up her cigarettes. Henry heaved the suitcase and a fold-away pushchair into the police car as Sally climbed into the back seat with the child.

The women's refuge was in Haslingden, a few miles away, and on the journey Henry tried to get some information from Sally about the whereabouts of Vlad and Bowman and what they had been up to, but she claimed not to know.

The refuge was a large old terraced house just on the periphery of the town centre, with nothing externally to identify it. It was discreet, anonymous, for obvious reasons.

They were greeted by a suspicious-eyed woman who peered through a gap in the triple-chained door and demanded that Henry – who was in plain clothes, even though he was driving a marked police car – identify himself. He did, flashing his warrant card, but wasn't allowed in – 'We don't allow men in here, whoever they might be,' he was told sternly. He gave Sally a quick wave as she entered and the heavy door was slammed firmly shut in his face.

Result.

'Sorry, boss, mercy mission,' Henry apologized to the portly, red-faced patrol inspector who had been trashing his office in an effort to discover the whereabouts of his car keys.

'Do that again, laddie, and you'll be on paper,' he warned Henry in his gruff Scottish timbre. He snatched the keys that were dangling from Henry's forefinger.

Effectively grounded for the time being, Henry – once again

– took the opportunity to get his head around his paperwork. Now that Sally was safe he didn't have to worry about Kaminski until next day, when he planned to get a fresh and detailed statement from her, then get her photographed by SOCO and examined by a police surgeon.

If Kaminski was arrested in the meantime, all well and good. If not, Henry would root him out after he had done Sally's paperwork.

He was looking forward to it and was just a bit pleased with himself that he was actually making a difference in someone's life. 'Freedom from tyranny and fear,' he said grandly to himself like the voice-over to a feature-film trailer. It felt kind of good.

But Henry had been extremely careless. Unwittingly, probably a bit cavalierly, and with the immaturity of age, the last thing he had expected when he loaded Sally Lee and baby into the back of the inspector's Maestro was to be observed – by Vladimir Kaminski and his brother Constantine.

Kaminski had been on his way back to Sally's with Constantine in a stolen Ford Granada fitted with legit number plates, a car stolen to order and which was in line to be used as the stage-two getaway car on the next, imminent armed robbery.

Kaminski had seen the police car driven by Henry – although he didn't know it was Henry at that time – turn onto the estate ahead of him. Not wanting to be spotted, he had dropped back and immediately lost sight of the cop car. He then drove cautiously into the estate and clocked the car parked up outside Sally's house, the front door of which was just closing as the officer was allowed in. Kaminski parked up a short distance away, giving himself a good but restricted view of the house from behind a couple of other vehicles and some bushes in a garden.

When, less than fifteen minutes later, Sally and the cop – who Kaminski now recognized as Henry – emerged from the house, luggage, pushchair and baby in tow, Kaminski's rage fired up instantly.

'I know him,' Constantine said. 'He was the cop in Manchester. I should've killed him.'

'I know him too. He meddles. We follow,' he said grimly to his brother as the police car set off.

He fully expected to tail the car down to Rawtenstall police station, so he was surprised and puzzled when at Queens Square the police car veered off left towards Haslingden.

Keeping his distance, he followed and without much of a problem he saw it pull up outside the three-storey terraced house. Parking up nearby to dash back on foot, dipping behind a wall, he watched Henry deposit Sally and baby Aaron through the front door that was closed firmly in the cop's face.

They saw the officer pause for a few moments, almost with his nose up to the door, then turn away, get into the police car and drive off. Kaminski and his brother drove slowly past the house, noting the sturdy front door and the bars over the ground-floor windows. Other than these features, which were actually fairly subtle, there was nothing really to distinguish it from the houses either side.

'What is it?' Kaminski wondered out loud, his heavy jaw rotating.

His brother knew instantly. 'Place of safety. Women's refuge.'

'Think so?'

'Is . . . yes . . . I'm sure . . . look at the bars, the door. Not kick that down.'

Kaminski drove past again, then pulled in a little further along the street. He started to get out of the car. 'I'm going to get that bitch.'

Constantine laid a restraining hand on his brother's arm. 'No chance. They won't even open the door for you.'

'Then I kick it down, drag her out.'

'Again – no chance, like I just said. While you kick, they get the cops. I bet there's an alarm straight to the cop station.'

Kaminski settled back and thought it through. 'Bitch is going to rat on me.'

'Looks like it.'

'I need to stop her.'

Constantine nodded agreement. 'Yes, but later. We have more important things to do first.'

'I need to speak to her tonight,' Vladimir insisted.

'You will not get in there,' Constantine said.

'Maybe there is a way, a subtle way.'

'You – subtle?' Constantine laughed harshly.

Vladimir's eyes moved sideways. 'As subtle as you blasting a woman cop with a shotgun. I am so jealous.'

Both men found this uproariously hysterical.

When they had settled, Vlad decided, 'I will see her tonight, but I need to do something first.'

Henry ploughed on with his Crown Court files. He actually enjoyed the paperwork side of being a cop – in that he took a great deal of pride in the reports he submitted. If one was ever returned he would be gutted. These files, however, were back with him so he could answer some queries from the barristers, which was OK.

As he worked through them, his mind often wandered to Jo Wade, the image of her last moments in his arms etched vividly in his mind. Once or twice he had to put down his pen and close his eyes whilst he wondered if he could have done anything more for her. In his heart, and in other people's reassurances, he knew he'd done what he could. She had been mortally wounded and would have died anyway, but he could not completely shake off the thought . . .

After a couple of hours he was done. He dropped the files into the out-tray in the sergeants' office. And his work day was over. He intended being very busy over the next few days but he was going to chill tonight. A pint and a curry with Kate seemed to be the way forwards, maybe watch a video, but not CCTV footage from a shop. He needed to forget work for a few hours and perhaps see if he could perform without agony, as his groin area seemed much less sore than before and his nose didn't hurt quite so much, even if it still looked a mess.

The four lighted cigarettes pushed down between the settee cushions started it. It was an old-fashioned piece of furniture and its innards were not fireproof. They smouldered for quite some time and soon the foam that had been deliberately torn from inside caught fire and once that happened it took only seconds as the flames crackled and roared.

At the same time, the dirty, well-used oil in the chip pan that had been placed on the hob, the gas turned up high, started to bubble and as the heat increased, there was a 'whoosh' as the oil caught fire and the flames licked the kitchen ceiling and raced along like an angry demon and thick, rancid smoke filled the room.

Two seats of fire were enough. Within minutes the whole house was ablaze. Not long after that, the building was gutted by flame.

Henry pulled on his jacket as he walked out of the door of the nick. He'd parked his car on a car park behind a row of shops at the back of the station, a walk of a couple of hundred yards, maybe.

His mind had switched off as the door closed behind him and was geared to the evening ahead. Working it all out: straight to Kate's to pick her up, back to his place for a shower and some canoodling (sex), then out for a pint. He fancied driving to the Deerplay pub out on the moors between Bacup and Burnley, one of his regular haunts. Then a takeaway and back to his with a video to watch Clint blow away a few bad guys.

A perfect evening.

He drove off the car park and a few moments later was at the traffic lights at Queens Square. They changed to green and he moved through but had to slam on as two fire engines bore down on him from the right, hurtling along Burnley Road from the fire station.

They jumped the red lights without even slowing down. If they had broadsided Henry, he and his car would have been mangled. As it was he stopped in time to see the two huge red beasts thunder past safely.

And, being curious, he wondered where they were going.

His instinct was to drop into their slipstream and follow. Had he been on duty he would have done so without a second's hesitation. Fire engines and ambulances were always worth checking out.

He held himself back, and turned slowly onto the roundabout and cut over the bridge behind ASDA. He saw them turn up towards the council estate and raising his eyes slightly, he saw the plume of smoke rising in the air from what was more than likely their destination.

Something nasty quivered through him.

He went after the fire engines.

FOURTEEN

2 a.m.: a good time to go burgling.

Not just because all right-minded people would be fast asleep but because this was the traditional changeover time for cops, when they would most likely be in the station, either coming in for refreshments or turning out, or finishing a tour of duty. And everyone knows that cops dawdle in police stations.

As did the burglar and, knowing it, always slotted his illicit night-time visits into this timeframe, which, even in the height of summer when the days were long and the nights were short, gave him the cover of darkness.

It helped that he was small, slim and could move unseen. A wispy ghost, dressed from head to toe in black, moving from shadow to shadow, keeping to the darkness even on well-lighted streets. He knew how to keep himself invisible by considering every move, every dash, stopping, listening, checking, not rushing. He knew his job.

Tonight was slightly different, though.

It was a break-in, but also a let-in.

He was on the street of the target house, just a normal East Lancashire street adjacent to an unremarkable small town centre. Terraced houses, nothing special.

He stood opposite, merged into the shadow in the doorway of a house, unseen by anyone passing in a car; even on foot a passer-by would have to stare hard to make him out.

His eyes roved the house, looking for a weakness.

Nothing.

So he moved and moments later he was in the alley running directly behind the house he was going to enter. Then he was at the high back wall of the property, at the door fitted within the wall that opened into the back yard. It was a solid, well-locked door. Still, he tried it, put his shoulder to it but it didn't even budge. As he had expected.

He looked up the wall, which was about eight feet high, two and a half feet higher than he was. Stretched across the top of it were strands of security wire with razor-like sections to it. Nothing he hadn't tackled before. Further down the alley he found a dustbin which he picked up and carried noiselessly to the wall.

He placed it down and climbed carefully onto it. He was light and it took his weight easily and now he could peer over the wall through the wire, into the back yard and the house. He immediately spotted a motion-activated security light fitted high on the back wall.

As good as he was at moving without being seen by the human eye, he knew he could not take the chance of the light coming on, so it had to be disabled.

Which was why he carried an air pistol. It was already loaded with a heavy, homemade lead pellet.

He pulled it out of the waistband of his black jeans and took aim at the lens of the security light, which was about six inches square, an easy target from about twenty feet.

Even in the dark he was confident he could smash the bulb. In his hands, the pistol was accurate up to about fifty feet.

There was a little bit of recoil because the airgun was quite powerful, but was also virtually silent, except for the muted 'phut' and then the sharp crack as the lens and bulb broke.

He took no chances at that point, though. He ducked back down, squatting on the dustbin, waiting patiently for any reaction, such as lights or voices.

Nothing.

He rose cautiously, slipping the gun back into his waistband, then from his self-modified builder's utility belt he reached for his next burglar's tools, a pair of protective gloves and some wire cutters no bigger than pliers.

In moments he had snipped the security wires and folded them carefully backwards to form a gap just wide enough for him to slide through without snagging himself, a stupid thing to do that could cause problems. The thought of being hooked there for the cops to find in the morning was something that made him even more careful.

He dropped silently into the rear yard, keeping to the shadow of the wall and pausing once more to check. Burgling well was a game of patience.

Then he crossed swiftly to the back door which was sturdy and, he assumed, alarmed. High up on the wall and out of reach to even him, unless he'd brought a thirty-foot ladder, was a covered alarm bell. If it had been in reach he would have ensured its silence by spraying it with hard-setting foam from the can he always carried with him. Which meant that forcing the back door was not an option, nor was entering through any of the ground-floor windows either side, which were covered by steel bars.

However, the first- and second-floor windows were not afforded such protection.

A thick soil pipe descended the outside wall. It was an old one, made of clay, but it was sturdy and pulling at it he could tell it was well fixed to the brickwork. Secure enough for him. Using a cord he also carried for such eventualities he slipped it around the pipe, wrapped the ends around his wrists and fists, then, like a man shimmying up a palm tree, he went upwards one foot at a time until he was alongside a first-floor window. He reached out with his leg and placed a foot on the window ledge and wedged himself between the pipe and the window like a mountaineer. He could now see through the window as there was no curtain and as he suspected, this was the first-floor landing, off which were three doors.

His eight-inch steel jemmy was the next tool from his belt and he used this to begin to prise right through the window frame, which started to crumble with rot as he worked the tool. He wasn't surprised by the poor state of the window. A place like this, run on hardly any money, mostly charitable donations, couldn't usually afford new windows.

But for the burglar this was the noisy and precarious part, wedged nine feet up and riving away at the window.

But he had been through many windows like this, old wooden ones, rotting, splitting. He liked them and he smiled grimly as he forced the jemmy all the way through the frame. Once this was done, he replaced the jemmy with a long-bladed screwdriver, which he inserted through the hole and used it to flick up the catch. He replaced the screwdriver into his belt and carefully pushed open the window, which opened with a faint creak of its hinges.

At this point he started to feel the tummy jitters.

He swung in and dropped noiselessly onto the carpet on the landing at the top of the stairs. He was in. He backed himself into a corner, keeping to the shadows, and caught his breath, tried to reduce his heartbeat, because as usual, he was bricking himself.

Breaking into property was actually terrifying. He had done hundreds but it never got easier and he had been forced to drop his pants at the entry point to many of the houses he had burgled and excrete on the floor. Tonight would not be an exception, even though he wasn't here to steal. The thought of what he was actually doing here was making him even more desperate for the toilet.

His guts churned. He slid his jeans and underpants down, squatted and released his bowels with a huge fart. It was over in seconds and he stood back up, fastening his jeans and feeling a whole lot better stomach-wise, though not emotionally.

The stairs in front of him led down to the ground floor whilst the ones at the far end of the landing would take him up to the second floor. The burglar moved silently along the landing, peering at the doors using his penlight torch, which cast a tight beam. He was searching for the answer to a question, but he didn't try the door handles because he could not afford to make a mistake. It had to be right.

The doors did not give him any indication of what he was looking for either on this or the next floor.

He went down to the ground floor, the stairs actually taking him to the front door, where he hesitated and checked the locks. Three sturdy bolts and a mortise lock, which, he saw with a grin, had had the key left in it.

Like so many places he had broken into, either domestic or commercial, security was often a joke. He turned away from the door and looked along the hallway. Directly facing him was a small reception desk, opposite which was a lounge, dining room and kitchen. There was a door underneath the stairs marked 'Private – Staff Only'. This, he imagined, went down to the basement accommodation for the live-in manageress.

He dipped behind the reception desk and flicked through the pages of an open A4-size diary, holding the torch with his teeth to read the entries. The one that interested him was the most recent and contained all the information he required.

His job was complete.

He closed the diary and went to the front door, sliding back the bolts and turning the key slowly, hearing the locking bolt move back out of its steel pocket. The door opened directly onto the street outside, the one in which he had been standing in a doorway opposite about fifteen minutes earlier, checking his target premises.

A figure standing in the same doorway sprinted out of the shadows and crossed the road. The burglar stood aside and allowed the man to enter.

'Room six, first floor,' the burglar whispered. The man nodded. 'You won't hurt her, will you?'

Vladimir Kaminski said, 'No, I promise. I only want to talk.'

'Good. I'm gone now,' the burglar said. He ducked out of the front door and disappeared into the shadows. Kaminski closed the door but left it unlocked. Then he went upstairs to room six.

FIFTEEN

'**N**o – you get your uniform on and you help us out. We're short-staffed and we need you.'

Though not the words Henry wanted to hear, he didn't allow himself a 'But, boss,' plea because he knew it would be useless to whine. The patrol sergeant's firm stance said it all and Henry knew his first responsibility was to the uniform section, not to go gallivanting off in the vain hope of catching robbers, murderers and escapees.

'Once you've done the court run, you can do whatever you had planned.'

'OK, sarge.'

Henry grabbed a set of car keys and skulked out of the police station, jumped into a car, envying the detectives who were rolling in for their morning briefing in the hunt for Jo Wade's murderers. He drove back to his rented house, chunnering to himself, annoyed he wasn't quick enough not to get cornered for the court run, the thrice-weekly jaunt to take prisoners in custody or on remand to Rawtenstall Magistrates.

He didn't get it.

The court run seemed to be a surprise to supervisory officers every time it happened, even though it happened three times each week. There never seemed to be enough staff on duty and they were always desperate to snatch officers from wherever they could to do the run. But it wasn't just the run, because officers had to remain with the prisoners in the secure room and then take them up to court for their appearance, and then bring them back afterwards unless they were fortunate enough to be released by the bench. It was a tedious, time-consuming chore that most cops tried to duck.

Henry had turned up for work in plain clothes, expecting to be able to carry on his illicit role as FB's private gofer.

But it was not to be.

The sergeant had descended on him as soon as he set foot

through the door, brooking no argument, and Henry avoided conflict by doing what he was told, for once.

He was back at the station in ten minutes, spic 'n' span with an ironed uniform and spit-and-polished shoes.

There were two prisoners that morning, for which Henry was grateful. It meant he wouldn't have to spend long hours at court.

One was a local town-centre drunk called Stuttard, one of those poor unfortunate souls who often became the target for young cops to practise their arrest skills on. Indeed, even Henry had once arrested him for drunk and disorderly just for something to do and regretted it later. He was easy to wind up and subdue, because there was no real fight in him. In reality he should have been in rehab or an asylum, but that would never be. He was destined to remain one of life's misfits and would probably drink himself to death.

The other, much to Henry's surprise, was John Longridge.

But he didn't have much time to enquire into that. The prisoners had to be at court for ten o'clock and it was the responsibility of the court escorts – Henry, in this case, and a young PC called Barnes – to sort out their breakfasts and get them washed and shaved.

Henry did all this with a scowl on his face.

The breakfasts were provided by a nearby pub and Henry went to collect them, managing to tease a bacon sandwich from the landlord for himself. By the time he returned to the station, PC Barnes had made the brews in the huge plastic mugs for the prisoners and the meals and drinks were posted through the observation flaps in the cell doors. This break gave Henry chance to make a tea for himself and slip upstairs to see FB, whose car he had seen in the back yard.

'I'll have half of that,' FB said, eyeing Henry's large bacon bap with hunger. Henry tore it across and gave FB a chunk which he ripped into ravenously, continuing to speak with an overflowing mouth.

'Why the uniform?' he asked.

'Roped in for court escort. Couldn't refuse, couldn't duck.'

FB grunted and snuffled.

'What's the score with Longridge?'

'Well, they don't really have anything on him . . . I, er, didn't mention the Kaminskis to the murder squad,' he said, slightly shamefaced.

Henry smirked.

'I thought we'd try and see that one through ourselves – if you ever get free from court that is.'

'I will . . . then I want to get a statement from Sally and sort out SOCO and a police surgeon for her. I think they have an interview room at the refuge for that sort of thing. Then at least we have something to speak to Kaminski about.'

FB looked at him curiously. 'What refuge?'

'Didn't I tell you?' Henry said in all innocence.

'No . . . but you better had.'

So Henry did and FB listened, pan-faced. When he'd finished, FB said, 'And you didn't think to tell me about this?'

'Uh, sorry . . . but it's a good thing, isn't it – under the circumstances?' Henry held his breath, ready for the tirade.

'I'll let it slide,' FB said not impressed. 'But don't do stuff without my say-so, OK?' Henry nodded. FB went on, 'Anyway, re Longridge . . . they're going for a three-day lie down so they can get into his ribs properly, so he'll be coming back here to lodge with us.' A three-day lie down was police jargon for a remand by the court to police cells for further questioning and when requested was rarely denied by the magistrates. 'I'll keep an eye on how it's going before I reveal what I know about the ID of Spiderman and his link to Vladimir and the gang.'

Henry smirked again. Knowledge was power. Henry didn't exactly know what FB's game plan was, but he surmised he planned to let the murder squad – of which he was no longer leader – struggle for a while with an uncooperative Longridge before suddenly helping them out and regaining his own credibility. Thanks to Henry, of course, although he doubted that his part in the proceedings would feature too highly. He wasn't bothered, just so long as he played some part in it.

'Presumably they do think Longridge is connected to the blagging team, even if they can't prove it?' he asked.

'Uh-huh – but he won't admit anything without hard evidence and even then,' FB shrugged. 'But I have a little something, don't I?'

So Henry was right. FB was playing his cards close. He corrected FB by saying, 'Yes, *we* do,' and turned to leave.

'Oh – you went up to the fire, I believe, at Sally Lee's place?'

'I did. Two seats of fire. Place was a mess,' Henry said.

'And?'

'No suspicious circumstances according to the initial assessment by the chief fire officer. Chip pan left on, and a discarded ciggie on the settee. I haven't crimed it – yet.'

'Kaminski, you think?'

'Well, the chip pan was off and Sally picked her fags up when we left yesterday – so, definitely Vlad.'

'And how is Miss Lee, liar, cheater and manipulator?'

'Miss Lee, the abused girlfriend, you mean? She was OK when I checked with the refuge last night. I didn't mention the fire, though. I didn't want to wind her up. She deserved a decent night's kip. But I'll tell her when I see her. Don't know how, but I will.' Henry glanced at his watch. 'Time for my court run.'

'Watch out for Longridge, by the way. He won't be averse to doing a runner if he can – and I know you've got form for not keeping hold of prisoners . . .' Now FB smirked.

Bristling and reddening, Henry spun out of the office.

The prisoners had eaten their breakfasts. Henry and PC Barnes supervised them washing and preening themselves, Henry believing this was one of the few occasions when Stuttard, the drunk, was sober, clean, presentable, affable – a completely different person to the one normally found rolling around the streets, inebriated on cheap cider mixed with vodka.

But Henry's eyes were mainly on Longridge.

That prisoner remained calm, quiet and within himself. He moved with tough confidence and maintained a look of distaste on his face, compounded by a half-smirk. Henry did not trust him and he didn't need FB's words of warning to tell him he was an escape risk. He had to be carefully watched.

When they were ready, Henry cuffed the prisoners to each other, Longridge's right wrist to Stuttard's left. Although Longridge didn't tower over his fellow detainee, he was bigger, wider and much more of a presence than the drink-ravaged Stuttard.

The call came over the radio that the section van had pulled up outside the back door of the nick. Henry told Barnes to grip the links between the handcuffs whilst Henry steered the prisoners out of the cell area into the back corridor. He took up a position just to one side, but slightly ahead of them and always walked at an angle so he was able to keep an eye on them and react to anything as necessary.

The preposterous nature of prisoner escort from Rawtenstall police station to the Magistrates' Court was never lost on Henry.

With the premises being just under a mile apart by road, it was always fraught with danger and Henry was surprised the cops hadn't been caught out more times than they had.

There were so many weak points in the journey it was laughable.

First of all, cops themselves did not make the best prisoner escorts. It was a task, without exception, they hated doing, but the idea of bringing in private security companies to do it usually appalled most police officers. The inbred culture of the service meant that they wanted to hang on to the task for as long as possible. Even so, they did the escort under duress and always moaned about it.

Next, the journey itself was a potential minefield.

The short walk from the back door of the nick to the van was a temptation for the baddies to make a break for it. The police vans themselves, although fitted with an internal steel door behind the back doors – though not an internal cage – were designed for transporting prisoners from the streets to the station. They were not prison buses and nor were they armoured.

The journey to court was a stop-start affair, usually in rush-hour traffic, giving serious villains plenty of opportunity to ambush the van and have a go at liberating their partners in custody if they so wished.

Once at court, things didn't get much better.

There was no secure garage or area for the van to reverse into because the old court did not have such a facility. The van stopped outside a side entrance which was also a public entrance, and the prisoners were unloaded and escorted in, often through bunches of milling, unhappy relatives or friends. A situation that had often resulted in nasty flare-ups. They were then put into a secure room at the top of the first flight of steps which only had a flimsy door and could be accessed by members of the public who constantly hammered on the door, demanding to see their loved ones either before or after their court appearances.

When the cases were called, the prisoners were taken up a narrow set of stairs leading to the dock in the main court where they faced the bench. If remanded, they came back down and the journey was reversed.

Much of the smooth running of the operation was dependent on the compliance of the prisoner. One who wasn't happy could make the whole thing a real nightmare. Henry was just surprised that most villains were so acquiescent and went along with it and that very few escaped or were sprung from custody.

But that morning he wasn't taking anything for granted.

They made it into the back of the van with the prisoners, climbing in and sitting opposite them on the fitted bench seats that ran on either side of the van.

Henry settled directly opposite Longridge, whose eyes never once left his. Henry returned the compliment, a slight smile on his face. He knew the type of intimidatory tactics that tough nuts like Longridge played with cops, but it didn't work with him.

The van driver, that morning's PC on section patrol duties, slammed the cage doors shut, then the rear doors, then climbed into the front cab and set off.

Longridge continued to survey Henry.

In a whisper he said, 'You and me.'

Henry felt the PC sat alongside him stiffen.

'You and me what?' Henry asked.

'Here. Now. You. Me.'

Henry shook his head, faintly amused. 'You live in fairyland, mate.'

'Chicken.'

Henry made a clucking sound.

The van lurched around a corner, then braked sharply, jerking the four occupants along the seats. Longridge used the momentum to pretend to come at Henry, his left hand bunched into a big fist, his face twisted into an aggressive snarl.

Henry didn't move, but simply folded his arms and gave Longridge a sad shake of his head. 'You're an idiot, mate.'

Longridge sat back.

Then the van stopped. Glancing through the rear window Henry saw they had reached the traffic lights at the junction with Queens Square. Not too far to go now.

FB had hoped to catch Henry but by the time he had finished the phone call, pulled on his jacket and legged it down to the back door, the section van was drawing out of the yard.

FB shrugged and jumped in his car, squealing the tyres as he accelerated out of the yard, choosing to go in a different direction to the van, cutting through Rawtenstall centre and gunning his car up Haslingden Old Road, his fingers gripping and re-gripping the steering wheel, beads of salty sweat dribbling from his scalp, down his forehead and temples.

He was a small man in height, large in girth, but he didn't often sweat. He was usually one hundred per cent cocksure of every course of action he chose to take and if he showed a misjudgement, or something went belly-up, he would use his bullying bluster, the sheer force of his personality and the general 'do not question' power that DIs exercised to bluff his way out of a bad decision.

Thing was, bad decisions didn't usually cost lives.

But this one had.

The section van went slowly through the lights in the heavy traffic, turning left onto Queens Square, moving across to the outer lane to circumnavigate the roundabout and then peeled off up to the Magistrates' Court.

Henry and Longridge continued to size each other up. Henry was a bit dumbfounded by Longridge's antagonism, directed at him for no real reason. But he knew that was how people like Longridge functioned. They lived in a sub-stratum of humanity where violence was offered and taken like currency, and a good payday included smacking a copper with or without reason – which partly explained Longridge's attitude to Jo Wade's murder. Nothing wrong with a dead cop. Henry enjoyed being on the outside of this knuckle-headed community, having to delve into it on a daily basis, but always leaving it behind at the end of a tour of duty to return to his normality. It was one of the things that Sally Lee had chided him about.

Sometimes bits of it came with him, such as bearing the mark of an assault, or the frustration at not being able to achieve justice, or being involved in something as tragic as the murder of a colleague. But on the whole, if he could, Henry left it behind and he hoped that as he progressed in the job in years to come he wouldn't be one of those cops who got depressed and took work home and then had, as they said in Lancashire, a 'shed collapse', meaning nervous breakdown. He didn't ever want to be one of them.

The van circled the roundabout, came off onto Haslingden Road, then bore sharp right across a traffic island and over into the steep side street by the court building. The driver cut left into the car park, stopped, then allowed the van to roll back. He turned and manoeuvred it alongside the steps leading up to the side entrance.

'Here we are.' Henry heard his muted voice on the other side of the toughened screen separating the driving cab from the rear compartment.

The driver climbed out, unlocked and opened the rear doors, then the inner cage door which had a metal bar handle on a fulcrum that looked like it could have been used to secure castle gates. It opened on its spring with a loud clatter and the driver looked inside, grinning.

'We've landed,' announced. He wasn't wearing his hat, which was unfortunate. Even his flat cap would have helped a bit.

His head suddenly jerked sideway and he stepped back. He had seen someone coming at him.

Fast. Low. Hard.

His right arm angled up in a protective gesture. Too late.

At which point Henry simultaneously saw and heard a Ford Granada screaming through the stone gateposts of the Masonic Lodge fifty yards up the street.

And the ski-masked, black-clad, baseball-bat-wielding man who had run up to the section PC brought the weapon around in a wide arc and smacked him across the skull, making a sickening noise as it connected. The PC did a full body shimmy like 10,000 volts of electricity had passed through him, his head split open and he disappeared from view as he collapsed.

The Granada slewed to a stop just feet behind the van.

Open-mouthed, Henry peered out, his heart pounding, as the back two doors of the Ford opened and two men, dressed exactly the same as baseball-bat man, jumped out. Dressed, Henry noted sourly, exactly the same as the gang who had violently robbed shops in Rawtenstall, shot at him and gunned down WPC Jo Wade.

The men from the car carried sawn-off shotguns and they ran to the van and pointed their weapons into the confined space, screaming almost indecipherable warnings.

Henry exchanged a glance with Longridge, who held up his handcuffed right wrist towards him, dragging Stuttard off the bench seat onto his knees.

'Do it,' he snarled at Henry.

Alongside Henry, PC Barnes sat petrified. Henry said to him, 'Unlock the cuffs, Dave.'

With his hands dithering almost uncontrollably, Barnes took out his handcuff key and inserted it into the cuff and released Longridge.

'Radios,' Longridge said, holding out his hand.

Henry and Barnes took their personal radios out of their harnesses and handed them to the prisoner, who dropped out of the van but turned to Henry. 'Tell your DI I'll be coming for him.' He then slammed the cage door and the metal bar self-locked.

Then he and his rescuers were gone, leaving two cops locked in the back of their own van and a badly injured colleague just surfacing into consciousness on the ground.

Henry bashed the back of his head against the van side in rage-fuelled frustration and creeping humiliation.

With a face that betrayed no emotion, Detective Inspector Fanshaw-Bayley was walked through the scene once more by the detective constable from Haslingden. They were at the top of the stairs on the first-floor landing of the women's refuge, looking down at two perfect turds on the carpet.

'Looks like he came in through the window,' the DC explained. The two detectives glanced at the entry point. In his head, FB was visualizing the MO and what he would have to write on the crime forms he would be submitting.

'Offender(s) approached rear of terraced house used as a

women's refuge during hours of darkness. Scaled wall after first breaking security light, believed with an airgun pellet, and cutting a gap in the security wire. Offender climbed soil pipe and jemmied open a window in order to gain access to the first floor.'

That's how it would begin. It would end in tragedy.

'Good climber,' the DC commented. 'Not many about these days.'

'Unh,' FB grunted. He could not stop his teeth from grinding.

'There's a few who still leave calling cards,' the DC said, looking down at the shit.

'Yeah, there are,' FB confirmed.

'So he gets in here, goes into the room . . .' The DC's voice faded.

'Let's have another look.'

FB was led along the landing to the second door on the left. It was slightly ajar. He pushed it wider with his fingernail, looking into the horrific tableau beyond.

A sudden feeling overwhelmed him as he looked at Sally Lee's body, naked and spread-eagled on the bed. He held it together.

'Battered to death,' the DC said.

FB took a step inside.

'Apparently Henry Christie phoned about ten o'clock last night and asked the manageress to check on her. Didn't her house go up in flames, yesterday evening?' the DC said, pulling a face. FB nodded. 'Anyway, Mrs Edge checked and she was fine, watching the box in here, baby asleep in the cot, whisky in hand. This morning the baby was heard crying but no one thought anything of it until the little bugger didn't shut up, so Mrs Edge checked up, noticed the broken window and the crap on the carpet, then when she couldn't get an answer at the door, she entered the room with her pass key. Found her, called us, I came.'

FB moved forwards. Already marked with tape was the route to the bed which anyone entering the scene would have to take from now on. He tried to keep the emotion out of his voice.

'Looks as though she was pinned down and pummelled. Blow after blow after blow,' he said bleakly. 'I'll bet he had his hand over her mouth.' He glanced at the blood splatters all over the bedroom, up the headboard, up the wall, across the carpet. There was a shoeprint in the blood.

Sally Lee had been pounded to death.

'Where's the child now?' FB asked.

'One of the other women's looking after it. Social services are coming.'

FB nodded. He looked at Sally, her face pulped and unrecognizable. That feeling almost had him again. But he steadied himself. 'Shit,' he said under his breath.

'Yeah,' the DC agreed. 'Who takes a shit and beats a woman to death?'

'Not the same person,' FB said. 'Whoever came in through that window let the killer in.'

'Y'reckon?'

'I know so.' Then under his breath, FB said, 'Shit,' again. And again.

SIXTEEN

'Judgement call my arse,' Henry Christie said bitterly, unable to remove the look of distaste from his face, or the taste from his mouth, even now, two hours after he had eventually finished work that day. It was 10.30pm, only half an hour to go before last orders, and he was hunched over a pint of Stella Artois accompanied by a Bell's chaser in the pub close to the street where he lived. It was his second pint. The first had gone down too quickly, but this one he was sipping. It was his first chaser but he had yet to taste that. He was in a mood to get drunk and mean, and somewhere at the back of his mind he knew he was bringing something home from work with him he shouldn't, despite his earlier thoughts on the subject.

But how could he leave it?

He was alone at a round brass-topped table. He had phoned Kate earlier and told her he wouldn't be able to link up with her that evening.

She sounded hurt.

He knew he should have cared but at the moment of phoning, and because of being fired up by what was going on all around him, he didn't. Which he knew was wrong.

His fingers continually curled into fists, his breath came in short bursts, his thoughts bleak and terrifying.

The thing that most cut him up was the fact that both of the big events of that day could have been prevented.

It would not have taken a person of any great intellect to have predicted them.

Firstly the escape from the court escort was just a very bad incident waiting to happen. Everyone knew it, no one did a damn thing about it . . . but they would now – now that it was too late. A dangerous criminal had been sprung by an armed gang and a cop had been whacked by a baseball bat.

He took a sip of his lager. It tasted bitter and unpleasant.

But at least no one had died. The cop had been hurt. His

head was sore and swollen and eight stitches now decorated his half-shaven skull – and the police just looked incompetent. But in the other case . . .

. . . Sally Lee had died.

Needlessly.

She had been treated as unimportant. That she didn't matter. That just because she was a bit of a girl, she had no right to be protected. OK, she was a bit of a girl, making complaints and then withdrawing them, but that was just a symptom of the life she was trapped in – and no one seemed to have seen that, except Henry.

And her killing could have been avoided.

Vladimir Kaminski, the prime – and only – suspect, was still free and, Henry thought despairingly, would probably stay that way. He would be well on the run now, Henry guessed . . . probably all the way back to Poland.

Henry felt utter shame for having followed orders. He had been told not to take her claim seriously and boot her out of the nick on that first occasion. *Following orders.* What sort of connotation did those words have? But yet, that was the way of things. Do what you are told to do, even if it's wrong and you know it. Questioning by subordinates in the cops at that time was stifled. It was the accepted order of things: the bosses knew what was right and their judgement should not be challenged.

Henry's only solace was that he had taken some steps to protect Sally, even if it was too little, too late. Ironically he had even mentally patted himself on the back for doing it.

She was destined to die at the hands of a violent madman.

'Fuck,' Henry said into his lager.

In the periphery of his vision he noticed a figure standing close to him. He raised his eyes. It was Steph, the landlady. She smiled sympathetically. 'Another tough day, I hear.'

'Kinda.' Henry swallowed and returned a washed-out smile. Steph arched her eyebrows.

'I could soothe your fevered brow,' she offered.

Henry considered the proposition. Was it too good to refuse?

'It's . . . kind of you . . . but I'm meeting someone,' he fibbed.

'Someone special?'

'Extra-special,' he said firmly and realized he really had

reached a major juncture in his life. 'She's called Kate, and I'm going to marry her,' he announced.

'Lucky girl.' There was a slight trace of disappointment in the words but they were supplemented by a nice, genuine smile. She turned and threaded her way back to the bar.

'Henry, you arsehole,' he admonished himself, 'turning *that* down!' He took a drink of the beer, but did not finish off the pint, nor even taste its golden companion. He pushed both drinks away, stood up and made for the pub door but came to a sudden standstill at the sight of the bulky figure coming in the opposite direction.

DI Fanshaw-Bayley.

They eyed each other malevolently.

'Buy you a drink?' FB asked cautiously.

'I'd rather you offered me out,' Henry retorted. 'Quite fancy punching your lights out.'

'I can understand that – but we need to talk.'

'What about?' Henry teased seriously. 'Me wrecking your career?'

'Let me buy you a drink.'

'To what end? Like I said, I'd prefer to screw a broken glass into your face, DI or otherwise.'

They were face to face, but their voices were not raised. To all intents, they looked like a couple of blokes having a reasonably friendly conversation.

'Let me explain things.'

'What? About judgement calls?' Henry's voice did rise. Other customers glanced in their direction. 'The bigger picture? You know, sometimes the bigger picture leaves the little, unimportant people out of focus, you twat.'

'I'll let that insult ride, Henry,' FB said. 'Siddown, let me buy you a drink.'

Henry relented and went to sit back at the table he had just vacated. FB eased his way to the bar and returned a short while later with two pints of Stella. He settled his wide backside across the round stool opposite Henry.

'Nice landlady,' FB commented. Henry merely raised a jaded eyebrow. FB took a sip of his pint as Henry observed him. To be fair, he looked drained, seemed to have lost some of his cocksure edge, maybe because he had discovered that sometimes he made shitty decisions and could be vulnerable. Or maybe he was just tired. 'I'll come straight to the point,' FB said. 'You and me need to sort out this shit.'

'Really?'

'Look, you're right, OK? But who could've known, eh? Who could've predicted she'd end up dead?'

Henry could not believe his ears. 'You want an honest answer to that? He regularly beat her up. Then he raped her because she didn't feel like having sex because she'd just had a kid. Then he beat her up again. Sense a continuum here? Sir?'

'There are two sides to every rape,' FB said.

'Do you really fucking mean that?' Henry was flabbergasted.

'Women usually get what they deserve.'

'NO – you're so fucking wrong. You live in the dark ages, mate. Men don't have a God-given right to violate women. I'm not saying there isn't a story to be told, but surely it's up to us to protect women and put those stories before a court and let a judge decide – not us! Surely.'

'We don't have time to be messed about,' FB said, sticking to his guns, 'by hysterical females.'

'I'm clearly not going to convince you. Y'know, just because it isn't a stranger abducting and raping a woman or a girl, doesn't mean to say it's not just as serious . . . and if we don't get our shit together on things like this, we'll come unstuck in a big way.' Rant over, Henry took a long pull on his lager, then, wiping his lips, said, 'Anyway, how come you're so soft on pond life like Kaminski, your informant – at least before you found out he was twirling you? He must have given you some real good stuff.'

'He got locked up a couple of months back for a town-centre disturbance, head-butted some guy. I talked to him the morning after when he was sobering up, like I do with a lot of prisoners because I'm always after intelligence and information and if it means a trade, then I trade – if it's worth it. He promised me something good and meaty if I got him out without a charge sheet in his back pocket and he came up with Jack Bowman for loads of burglaries. Obviously knew him and what he was up to through Sally Lee. When you pulled him for raping Sally, he offered me more.'

Henry's face remained impassive. 'What did he offer?'

'Another burglar. Y'know, it's rife in the valley.'

'And you're going to make your name by detecting a shed-load of burglaries rather than arresting a rapist?'

FB did not respond, but the answer was yes.

'He was playing you,' Henry said. 'His freedom in return for a phantom burglar while what he really wanted to do was get out because he knew a robbery was going down that day and he was involved somewhere along the line.' Henry had a thought. 'Know what? You've killed two women now, FB.'

The colour drained instantly from FB's tired face and his bottom lip sagged. 'What're you saying?'

'Kaminski would have been in custody and maybe the gang wouldn't have hit the shop that Jo walked into.'

'Tenuous . . . and don't you dare ever voice that, or I'll kneecap you for ever,' FB warned ferociously.

'No smoke without fire,' Henry said cheekily, enjoying himself in a perverted way. But he realized he could not take it too far. He wasn't naive enough to think that FB didn't have friends in high places and that he had the power to crush Henry's career like a bug under his winkle-pickers. It would be no contest and would be done in a subtle, underhand way. Henry's aspirations would be poleaxed and he'd be a cop on the beat for the next twenty-six years, though from where he sat in the here and now, it seemed a pretty good career choice.

Henry also understood FB's dilemma. A good grass was worth his weight in gold and there was always a trade-off because all informants were in it for selfish reasons – money, revenge, power – not altruistic ones. That was the way it worked. The hope was, it didn't go wrong – as in this case.

Henry also knew that if any shit should fly, none of it would splat FB because he was a sneaky reptile and would just claim that he'd been the one to get Sally Lee in the women's refuge. It wasn't his fault that the security in the place wasn't up to much.

The two men regarded each other.

Henry had finished teasing.

'Question being – what's the next step?' FB said.

'Catch Vlad.'

'I don't think it'll be a simple job. He won't be hanging around Rossendale if he's any sense. Been trying to pin the bastard down all day as it is. No luck. But I do have an idea that might be worth exploring.'

'That would be?'

'Well,' FB drawled, 'if we ID the burglar who broke into the refuge, we might also find the link to Kaminski and his whereabouts.'

'If we knew who the burglar was, that would be logical.'

'Well,' FB drawled again. 'It's someone who's good at climbing. Must be a beanpole of a chap. Very experienced. But when he gets into the property, he shits.'

'You've been keeping that under wraps,' Henry accused FB. He had heard the theory that someone else had let Vlad into the women's refuge to murder Sally, but no names had been bandied about. Nor had it been written down anywhere about the excrement at the point of entry, something else that FB had been holding back. Henry had not even had time to think who it might have been because he'd not been involved in anything connected with Sally's death, having spent his day dealing with the fallout from the custody break – which had included a visit to the subdivisional superintendent's office for a very serious bollocking.

'All day,' FB admitted.

'It's Jack Bowman, isn't it?'

'It fits his MO – as you know.'

'Why would Jack do that to his own sister, or whatever relation he is to her? And why tell me? Why not go after him yourself, cover yourself in glory. That's your MO.'

'Because . . .' FB's eyes narrowed, then he sighed, 'Because it's only right to include you. You deserve a chunk of it.'

'Or is it to buy my silence?'

'That too, obviously.'

'What's the plan?'

FB checked his watch. Henry noticed it was a Rolex, a make of watch he had always coveted and had promised himself he would own one day . . . he hoped. 'How drunk are you?'

'Stone-cold sober,' Henry said.

'No time like the present, then.'

*   *   *

They climbed into FB's Jaguar XJS in the car park, Henry's backside slithering on the leather upholstery. FB fired it up, pumped the accelerator and the engine gave a throaty feline growl.

'Nice motor,' Henry commented.

'Ta.' He reversed out of his spot and then motored effortlessly towards Rawtenstall.

'Where we heading?' Henry asked.

'Might try Sally's house on the estate. It looks like she'd been harbouring Jack there so he might've sneaked back to get his head down,' FB suggested. 'Even though we've been in and out of there all day, there's no one guarding it now. Plus, it's almost burnt to a cinder, but even so he might see it as safe. From what I know of him, he has nowhere else to crash.'

FB drove along the quiet roads, then up onto the estate which they cruised around for a couple of minutes. It wasn't particularly late but there wasn't much happening. Most Rossendale estates closed for business after the pubs kicked out and there wasn't always much activity on the streets themselves. It was a time for domestic disputes and often the only people out and about were the ones who couldn't easily be spotted, such as burglars and thieves.

They drove past Sally's house a couple of times. It was a sorry sight, the windows boarded up by the council, black scorch marks fanning up the brickwork above the living-room window. Henry felt very sad.

There was no obvious activity, so FB parked up a little away, but with a view of the front of the house. He switched off the engine and lights.

And waited.

Ten minutes later Henry had sunk low into the comfortable seat and was having major problems keeping his eyelids from slamming shut. The low point came when his chin dipped onto his chest, he started dreaming in very odd, disconnected images, then woke with a start as if he had been prodded. He had – by FB, who had jabbed him in the ribs.

'Wake up.'

'Why? Why?' Henry said gloopily. For a moment he couldn't quite work out where he was and tried to recall the dream, but it had gone. Then he realized. 'You seen something?'

'No – but I do have the house key.'

'Now you tell me.'

'We could wait inside.'

'What about the car? You wouldn't want to leave it parked up, would you?'

'When I said "we", I meant "you".'

'Ahh. But I don't have a radio.'

FB dipped his hand into the driver's door pocket and came out with a PR that he handed to Henry. 'Boy scout,' he said, and also gave him a Yale key and a penlight torch. 'You might need that – the electric's off.'

Henry took the items reluctantly.

'The PR has fresh batteries,' FB said. 'It'd make more sense for you to be in there and I'll be back at the nick in my office. That way, if he reccies the place, there won't be anything around to spook him. And you're right, this car is just a bit too conspicuous in this neck of the woods. And you can be inside, waiting to grab him.'

'I feel as though this was planned.'

'No, honestly – spur of the moment,' FB assured him.

Henry was unenthusiastic. 'One hour, and that's it.'

'Fair enough. If he doesn't show, we'll start looking for him again tomorrow.'

Henry climbed out, and realized as the cool wind whipped off the moors that where he should be was in bed, not looking to spend an hour in a fire-gutted house waiting for someone to show up – or not. Shaking his head at the absurdity, he set off to the house, entering through the front door, having to fold himself through a crisscross of crime-scene tape pinned across the door frame.

It was pitch black in the hallway and immediately Henry was hit by the overpowering stench of the fire. He turned on the torch and played it over the floor, walls and stairs, seeing how the fire had spread rapidly through the house, searching and destroying it. The repair bill, if it was ever so lucky as to be repaired, would be astronomical. And the damage was not assisted by the complete but absolutely necessary drenching handed out by the fire brigade.

Stepping down the hallway was like treading through a Grimm's fairy tale swamp.

Henry swore.

He glanced into the living room, the seat of one of the fires.

It had been decimated, leaving only blackened springs and part of the metal frameworks of the settee and chairs.

'Bastard,' Henry muttered. It looked far worse in the dark, playing the torch beam over it, than it had done in the immediate aftermath of the fire itself, at which he had been present the evening before. Then he went rigid, thinking he had heard something. Like a dull, moaning sound. Possibly it was the wind. He relaxed, and continued to flick the torch beam around the room, wondering where best to lodge himself for the next hour on this wild-goose wait. There was nowhere in here.

He remembered that the dining room had escaped most of the devastation because the door had been closed and the fire brigade had landed within minutes. It was in here he would stay.

Stepping back into the hall, he heard that same noise again.

A moan. Could have been the wind, but sounded almost human.

A shiver of apprehension went down his spine. It was a bit ghostly. Maybe Sally was back already, haunting the place.

He heard it again.

Not the wind. It was coming from behind the dining-room door.

He trod carefully on the burned, sodden carpet that squelched as his weight came down on each foot. His hand went to the door knob, which he gripped.

Again, the moaning sound.

His heart whammed and his mouth was dry as he turned the handle and opened the door. The room had suffered only superficial smoke damage, leaving its fixtures and fitting more or less in one piece.

His torch beam picked up the source of the noise, two eyes glinting in the darkness.

'PC Christie to DI Bayley,' Henry said into his radio. 'You need to return to the house as soon as possible.'

It was an eight-inch carving knife and had been driven deep into the table top by a huge force, the point of the blade probably a whole inch into the wood.

The only problem was that the knife had also been driven

through the back of Jack Bowman's right hand which, palm down, fingers splayed, had effectively pinned him like a butterfly, and sliced through the spread of delicate bones that radiated out from his wrist to his knuckles.

Bowman was kneeling by the table and looked as though he had been caught reaching for something on the table and suffered a terrible consequence for it.

He was still conscious as Henry entered the dining room and looked at him pleadingly through pain-ravaged eyes.

An expression of relief crossed his face.

'Help me,' he whispered hoarsely. 'Help me . . . I can't . . . can't . . . move,' he tried to say.

Henry crossed quickly to him and inspected the situation and gave a little whistle of appreciation. It looked as though a shaved, five-legged tarantula had been skewered by the knife. Bowman's palm rested in a pool of bright red blood. His fingers and thumb twitched involuntarily.

'I can't . . . I daren't . . .' Bowman gasped.

Henry reached for the knife, his initial instinct being to release a fellow human being from suffering. But just as his fingers were about to wrap around the handle, he stopped and shone his torch into Bowman's face, then took his hand away and slowly squatted down on his haunches so his face was level with Bowman's.

'Looks like it's stuck.'

'I tried to . . . I couldn't . . .' Bowman cringed. 'Oh God, please get it out. I . . . every time I move . . . Christ, it hurts.'

'Who did this to you?' Henry asked, making no effort to release him, staying exactly where he was.

'Get it out, get it out,' he begged. 'Please, please.'

'You need to tell me who did this,' Henry said reasonably.

'Please, man . . .'

'You won't be running away this time, will you?'

The implication of Henry's words and lack of action sunk in and Bowman's grey face turned to horror.

'Does it really hurt?' Henry asked cruelly.

'Yeah, yeah, oh God, please.'

'How much does it hurt?' Henry said – cruelly again – but the tone of his voice sounded soft and caring, as though he was concerned.

'A lot. I daren't move. Each time I move it cuts me even more.'

'Yeah, a lot of nerve endings in the hand,' Henry said knowledgeably.

'Please help me.'

'I will, course I will.' Somehow Henry knew that if he hadn't had a drink, he would have instantly released Bowman and called for an ambulance. But those few drinks had made him reckless and cruel, made him realize he could get something out of this situation. 'But first you need to talk to me, Jack, boy.'

Henry's head tilted slightly. Outside he heard a car pull up, a door slam, footsteps approaching. Then FB appeared at the dining-room door, a big torch in his hand, flashing it onto the tableau in front of him. An evil smile of opportunity creased his face. He had realized instantly what had taken a minute or two to dawn on Henry.

'Well, well, well, what have we here?' He strode across, Henry and Bowman watching him.

He peered at the knife and the hand and the blood-covered table. He inhaled a sharp whistle of breath. 'Now that must hurt.'

'Apparently it does,' Henry confirmed.

'You bastards, you utter bastards,' Bowman hissed, gripping his right wrist with his left hand and starting to tremble. His skin was drawn tight across his features.

'He was just going to tell me something,' Henry said.

'Was he now?' FB reached out and touched the top of the knife handle with the tip of his forefinger. 'Looks like it's in deep. I'm not certain we could actually remove this without destroying evidence. Fingerprints, y'know?'

'I was thinking the same thing.'

'But we could, I suppose, wiggle it a bit to see if we could get it free. But I reckon that would hurt a hell of a lot.'

FB tugged up his trousers by the front crease and squatted down on the other side of Bowman to Henry. 'Now then,' he cooed softly, 'we are normally decent, sympathetic people, Jack, but at this moment in time, we're not.' He shone his torch beam directly into Bowman's face.

Sweat dribbled from Bowman's hairline. His nostrils dilated constantly as he tried to deal with the pain and the situation.

'Y'see, I'm investigating your stepsister's brutal murder and the equally brutal murder of a young policewoman and several armed robberies.' FB's bushy, untrimmed eyebrows arched, and then dropped back into position. 'And your part in them,' he added.

'I had no part.'

'Listen to me, Jack . . . you did play a part in Sally's murder, didn't you?'

If Bowman's skin could have tightened any more, he would have looked like a skull. He shook his head.

'I'm going to stand up now and see if I can loosen this knife, Jack,' FB said. He put his left fist in front of Bowman's face and made a waggling gesture. 'I would guess that me riving it backwards and forwards and side to side in an effort to free you would certainly make the wound more serious than it already is and would cause you a great deal more pain. And it still might not come out. In fact, the point might accidentally go even deeper into the table.'

'You wouldn't. That's torture.'

'Merely me trying to release a man whose hand is pinned to a table by a carving knife and who was begging me to do just that.' FB stood up, his knees cracking.

Henry was still at Bowman's eye level. 'Speak,' he urged quietly.

FB's right hand, fingers outstretched, reached for the hilt.

Bowman watched in disbelief as FB curled his hand around it. 'What about the evidence?' he gasped.

FB pulled his face. 'To be honest, I don't think we'll get prints off the surface of the knife handle.'

'Speak,' Henry urged again, his lips not far from Bowman's ear.

'OK, OK, I broke into the women's refuge place,' Bowman gabbled quickly before FB could start to move the knife.

'Why?'

'For Vlad. He said he wanted to speak to Sal, said he wanted to chat things out with her.'

'Mm, interesting,' FB said. His hand hovered close to the knife. 'That makes you a murderer.'

Bowman blinked, the words penetrating through the haze of pain. 'I didn't kill her.'

'No, but you're part of the murder plot. An accessory. A co-conspirator. A co-accused . . . all those things . . . Looks like a life sentence for you, my lad . . . No more running away from cops. Screws, maybe. Other inmates, definitely, sex offenders and the like . . . Lad like you would be catnip in prison.'

'He said he wanted to talk to her, needed me to let him in, that's all,' Bowman blabbered quickly.

FB frowned. 'A court would convict you like that!' He clicked his fingers with a snap. 'Which means you need to talk – now.'

'I let him in. I swear I didn't know he was going to kill her. I wouldn't have let him in if I'd known what was going to happen, would I?'

'I don't know, would you?' FB asked.

'No, no, no.'

'So you broke in, then let him in – is that correct?'

'Yes, YES! Now call an ambulance, please.'

'In a minute,' FB said tantalizingly.

'Shit.'

FB stepped back thoughtfully. 'I'm not convinced.'

Henry looked at FB sharply, frowning. He thought this had gone on long enough now. He thought they had enough.

'Convinced by what?'

'By you, Jack . . . How come Vladimir grassed on you.'

'What do you mean?'

'About all the burglaries you committed.'

'What? He grassed on me?'

'How the hell do you think I knew about you? He told me everything you'd done.'

'I didn't know.'

'He's shagging your sister and, basically, butt-fucking you, too,' FB said. 'So what's this about – the knife through the hand?'

'Like I said,' he breathed dully. 'I didn't let him in with the intention of killing Sally, I didn't know he'd do it – honest! I sneaked back in here to get my head down after you lot'd gone, but he must have followed me, OK? He knew I wasn't remotely happy with him. I'd argued with him, said I'd go to the cops . . . yeah, like I meant it. Not. You don't cross a crazy psycho like him. You don't even threaten to cross him, even if you don't mean it. But I did and he stuck me to the fuckin' table. Now, please will you call an ambulance? It really, really, really hurts and every time I move just a bit, it creases me and I'm bleeding and I want to faint, but I daren't just in case I fall over and my hand gets sliced in two. And pull it out – quick.'

FB didn't move. 'Where is he?'

'I don't know, Christ I don't.'

'I said, where is he?'

'I don't know . . . but I do know one thing . . .'

'And that would be?' FB said.

'There's a big job being pulled tomorrow and Vlad's in on it and when it's done he's outta the country, going back to Poland with his equally freakin' psycho brother.'

FB gripped the knife.

Bowman froze, watched terrified.

Henry's breath stopped.

FB counted: 'One . . . two . . . THREE!'

SEVENTEEN

By the time the two compassionate cops had accompanied their wounded prisoner to Bury General Hospital – the nearest casualty department to Rossendale – and stayed close to him during treatment (Henry hovering even during the stitching process because there was no way he was going to let him run a third time) and then taken him back to Rawtenstall nick under arrest in the section van, it was almost 4am.

FB took the honour of claiming the arrest – suspicion of murder – ensuring that his name was emblazoned on the back of the charge sheet in big, bold capitals, whilst Henry watched on with mild amusement. It wasn't said in so many words, but FB was clearly going to shove all this firmly up the force's backside for the sin of dislodging him from the helm of the murder investigation, which had so infuriated him.

He did, however, allow Henry to put the heavily bandaged and drugged-up Bowman into a cell. Some compensation, perhaps, for something he should have done a couple of days earlier.

When Henry walked back into the charge office, FB crooked a finger at him and led him upstairs to his office where the heavy detective slumped into his office chair and Henry took a seat opposite.

Both men exhaled heavily.

'Where do we take this?' Henry asked.

FB spun on his chair, thinking. Then he said, 'We don't have much to go on, really. Bowman needs to be wrung dry of everything he knows in the morning, which will implicate Vladimir to the hilt, if you'll pardon the expression.' He chuckled at his own humour.

'But we still have to find him,' Henry said. 'If he's gone to ground in Manchester, it won't be easy.'

FB pinched the bridge of his nose.

Henry felt a throbbing headache coming on from a combination of tiredness, a bit of excitement and the alcohol wearing off. 'And on top of that, if Bowman is to be believed, then there's a big job coming off,' he checked his watch, 'sometime today.'

'The questions being, what, where, when and how?' FB said. 'And if we don't know these things, or can't find them out, should we just try to disrupt it?' He paused, counting off on his fingers as he spoke. 'Flood the place with uniforms, lots of them. High-visibility patrols, checkpoints, pulling everything coming into the valley from *that* direction' – FB jerked his thumb towards Manchester – 'and just put the buggers off.' His eyes narrowed conspiratorially. 'Or do we let it run, keep our resources hidden and hope we catch 'em?'

'We could compromise,' Henry suggested.

'How?'

'Y'know – meet in the middle.'

'I know what compromise means, you jack-ass.'

Henry grinned. 'How about we get all the unmarked divisional crime cars in and get them patrolling and stop-checking with a bit of subtlety, maybe with some help from the traffic department.' He saw FB's face scrunch up tight at the mention of traffic, referred to by the CID as 'gutter rats'. Like most detectives he had an unhealthy dislike of the traffic section, but for no real reason. 'It's just, if we let it run,' Henry said thoughtfully, 'and someone gets hurt and it's discovered we knew about it but didn't do anything, then you could be in big bother.'

FB's face reacted to the change from the royal 'we' to a finger-pointing 'you'.

'You are the senior officer, after all,' Henry said. 'You might have Teflon shoulders, but maybe not in this case.'

FB made a 'harrumph' noise.

'And while that's happening, the search can still be going on for Kaminski and Longridge and some enquiries could be made to try to pinpoint the potential target for the robbery . . . and we could have a firearms team on standby.'

'You've thought this through,' FB said.

'Just winging it,' Henry admitted, 'but at least we cover most things with that approach . . . I think,' he concluded unsurely. A flood of tiredness swept through him and he stifled a yawn and the urge to fall asleep with his forehead on FB's desk.

FB tilted back in his chair, blinking like a fat frog, staring at the ceiling for inspiration. 'It's a plan,' he said.

'I need some sleep,' Henry said.

'Ditto – but before that, let's go down and visit our prisoner, shall we?'

'To what end?'

'Just to make certain he's really telling us everything he knows. I'd hate to think he was holding stuff back.'

'Such as?'

'Don't know . . . but I have an urge to shake his hand – tight.'

The station sergeant handed the cell keys over to FB without a murmur. Henry followed the DI down the corridor, noting that two more cells were occupied, one by a singing drunk, the other by a sleeping thief. Bowman was in the cell furthest away from the charge office. FB put his eye to the peephole before inserting the key and pulling open the heavy door.

He stepped inside.

Henry hung back a couple of feet.

Bowman was flat on his back on the concrete bench/bed, a coarse blanket tugged up to his chin, his heavily bandaged right hand outside and resting on his chest. He was sleeping and dribbling.

But not for long.

He was lying on a reinforced plastic mattress. FB tipped him off. He hit the cell floor hard and rolled onto his injured hand.

Henry winced.

When he had joined the police in the late seventies, a prisoner being smacked around the cells was not uncommon. It wasn't that he'd never had confrontations in cells and he'd had to whack a couple of extremely uncooperative drunks who had attacked him, but those occasions had been moments in a chain of consecutive events, explainable and defensible. He had never arrested anyone, put them in a cell, and then gone back and cold-bloodedly given them a beating, even if he might have wanted to, either for revenge or to extract a confession. It just wasn't in him to do so. He knew that whilst he was a ruthless hunter of the truth – that was a trait of his personality – he wanted to do it without compromising his own integrity and pride. If he had to beat someone up to get an admission, then it probably wasn't worth it.

Not that he didn't want to beat the crap out of some of the vile, nasty, perverted and obnoxious pieces of work he'd come across, and he didn't rule out that sometime in the future it might happen.

But a callous visit to a cell in the middle of the night would not be on his agenda – ever.

Using a situation to his advantage was one thing. Such as finding Jack Bowman pinned to a table. Henry had only intended to tease Jack for a few moments before pulling out the knife and calling an ambulance. But FB had shown, was showing, he was prepared to do things the 'old school' way of coppering and take everything to its limits in his own way of pursuing justice.

Henry observed with unease as FB crouched down next to the prostrate and confused figure of Bowman, place a hand over the young man's mouth, and lift up his injured arm with the other.

'Now it's time to talk properly,' FB whispered.

And with that, FB smacked the injured hand against the top corner of the bench, making a dull thump. Henry winced.

Bowman would have screamed, but the palm of FB's hand was clamped over his face like an octopus, effectively pinning the slender lad down and the floor, despite his wriggling and efforts to get free. FB's face hovered a couple of inches over Bowman's. 'I want to know everything about Kaminski, where he is, what he's going to do . . . Everything, lad.'

To reinforce the demand, he repeated the move with the hand, striking it against the bench. Bowman, red-faced, wide-eyed and terrified, struggled futilely. FB had him pinned down.

Henry could see the pain jolting through him and something told him that this was one of those pivotal moments in his career, in his life.

This was about him being a decent human being first and cop second.

If he was comfortable watching this happen, then so be it. His fate was sealed.

But he wasn't.

Inside he was squirming. Not simply because of what he was

witnessing in front of him, but by the complicit nature of the sergeant who had handed over the keys without question, and thus, by definition, the complicit nature of the organization that would allow this sort of thing to happen. It should be better than this.

'Stop it,' Henry blurted. He had seen enough.

FB's head turned slowly towards him, his eyes burning like a malevolent demon. 'What?' he growled.

'Stop this,' Henry said. 'This isn't happening.'

'Get out of the cell,' FB said. 'Like you did before – remember? Leave him to me, if you don't have the guts to see this through. There's a lot at stake here.'

'No, I won't go,' Henry said. 'Not this time.' He stood firm, even if inside he was quaking.

'Did you hear what I said?'

'You know I did.'

Their eyes locked. FB must have expected Henry to back down, but he didn't. He almost did, almost ran like a puppy, but he held fast and FB knew that it was over.

He got up slowly, leaving Bowman on the cell floor, and shouldered his way furiously past Henry, who waited, listening to FB's fading footsteps.

'What's this? Good cop, bad cop?' Bowman said, groaning as he stood up and threw the mattress back onto the bench.

'I'm not a good cop,' Henry said. 'But as soon as I turn my back, he'll be in here and I won't be around to stop him.'

Nursing his hand tenderly in the crook of his arm, Bowman sat on the edge of the bench. 'Is that supposed to shit me up?'

'No, it's the truth, Jack. He's searching for a killer and he thinks you have the information he needs and he'll wring your neck to get it.'

'Wring away. I don't know owt more than I've already said.'

'Thing is,' Henry speculated, 'I think he's probably right. People like you always hold stuff back. Matter of pride.'

Bowman swung up his legs and pulled the blanket over them. 'I don't know anything else.'

'What if I can get you off a murder charge?'

Bowman squinted at Henry.

'At the moment you are as implicated as Kaminski for Sally's murder – and to be honest, Jack, you haven't shown much sorrow at the terrible death of your sister. So maybe it shows you were in on it, knew what Kaminski had planned. You'll have to work damn hard to convince a jury otherwise.'

'I let him in, that's all,' he cried. 'He told me he wanted to talk to her, not murder her. I've told you this already.'

'And still no grief or remorse,' Henry said. 'Just trying to protect yourself.'

'I haven't had time to grieve. I've been pinned to a fucking table for hours.'

Henry shook his head sadly. 'Some brother . . . Look, final offer . . . Start blabbing now or you'll be in the dock next to Vlad facing a murder charge. Tell us all you know and we'll look after you . . . otherwise, you're screwed for the rest of your life.'

'How can you look after me?' he sneered.

'You'll have to trust me.'

'I don't know anything more than I've already told you . . . well, not much anyway.'

Henry beckoned him out of the cell. 'Let's have a proper chat.'

He opened FB's office door to find the DI on his chair, legs swung up onto the edge of his desk, crossed at the ankle. FB glared.

'Who the fuck do you think you are?' FB demanded. 'Holier than thou.' He made a spitting gesture.

Henry jarred to a halt. 'I didn't join the cops to twat people around the cells, nor do I want to be a party or witness to it. I'll do what I have to, but . . .'

'You're prepared to let vicious crims go, or let armed robberies happen, just for the sake of a good smacking?'

'I'll do it the right way, the only way.'

Henry knew this was a claim of youth. A claim made when everything seemed to be clear cut, the division between right and wrong. He knew life became foggy and complex and he knew that someday in the future, if he ever found himself face to face with a sneering child-molester, he would probably eat those words. But for now, that was how it was. He was high-principled and he didn't want to be woken up by the knock on his front door from the rubber-heel squad, the cops who investigate cops.

Henry thought for a moment that FB eyed him with some degree of admiration . . . maybe just for a second. Or was it ridicule?

'So where does this leave us?' FB asked, then answered his own question. 'With a killer still at large, us without clue to his whereabouts and a big job about to go down on our patch and no idea on that either.'

For a moment, Henry considered playing the DI, but dismissed it, fearing for his life if he did. Instead he said, 'You were right about Jack Bowman.' FB continued to stare at Henry. 'He does know more than he let on.'

'I knew it.' FB's heels came off the desk and he shot forwards as his hands slapped his blotter.

'But I had to schmaltz it out of him and make him a promise.'

FB's face of triumph waned slightly. 'What promise?'

'That we'd drop any murder charge against him.'

FB's slug-like eyebrows met as he frowned. 'You what?'

'I'm certain he didn't know what Kaminski intended.'

'And you promised him he won't face a murder charge, or whatever the appropriate charge is, because he told you what, exactly?' His incredulity was almost tangible. 'It's all right being high-minded, Henry, but being naive as well? Double-dumb. He's lying to save his arse.'

'Don't think so.'

'Well, that looks like another point on which we'll be begging to differ. I need my bed.'

'It's a cash in transit job,' Henry said quickly. 'Not a shop or other retail premises.'

FB sat upright at this revelation.

'It's a bank job,' Henry went on. 'Apparently Kaminski's been scouting for the gang with regards to all the shops that have been hit and stumbled across something else very tasty.'

'I'm listening.'

'Each third Friday of every month – and that's today – a security van delivers cash to the Rossendale Valley Building Society, the branch in the shopping centre, here.' Henry pointed towards the town centre, less than a hundred yards from the station. 'Vladimir discovered it by accident, he's been keeping nicks on it and they're going to hit it tomorrow – today, actually. And it's a lot of money.'

'And Bowman told you this? Without you having to beat it out of him?'

'Yeah – amazing, eh?'

'How does he know?'

'Overheard Vlad and Constantine talking last night when they were waiting in a car before they dropped Jack off to break into the refuge. He was pretending to be asleep.'

'And he told you this?'

Henry nodded. 'And he admitted breaking into old Mrs Fudge's house, but that's another story. And he said sorry for escaping. And I didn't hit him once.'

As shattered as he was, and flabbergasted he was still functioning – though barely – Henry knew it would be impossible to get to sleep even though FB ordered him to go home and get his head down for a couple of hours, then get back to work for nine. That gave him three hours – and Henry knew exactly what he was going to do with that time, and it wasn't sleep. And his testicles felt so much better.

He drove to Kate's house, turned into her road, switched the engine off and cruised his car to a soundless stop outside the house and got out, closing the door silently. He looked up at the house, knowing her parents were back in residence but undeterred.

He crept up the driveway, sprang over the gate and made his way along the side of the house to the rear garden, stepped back and looked up at Kate's bedroom window. There was no way of contacting her without alerting her vigilant father, the only phone the family had being in the hallway on a stand at the foot of the stairs, so, frustratingly, he was reduced to this primitive, time-honoured way of waking her: stones thrown against the bedroom window, like some suitor in an Edwardian stage farce.

But he didn't want to break the windows, which were single-thickness glass, not double-glazing, set in old-fashioned iron frames.

He used what he could find in the garden, a handful of chippings, and took a couple of practice throws just to get the height right, before actually going for his target.

Four hits, four taps later, and no broken glass, and the curtain twitched and parted. And there she was, a sleepy-faced, hair-mussed, but beautiful young woman, looking down at him uncomprehendingly. Her face cracked into a smile of joy before she took control of herself, folded her arms across her nightie and gave him a stern look of disapproval.

'Open the window,' he mouthed.

Kate shook her head. 'Why should I?' she mouthed back.

'Because I love you,' was his mouthy response.

Her features softened. She shook her head again and opened the window. 'Henry, what are you doing?'

'I just needed to see you,' he whispered up to her.

'Right – you've seen me, now go.'

He opened his arms. 'Need a kiss.'

'Do you know what time it is?'

'Yep. Let me in.'

'What about my parents?'

'I don't want to kiss them. Be sneaky.'

Unable to believe she was actually going to do this, she closed the window, pulled the curtains together and disappeared from view. A long minute later the back door opened and she was there in fluffy slippers, a towelling dressing gown over her almost ankle-length nightie.

Henry surged in, hardly able to contain himself. He took her in his arms and danced her around the kitchen as he kissed her passionately, lips, face, neck, pulling her dressing gown open, his hands finding her lovely breasts over the nightdress material.

And despite herself and the slightly scary situation, she responded and pulled at his clothes, returned the passion.

Within moments, Henry's jeans and underpants were around his ankles, Kate's dressing gown had been discarded, her nighty pulled up around her midriff. Henry backed her against the oven and she wrapped her legs around him and they made urgent, but quiet, love in the kitchen, Henry holding her up easily.

They twirled thus engaged around the kitchen bouncing off the appliances, rattling the contents of the fridge, like a ball in a bagatelle gathering points, until both of them reached a stage where they really had to let go. Sensing forthcoming screams and load moans, Henry clamped a hand over Kate's mouth, she clamped one over his, and so connected, they held each other's sparkling eyes as they came together in muted silence with Kate's bare bum perched on the edge of the sink.

'*Kate!*'

Suddenly both tensed up at the sound of her father's voice hollering down from the top of the stairs.

'Kate? Is that you?'

Passionate stares were replaced by horror tinged with amusement. She called back, 'Yes, Dad, just getting a glass of water.'

'Are you all right, my love?'

'I'm fine . . . just needed a bit of something.'

'I thought I heard a crash.'

'It was nothing.'

'OK, love.'

The lovers, still entwined, waited tensely and silently until they heard a bedroom door click shut. Then they giggled into each other's shoulders.

'Oh God, Henry.'

'Nothing like living dangerously.'

Slowly – unwillingly – they disengaged and Henry allowed Kate to stand on her own two feet. They rearranged their clothing and fell into a long, tender embrace before Henry stood back.

'I'd better go,' he whispered. 'Got to be back in work by nine . . . been in all night, too . . . long day ahead, I think. Things are moving fast.'

'OK.'

'But I'll see you tonight. Pick you up at seven? Let's go for an Italian at that place on Grane Road.'

'Sounds good.'

They kissed one more time and Henry stole out of the back door and made his way back to his car, now facing the slight problem of starting it. Henry's motor was not a discreet car. The exhaust blew. The tappets needed adjusting. He thought that by turning the ignition slowly and bracing himself it would fire up quietly. It didn't.

He glanced at Kate's house.

She was framed in the downstairs lounge window.

Directly above her was her father's thunderous face at a gap in the bedroom curtains.

'Shit,' Henry said, and with a forced smile and a nice wave, he gunned the Marina away.

He slept for two hours. Deep, solid, exhausted, dreamless sleep. He made certain he was up in time to shower and then have a decent breakfast, thinking that he would probably be eating rubbish food on the hoof for the rest of the day. He made scrambled eggs on thick toast and had fresh coffee and orange juice. Despite the lack of sleep he was buoyed up for what was to come – getting involved in a big police operation and hopefully catching some very bad men. The prospect thrilled him, not least because he'd had a major hand in generating what was to come.

It was a proud day for him, one which he hoped would be the first stepping stone on his faltering way to CID which had been blocked by his ignominious secondment in Blackburn.

He found a parking spot in the usual place and made his way on foot to the back of the nick. As he turned into the yard he had to back-pedal a few steps out of the way of a stream of police vehicles hurtling out. A personnel carrier, two plain cars and two liveried cars, all crammed with cops, one behind the other, clearly on a mission.

Henry watched them all whizz by, his forehead creased, an uncomfortable sensation in the pit of his stomach.

When the way was clear, he headed into the station.

Inside, it too was bursting with cops and even a couple of police dogs.

Something big was going down.

Increasing Henry's bad feeling.

He twisted up the back stairwell and made his way along the corridor to FB's office. It was empty, but the phone on his desk was ringing continuously.

Henry's lips pursed. He pushed himself off the door frame, feeling anger building inside him, and strode to the lecture room that had been converted into the incident room, easing through the door.

DI Fanshaw-Bayley was sitting at a desk at the far end of the room in his shirt sleeves, tie askew, surrounded by four detectives to whom he was giving instructions, nodding at queries, asking questions. Other detectives worked on the flip charts and a time-line that had been pinned to the wall behind FB. Another detective was working head down at another desk, surrounded by 'in', 'out' and 'pending' trays stacked high with paperwork. Another pair were in deep discussion over some file or another.

The air had a palpable tingle of excitement to it, but it only served to rile Henry, who was coming to a very clear conclusion as to what was happening.

He walked slowly across the incident room until he stood behind the detectives milling around FB. He wasn't really listening to anything that was being said, it was just white noise, kept at bay by the pulse now beating in his ears.

The detectives, having apparently been briefed, peeled away one by one until just Henry stood in front of FB.

FB suddenly became engrossed in sifting very important paperwork, reckoning he hadn't seen Henry at all.

Henry went along with this psychological game for a few moments until he could stand it no longer.

'What's going on?'

'Uh?' FB still didn't bother to raise his eyes.

'I said what's going on?'

Then he did look up, a pained expression on his face at the interruption to his thought process. 'What do you mean?' he asked innocently.

'All this.' Henry gestured.

'All what?' FB continued to play dumb.

'You told me to come in at nine.'

'And you're here, aren't you?'

'And you've kicked everything off without me, or so it seems.'

'Yeah – I've kick-started a large police operation intended to round up some big villains,' FB said, matter-of-factly.

'What about the info about the robbery at the building society?'

'I decided to disrupt and arrest, rather than take the chance of getting an innocent bystander injured in the crossfire.'

Henry blinked and swallowed drily, his bubble bursting spectacularly. 'And my part in this is . . .?'

FB held his gaze. 'You don't have a part.' He collected up some papers and rose from the desk. 'And now if you'll excuse me, I have an operation to coordinate.'

Lost for words, Henry watched him disappear through the door. But then something galvanized him. He caught up to FB as he entered his office. Henry framed himself in the doorway.

'How can you do this?' he demanded.

FB sat at his desk and coolly gestured for Henry to come in, close the door.

'Sit.'

Henry sat slowly.

'You gotta learn some moves in this job, Henry. I'm now back running the investigation into Jo's murder, where I should be.'

'How have you pulled that off?'

'You know the sportsman who stays behind, practising when the rest of the team goes home, the one who wants to be the best? Or the swot who stays up till all hours because he wants the best grades? Well, that's me. I work hard. I stay at work longer. I lobby. I forge meaningful relationships, so that when all the others have tootled off home, I'm the one still at the grindstone. And that's what I did after you went this morning. You know – when you went to bed? I stayed here and picked up the phone and that's how you get on. And suddenly that completely useless detective super is binned and I'm back in charge.'

'Why didn't you call me?' Henry whined. He knew it sounded pathetic.

'On what? Do you carry a phone around with you, or something? No, because such things don't exist . . . and because . . .'

'Because you want all the glory for yourself?'

'Something like that,' FB admitted with a proud pout.

'You used me. Everything I put together, you nicked. Just to feather your own nest.'

FB guffawed. 'Team effort, Henry. No "I" in team and all that shite. Within half an hour of bending the ACC Crime's ear, I had it all sorted. GMP and us, hitting eight addresses as we speak, rounding up all the usual arseholes and preventing a robbery and probably arresting Jo's killer in the process, and hopefully Sally Lee's, too. And a high-profile operation around the valley to discourage any possible robbery – just in case.' He sounded smug. He gave Henry a half-smile and a wink. 'Man up and look upon it as a learning process.'

'Well, at least I've learned what FB really stands for.'

'You be very careful about what you say, Henry.'

EIGHTEEN

Henry rejected the offer of getting changed into uniform, putting on his big hat and patrolling the town centre, the only role that FB could come up with for him. Instead he retreated into the shell that was paperwork. Deflated, he didn't even bother to book out a PR because he didn't even want to hear if anything was happening. He went to his tray and found that another Crown Court committal file had appeared and needed some attention, made a mug of tea then found a quiet corner in the report-writing room and sat down granite-faced at a desk and began leafing through the file. At the back of his mind he tried to work out what had just happened and how he could bounce back from it.

He was gutted.

He had worked hard, produced results, and then been sidelined.

He would not have minded so much if FB had simply called him in and made him an integral part of what he had decided would happen. But no. FB had used the information that they had unearthed together – with Henry having done most of the digging – and applied it to his own career.

Henry gave a short laugh, mainly at himself. A lesson well learned, he thought. The price of an education.

And although that lesson might be 'screw others', Henry wasn't prepared to do that. It wasn't in his nature.

He began to work on the file.

At noon he had boxed off the paperwork. He leaned back and stretched. There was other stuff to do and he decided to do it after grabbing some lunch. He piled it all together and walked into the sergeant's office, where his tray was located.

Emerging and looking down the back corridor, he saw the rear doors of the nick burst spectacularly open. Three cops crashed through, wrestling with one prisoner that Henry instantly recognized:

John Longridge, the second person to have escaped from his clutches recently.

He braced himself to step in and help if necessary.

The four of them tripped and rolled, but Longridge ended up pinned face down on the tiled floor, blood flecking out from a busted nose and split lip. He squirmed like a trapped leopard, kicking, spitting blood and saliva, and cursing vehemently. His hands had been cuffed behind his back, so the damage he could inflict was fairly minimal, but he fought all the way as he was carried and dragged straight through the charge office and heaved bodily into a cell where the officers, with the station sergeant – PS Ridgeson – barking instructions above them, immobilized and searched him. He was then left in the cell, still handcuffed, shouting, swearing and head butting the door. Not a happy person and completely different in demeanour to how he had been on his previous arrest, all cocksure, cool and arrogant. This made Henry wonder if he'd been caught in the act of doing something he shouldn't.

As soon as this was done, the next prisoner arrived, this one a bit more dignified in his lack of liberty. At first Henry thought it was Vladimir Kaminski, but as he was brought closer, he recognized Constantine, the slightly younger brother, who Henry had tackled in Manchester and come off worse. The sight of him made his balls ache. He was not exactly compliant, but not as violent as Longridge, just awkward. He was flanked by two officers and a third behind, gripping his jacket collar and holding his cuffed hands as he was manhandled firmly along the corridor. His eyes caught sight of Henry and he raised his chin with a smirk, giving Henry an unobstructed view of the tattoo across his throat – the serpent wound around a rifle. Henry smirked back . . . so Constantine was definitely the one who had scaled the walls and then assaulted him.

He was compliant enough, the sergeant decided, to be uncuffed, searched, booked in and then taken to a cell.

After this flurry of activity Henry stepped into the charge office where Ridgeson was completing the paperwork for the detainees.

'How's it going?' Henry asked. He was unable to contain his curiosity, despite himself.

Ridgeson glanced up. 'Oh, hi, Henry. Well, I think.' Then he frowned. 'You not part of this?'

'Don't ask.' Henry waved his hands and tried to keep his body language neutral, but a knowing look came over the sergeant's face. 'Are these the only arrests?'

'No, there are others but we're using Accrington and Blackburn cells, too. Keep them apart a bit.'

Henry nodded and stood aside when FB came into the room. 'Hi, sarge,' he said breezily to Ridgeson, giving Henry a quick, guilty glance.

'They're trapped up,' Ridgeson said, anticipating the question. 'Longridge kicked off and hark' – he cupped a hand to his ear – 'you can still hear him. He's on speed, I'd say.'

From the cells came the dull thud-thud-thud of Longridge's head as he beat it against the cell wall.

'Great stuff,' FB said 'Property searches are going on as we speak and when I know where we stand, I'll let you know, sarge. Good signs so far, I hear. Shotguns and ski masks . . . looks like we grabbed the bastards just in time – and we know the cash drop to the building society has been made without incident, so that's good news, eh? But whatever happens, neither of these two will be going anywhere. Longridge is an escapee and Kaminski assaulted our Henry here,' he said mock-affectionately and looked at Henry again who, for a moment, thought of saying he wasn't going to pursue a complaint – just to annoy FB. He didn't.

'What about Vlad?' Henry enquired. 'Has he been locked up yet?'

'Not so far, but it's only a matter of time,' FB said with certainty. He then swung away happily and disappeared, leaving Henry and the sergeant, who gave Henry that knowing look again.

'He cut you out?'

'To some tune.'

'He's very focused.'

'And selfish.'

'Learn from it,' the sergeant advised. 'That man will go far.'

'Not far enough,' Henry grunted, 'but cheers anyway.'

Henry hesitated, desperately wanting to be involved – at the very least to interview Constantine – but he didn't want to be seen to be begging. It was unbecoming. Already he was thinking ahead, planning how he would move on and get onto CID. He would not be battered down by this, no way.

He walked back to the report-writing room and put on his jacket, which he'd left slung over the back of the chair.

There was a little errand to make in the town centre, then he'd drop by to say hi to Kate in the insurance brokers, though he doubted if he'd be able to entice her to repeat their sexy encounter in the consulting room. Even Henry had to admit that, at least for today, he'd had enough sex in a scary place, that being Kate's kitchen. He didn't want to push it. After that he would have a brew and a toastie at a town-centre cafe, then go home, creep under his duvet and sleep.

That was his short-term plan.

He left the station via the back door and strolled into town.

As ever, Rawtenstall was fairly quiet and reasonably pleasant to saunter through. He dropped by Kate's workplace. She was busy with a client at the counter and although he caught her eye, it was clear she was unable to extricate herself, so he gave a wave and left, walking up Bank Street to complete his errand at another shop. The result was excellent and he thanked the manager, who shooed him away without having to pay, even though Henry did genuinely offer.

'No,' the man insisted. 'You're doing a good thing here, so I'll play my part in it.'

Henry thanked him and took the item which the man had slipped into a strengthened envelope. He then walked further along Bank Street to a cafe where he found an empty seat on a stool at the bar by the window and ordered a milky coffee and cheese-and-onion toastie. He sipped and ate whilst considering life, death and the universe.

He didn't manage to reach any firm conclusions about any of the subjects. He wasn't such a deep thinker.

But he enjoyed his coffee and food and watched life go by, including the slow cruise past of a couple of traffic cars and a couple of cops he recognized as authorized firearms officers in a plain car, no doubt part of FB's cunning plan for today's operation to discourage violent crimes. And it would seem that, with the success of the op so far, there wouldn't be an armed robbery.

'Git,' Henry said between gritted teeth as his mind spun to FB. Again. The man infuriated him, but he could not stop thinking about him. Henry was pretty sure that Bill Ridgeson's prediction about FB's future would come true. Based on the way the man operated – if advancement came from stepping on others' heads – he was definitely going to be chief constable one day. A chilling thought.

Time for bed, Henry thought.

He finished his coffee, picked up his envelope, paid, and stepped onto Bank Street, pausing at the door for a few moments before setting off to his car. He didn't plan on showing his face in work again that day, nor the next, because it was a rest day.

Then he quickly stepped back into the cafe doorway.

The man across the street was wearing a green parka jacket, with a grey hood pulled up over his head. His left hand was tucked into the pocket, right arm hanging stiffly down by his side, the hand hardly visible, covered by the hem of the coat sleeve. He wore grey tracksuit bottoms but it was the blue and white Adidas trainers on his feet that clinched it, because not many days ago Henry had held them in his own hands and given them back to the person who was now walking down the main street.

His head was tilted forwards and he seemed to be staring at the ground as he walked up the opposite side of the street to where Henry stood. Not that there was anything bad about that. Lots of people walked with their heads down, looking at their feet, avoiding eye contact. That was just the way people were.

Henry knew this man was doing it for a specific reason. He knew that normally this individual would be lording it along, swaggering and cocky, hoping someone would be daft enough to bump into him or look into his mad eyes and give him a reason to start an argument that would lead to a fight.

Not today.

Because today, Vladimir Kaminski wanted to hide his face.

Henry hadn't clearly seen the face, only a sliver of it. It was the overall body shape, broad, stocky, muscled, that Henry recognized and could not be hidden underneath a parka that looked a size too small anyway . . . Henry's mind flashed back . . . Could it be the parka he had seen hung in Sally Lee's hallway that first time he had met her?

And the trainers.

Henry remained where he was for a moment, then went back into the cafe and asked a waitress to look after the envelope for him, stepped out of the cafe onto the pavement and started to follow Kaminski at a discreet distance, about fifty yards behind him. Then Henry crossed over so he was on the same side as Vlad, having decided that he would be tackling him within the next few seconds. He plotted it through quickly: upping his pace, keeping as silent as possible, then a final surge – the shoulder smashing into the small of Kaminski's back to flatten him, knock the wind out of him, keep him down and then scream for someone to call for help.

Excitement shuddered through him – not just at the prospect of the physical encounter, but at the thought of seeing FB's face as he marched his prisoner into the charge office. A dream.

He turned onto autopilot as he surveyed Kaminski's broad back, working out exactly where his shoulder would connect, just at the base of the spine. Then he noticed the very stiff right arm again, hanging by his side as if it was false, or as if something was secreted up the sleeve and he was holding whatever it was in place with his fingers like a shoplifter hiding a bottle of stolen whisky.

Kaminski's pace increased slightly but noticeably.

Henry was certain that the guy had not spotted him.

Still heading along Bank Street, he crossed the junction with Grange Crescent, then the next one with Kay Street, the shops to his left as he walked.

Henry began a half jog, starting to speed up his pace. When he hit him, he wanted it to be as hard as possible and at full pelt and bring him down in one.

Kaminski then did a sharp left into the square that was the main shopping centre, sending a cold feeling of dread through Henry who hoped that he was wrong as he slotted things together, his thought processes working in parallel. Located on the square was the Rossendale Valley Building Society which had, earlier that day, successfully received a very large cash infusion. And suddenly Henry began to wonder just what the hell Kaminski had secreted up the right sleeve of the parka. A sawn-off shotgun? It could just about fit. Was Kaminski about to try and do a solo job on the building society, a rash act driven by several factors, his desperation to leave the country, that he could guess he was wanted for murder, would probably also know that Jack Bowman had been arrested and could be grassing on him at that very moment (such an irony, Henry thought) and the fact that the cops had started to round up his associates? The cash they'd planned to steal was now with the rightful owners and all it would need would be to shove the shotgun – if that's what he had – into the face of one of the tellers and get her to fill up a bag with nice new notes. About thirty thousand pounds' worth.

Rightly or wrongly, that was how Henry put it all together in those fleeting moments.

But it didn't actually matter what Kaminski's intentions were. What remained a necessity was to arrest him.

He was now about thirty yards ahead of Henry, almost outside the door of the building society.

And then he was at the door.

Kaminski stopped suddenly, pivoted ninety degrees and jerked his right arm a couple of times, and proved Henry right.

A single-barrelled sawn-off shotgun slithered out. He caught the stock with his fingers and his left hand came up to grip the short barrel as he flipped off the hood of his parka with a backwards jerk of his head, revealing for the first time that his features were distorted by the stocking mask pulled tight over his face. Old hat, maybe, but it was still one of the scariest sights ever, an armed robber with such a mask over his face, skewing the facial features grotesquely. Great, tried and tested psychology.

Then he set himself with a roll of his broad shoulders and charged to the door.

He had been so tunnel-visioned, so deep in getting himself in the right frame of mind to commit this act, that he did not see or hear Henry's approach from the side until it was too late.

Henry had been moving from the instant that Kaminski turned to face the door of the building society.

He had seen the shotgun slide down the sleeve, the hood get flicked off, all in the time he started to run at him, and had to completely reappraise his approach as he was now going to have to hit him sideways.

His arms pumped like pistons.

When he was about ten feet away from Kaminski he pitched himself into a low dive so his left shoulder would connect just above the villain's left hip whilst aiming to grab the shotgun at the moment of impact and keep his own head down and safe behind him, tucked into the small of Kaminski's back, and take him down.

Yet at that very last moment, Kaminski must have registered the blur and bulk of Henry flying at him from the corner of his eye and that he was coming through the air at him. He half-twisted, the shotgun swinging around at hip level.

And then Henry's mind's eye picture of what should have happened in the ideal world got smashed to pieces.

As Kaminski turned, the two men were now almost directly facing each other.

Henry in mid-air, Kaminski three-quarters turned, his finger on the trigger.

Henry's left shoulder connected at lower gut level. He was flying hard and anyone else would have been winded and possibly quite badly hurt, but Kaminski's steroid-assisted physical regime had moulded his stomach muscles into ridges of rock.

He didn't even overturn him.

Kaminski merely staggered backwards a few steps on his tree-trunk-thick legs, but fortunately the shotgun did jolt skywards as Henry, his whole body jarring, slammed onto his knees. A flash of memory recalled how hard it had been to overpower Kaminski after he had chased him from Sally Lee's house on that morning which now seemed a million years ago. With that thought was the realization that he had only been successful then probably because he had stamina and Kaminski, despite his physical prowess, had easily run out of breath. He was built for brute strength, the 'here and now', not the long haul.

This troubled Henry.

In a fight in which Kaminski didn't start off exhausted and was probably on stimulants, he had to be the favourite. He had immense muscle power, and whilst Henry wasn't short of muscle and strength, his fitness was of a different type. He had more stamina and was rangy.

There would be no beating up the cock of the town that morning.

And because of the circumstances, for Henry this would be a fight for survival.

Kaminski wobbled back but kept his balance. And Henry, having failed to connect properly and keep a grip, hit the concrete with a thud, trying to get the gun at the same time. Kaminski kept the weapon out his reach, then twisted back, bringing the gun round as he did with the intention, Henry assumed, of blasting him at point-blank range.

Henry saw the gun arcing round and, thus motivated, scrambled like a runner starting a race on a muddy track and flung himself at Kaminski's thick legs, keeping his head low and wrapping his arms around his shins like a lasso, tightening the hold and heaving backwards.

This time the big man lost his balance and toppled like he'd walked backwards into a coffee table and in so doing, the gun jumped skywards again and his finger jerked the trigger back, firing it with the sound of a metal tray being whacked on a table top.

He fell over, but as he did he tried to crash the barrel of the gun across the back of Henry's head, catching it, but only with a glancing blow. It hurt, sending a shockwave through Henry's skull, but he held on tightly, keeping his head tucked in and shouting, 'Call the police,' uselessly because his voice was muffled as his face was crushed into Kaminski's tracksuit bottoms.

Kaminski writhed, desperate to free himself from Henry. He felt incredibly strong. Henry could feel the outline of his huge iron-hard calf muscles, and could not prevent Kaminski success-fully extracting himself from his clutches.

There was another blow from the gun which Kaminski was now using like a baseball bat, hitting Henry's back – but still he held on tight.

But with one huge surge of strength, he broke free and kicked Henry violently away, then he was up on his feet. But he didn't run. He came at Henry with a snarl and kicked him hard in the side, twice, and tried to stamp on his head.

He was still holding the shotgun in his left hand as he did this, and his right hand delved into his parka pocket, fumbling for something. A shotgun cartridge.

Henry rolled away, his hands covering his head. Kaminski

silently and remorselessly pursued him, kicking, whilst at the same time he flicked open the breech of the shotgun, ejecting the spent cartridge and slotting the new one in place, then slamming the gun shut.

As Henry reeled whilst being assaulted, he had a rushed, unfocused vision of other people in the shopping centre who were witnessing the incident. As usual in Rawtenstall, there were not many folk about.

Two old women, scarves on their heads, old-fashioned wicker shopping baskets in their hands, stood rooted to the spot, mouths agape.

A man turned and ran away.

Another man cowered. Henry heard a scream.

But that was all he saw as he rolled away and came to a stop on his back, looking up at the cloudy sky, feeling a spit of rain on his face. The beating was over. Kaminski towered into his vision, blocking out the sky, standing over him with his legs apart. The shotgun, reloaded, was pointed at Henry's upper chest. There was a wild, breathless expression on the man's face as he slowly aimed the gun at Henry's heart and looked down the shortened barrel at him.

The young cop braced himself and held his breath.

Kaminski smiled grimly. 'I knew I would kill you,' he said, his face squashed and contorted underneath the stocking mask.

Henry saw the finger on the trigger, the single barrel and the rough hacksaw marks across the muzzle.

Then the sound of the shot, then a second one.

Suddenly Kaminski's right shoulder jolted forward, then his left shoulder exploded in a splatter of blood. Henry saw a look of total surprise on Kaminski's face as he slumped down onto his knees and dropped forwards across Henry like a log, smashing his face into the concrete, the shotgun skittering out of his grip across the ground. Henry scrambled from underneath him and snatched up the gun as he came up onto one knee, holding the weapon out, away from himself like he'd caught an angry cobra.

He watched as the two firearms officers in the combat position, their weapons – four-inch-barrelled Smith & Wesson Model 10 revolvers – pointed at Kaminski, came towards him.

One said to Henry, without taking his eyes off Kaminski, 'You OK?'

He nodded.

With their guns unwaveringly aimed at him, the officers circled the prostrate Kaminski, who was writhing and screaming deafeningly in pain from the bullet wounds, one in either shoulder, blood pumping from each entry, drenching the parka to a dirty shade of black.

Henry stood up shakily and watched, breathing deep, trying to bring himself back down from where he was and wondering where the hell the firearms officers had suddenly appeared from.

Moments later the shopping precinct seemed to be filled with cops under the control of a uniformed inspector. The shotgun was prised from Henry's grip by that officer who said, 'I think I'll have that, son.'

Henry stepped back, observing it all in a haze of slow motion and unreality.

He was brought back to thumping reality by the appearance of FB standing in front of him, a look of accusation on his face.

The DI snorted, 'You ever heard of a police radio? A call for assistance? Anything like that?'

'No,' Henry retorted.

FB shook his head. 'Bloody good job these two firearms officers were in the building society, isn't it? Otherwise, you'd be a dead 'un.'

'That's where they came from,' Henry said. He'd been wondering.

'Yeah. At my behest, they'd been checking up to see if everything was all OK.'

'I didn't know that, did I?'

FB continued to shake his head. In the distance was the sound of ambulance sirens. Police cars pulled up on Bank Street, blue lights flashing.

'Are you all right?' FB asked. It was his first – and only – but genuine show of concern.

'I'm great,' Henry said dully, feeling his skull.

A crowd had gathered and were being eased backwards by the police. Henry shouldered his way through the onlookers and glanced up to see Kate running towards him.

*   *   *

Henry handed his written statement over to the DI.

'My version of events,' he said.

It was six o'clock. At last the police station was reasonably quiet, but FB's normally pristine desktop was awash with paperwork and the man himself looked stressed and harassed. He snatched Henry's statement and dropped it wearily into a tray.

'How's it all going?' Henry asked.

'Ugh, manic, a nightmare,' FB moaned.

'Any more progress?'

'Well' he said placing down his fountain pen, 'Kaminski's in hospital not in any real danger, the Police Complaints Authority are curious as to why a firearms officer shot a man twice in the back . . . the chief constable's crawling all over this like a . . . dunno, just crawling . . .'

'I was thinking more about admissions and the like.'

FB sat back now and steeped his chubby fingers. 'Constantine has admitted shooting Jo . . .' A surge of blessed relief coursed through Henry at this, and he suddenly went weak, though did not show this to FB, other than to bunch his right hand into a fist and punch low. 'He's also admitted firing at you in your car when you were chasing the gang, but insists they were warning shots, not intended to injure. He's also admitted head-butting and kneeing you in the balls in Manchester . . . He's a pussy cat, actually. Can't stop blabbing.'

'Brilliant . . . What about John Longridge?'

'Nothing from him yet, but he was found in possession of a mask, dark clothing, a shotgun, a street map of Rawtenstall,' FB shrugged. 'So he's nailed to the wall . . . He does seem to have a bit of a downer on me for some unaccountable reason.' He smiled knowingly. 'He was also in possession of several passports, one for him, and one each for the Kaminskis – all forged, incidentally. Looks like they were all going to skip the country after the robbery, as Bowman said. Anyway,' FB stretched, 'he's goosed and we've got two other gang members locked up elsewhere. They were definitely going to hit the building society, so good result all round.' He checked his watch. 'Vladimir is being operated on as we speak and I'm certain we can prove he killed Sally.'

'Mm . . .' Henry had been going to ask a question about Jack

Bowman, but suddenly he didn't care about him one way or another, and instead he could not stop himself from saying, 'Sally didn't have to die, you know? We could have prevented it.'

FB stifled a yawn. Henry couldn't say if it was genuine or out of boredom. 'So you say, but I think you're wrong. She would have backed out of court proceedings against Vlad sooner or later and they would've got back together . . . *they just would*. And he would have killed her eventually . . . Sometimes you can't help people like her, Henry.'

FB shrugged, a gesture that Henry found incredibly uncaring. If his head hadn't hurt so much he would have dragged FB across his paper-strewn desk and smashed his face to a pulp. Instead, he simply said, 'But at least you can try.'

With that he spun on his heels and left.

Henry knocked for the fourth time before he heard movement behind the door.

'Who is it?' the shrill old voice called.

Henry bent to the letterbox. 'Mrs Fudge, it's me, PC Christie . . . I came to your break-in a couple of days back, remember?'

Silence. Then he heard the door being unlocked. The door opened on the security chain and the old lady's face appeared at the crack.

'Where's your uniform?' she demanded.

'I'm off duty . . . I just called round . . . got something for you.'

The one eye he could see squinted slightly as it looked at him, then the door closed and the chain slid back and the door opened again.

'What?' she asked.

'Could I come in?'

'I'm havin' me tea.'

'Won't take long, honest.'

'All right, then.' She turned slowly and went back down the hallway and into the front room and lowered herself into an armchair. Henry followed her.

'How are you doing?' he asked.

'I'm all right . . .'

'Good. Erm . . . got you this,' he said. 'I managed to recover the picture frame you had stolen.' He held up a slim, wrapped parcel, A4 size. 'Unfortunately the photograph in it had been ripped up.'

'Oh no,' she said sadly.

'But I managed to find all the pieces and I took it to a photography shop in town and asked the man there if he could do anything with it, you know, try and restore it? Anyway – this is the result.'

He handed her the package which she took gingerly, a very puzzled expression on her face.

'Go on, open it,' he encouraged her.

Her bony old fingers slowly tore off the brown wrapping paper, revealing the contents, the silver frame and the reconstituted photograph in it – the wedding photograph. The woman's eyes looked at the picture and started to moisten.

'I know it's not as good as it was,' Henry began to say apologetically.

'No . . . no, it's not . . . it's better, this is wonderful,' she said. 'I don't know what to say . . . My God . . . I never thought I would see this again, ever. How, how much do I owe you?'

'Not a penny,' Henry said.

'Thank you, officer, this means everything to me.' She looked him in the eye and Henry could see that the words came right from her heart.

Henry Christie was not renowned for his sartorial elegance. He was more a jeans and T-shirt kind of guy. Having to wear a uniform every day for work made him tie-and-smartness averse when off duty.

However, that evening he had been instructed, if not ordered, to make an effort to make himself presentable. This directive had come from Kate and just showed exactly how much she was pretty much taking over his life both emotionally and practically and he seemed unable to resist this march of the inevitable. Thing was, much to his chagrin, he was coming to love it.

Henry had once tried to read a Lawrence Durrell novel called *Justine*. He'd convinced himself to read it after having read *My Family and Other Animals* by Gerald Durrell, Lawrence's younger brother, thinking it would be much the same sort of thing. It wasn't anything of the sort and he had found it quite hard going, especially for someone like him who feasted mainly on fast action thrillers. He persevered and got through it, disappointed by the lack of creatures, but one small section of it really resonated with him. Near the beginning, the main character described how his life had been before meeting a woman who became his lover.

The character said that although he wasn't unhappy as such, bachelorhood had sickened him because of his domestic inadequacy, his hopelessness over clothes, food and money and the cockroach-haunted rooms in which he lived.

When Henry read that bit, he exclaimed, 'That's me!'

Although by no means unhappy, nor poor or ill-fed, he was starting to find his single-man existence a little tedious and vacuous, though he maybe hadn't realized it until he met Kate and his relationship with her had altered his outlook on life.

It wasn't an overnight Hallelujah, a blinding-flash insight, more a gradual simmer of a soup to which ingredients kept being added whilst others were fished out and disposed of.

Quitting the life wasn't easy, but even at the ripe old age of twenty-three, he wasn't far from becoming an old swinger about town, though not in the wife-swapping sense, more in the Frank Sinatra way. Some of the people who he joined the cops with were now married, were taking their sergeant's exams, buying houses, having kids even and sex once a week. What did seal his resolve to change his ways was, yes, that gradual build-up of his feelings for Kate, his occasional musings about what it might be like to settle down with her, but the final thing that did it took place in the moments after he had tackled Vladimir Kaminski in Rawtenstall town centre.

He had faced death, and that was certain. The image of the muzzle of Kaminski's shotgun would remain with him for many a night to come.

If Vladimir had managed to pull the trigger, Henry knew he would have died there and then. His heart would have been blown out and death would have been very quick indeed.

But Kaminski had been taken down by a firearms officer, who Henry had thanked for saving his life by doing something and making a tough decision that would lead to a few difficult months ahead for the guy in terms of the scrutiny he would have to endure – and Henry had lived, when he could easily have been dead.

Then he had seen Kate running towards him. She had forced her way through the gawping onlookers and rushed to him – and he experienced something amazing.

His mouth went dry. His heart hammered. His guts flipped, not just because of what had taken place. It was the realization that when it came to dying, when it happened, when he was teetering on the precipice, he wanted it to be in Kate's arms.

The moment stunned him.

He had refused hospital treatment even after one of the ambulance men recommended that he should go, just to be on the safe side. Sure, his head hurt, but he'd whacked it harder on his car boot and survived, and was sure he would this time, too. He promised that if he felt sick or dizzy he would get to casualty.

Kaminski had been stretchered into the back of the ambulance and two uniformed officers climbed in with him and the ambulance had sped off, leaving nothing to look at but bloodstains on the ground and a few cops sealing off the scene, so people drifted away quite quickly. Despite FB insisting that Henry should get to the station 'this instant' and write his witness statement, Henry shook his throbbing head and said, 'A bit later.'

The expression on his face made FB back off.

Henry and Kate then walked arm in arm to the insurance brokers where she took him into the staff room at the back of the shop and made a mug of tea for each of them which they drank sat at the table and Henry poured out his heart for the first time in his life . . .

The result being that he was now dressed in khaki chinos, brown brogues and a red-check short-sleeve shirt, pulling up outside Kate's house in Helmshore and climbing out with two bouquets of flowers in his arms. Kate, who had been waiting nervously at the front window, hurried out to meet him, giving him the once-over with a critical eye.

'You scrub up well,' she observed.

'And so do you – you look gorgeous.'

'Thank you . . . Look,' she said seriously, 'you don't have to do this.'

'I think I do . . . Anyway, I've bought your mum a bunch of flowers, don't want to waste them, do I?'

'What about Dad?'

'I had planned to give the other bunch to you,' he admitted, 'but if you think I should give it to him, then so be it,' he said flippantly, but with an undercurrent of panic.

'You know what I mean,' she said, stern-faced. 'Are you ready to face him? Mum's not the problem, she sort of likes you.'

'To be fair, I'd rather tackle an armed robber – but I'm up for it, if you are.'

They locked eyes and she said, 'Yes I am.'

'Then so am I.'

'Well, he's waiting in the dining room . . . all you have to do is go in and ask for my hand in marriage.'

'Jeez . . . is that all?'